INVICTA
FALL of ROME

CHRIS HACKETT

"Rome fell, and with it, the world."

Augustine of Hippo

North Sea
Picts
Scots
Britons
Angles
Saxons
Jutes
Jutes
Angles
Saxons
Warni
Thuringians
ATLANTIC
OCEAN
Britons
REALM OF SYAGRIUS
Soissons (486)
Alamanni
Strasbourg
KDM. OF THE RUGII
Bay of
Biscay
Vouillé (507)
KDM. OF THE BURGUNDIANS
KDM. OF THE SUEBI
Basques
Verona (489)
Isonzo (489)
ODOACER
Adria
KDM. OF THE VISIGOTHS
Tyrrhenian Sea
MEDITE
KDM. OF THE VANDALS
Europe
476 AD

Europe at the Fall of the Western Roman Empire in 476 AD
Western Roman Empire to 476
Germanic peoples
Celtic peoples
KDM. of ODOACER
Alamanni
Britons
Frankish victory
Ostrogothic victory
Baltic peoples
Slavic peoples
Alans
Huns
Huns
KDM. OF THE GEPIDS
Crimean Goths
Alans
Huns
CAUCA
REA
Black Sea
EASTERN ROMAN
SASSA
EMP
EMPIRE
SEA
Ghassanids

I

A.D. 493, Chalcedon Estate, Southern Gaul

The metal orb atop his prayer staff shimmered, reflecting wisps of candlelight. It was enough to make Orephes forget about the chaos outside. Enough to make him forget that war had finally arrived.

For years, he had believed his father's insistent confidence that everything would be OK. The time for allowing himself such naïveté had passed. Orephes knelt before the lifeless statue in front of him, gripping his prayer staff tighter at each rumble in the distance. They were getting closer.

"Father Mars, I pray that you will be gracious and merciful to me, my house, and my household," he appealed, beseeching the Gods for protection from the horde outside his walls. The quiet echo of his own voice was the only reply. For a moment, ever briefly, he had held out hope of hearing something else.

"Orephes," his brother, Gargarus, shouted from somewhere outside. Not exactly the voice he had meant to hear. Gargarus appeared in the open doorway behind him, holding armor and a sword under his arms. "What are you doing?"

"Praying," Orephes replied coolly.

"There is no time for that," Gargarus chided. He stepped forward and tossed the armor and sword into the temple. It was a small, intimate building, compounded by the amount of room taken up by statues and shrines. The few steps his brother had taken toward him gave him a good look at his face. His brown eyes looked worn and battered, the dark circles under his eyes contrasting against the even darker complexion of his skin. He hadn't been sleeping. "Eschelus is preparing the forces on the wall, but every able-bodied man in this villa will be fighting today. Even you."

Eschelus. The famous Roman general who defied the odds as the Imperial world ceaselessly collapsed around him. A living anachronism, in an era where the average "general" was whomever managed to gain the most loot from the last raid. Yet, also a living legend—one who dared to stare the collapse in the face and attempt to deny it further ground, even as emperors and senators alike simply embraced it.

Orephes put on the armor and grabbed the sword, taking care to blow out every candle in the temple before departing while Gargarus paced impatiently outside. He shut and locked the door behind him, believing it to be the last time he would see it. He didn't want to make it an easy target for pillage. At the very least, they would have to kick down the door to get in, though he admitted to himself how stupid the thought was.

"Why do you still bother?" Gargarus asked. "It is all nothing but superstition."

Orephes didn't respond. Truly, he had no response. As much as everything in him believed that they had to be more than superstition, nothing he had lived through had proven his brother wrong. The brothers were silent as they walked briskly on the well-maintained trails through the northern fields of their estate, a veritable green sea punctuated only by the occasional old tree and the lone temple they had just departed. The fleeting moment of silent serenity changed as they approached the northern hill that overlooked their home. All around them, residents of the villa were scurrying about, some in armor and others in robes. There were more than there used to be. Hundreds had flocked to the Chalcedon Estate over the years from the surrounding areas of Gaul after Eschelus's forces arrived, thinking it was safe. Thinking they would be safe.

As the brothers reached the crest of the hill, they could see the torches of the incoming army over the stone walls in the distance. Their numbers were staggering.

"By the Gods," Gargarus whispered. He ran his hand through his graying hair. "Brother, you better hope Mars listens. For all our sakes."

"Father!" A little girl came running toward them, meeting them halfway between the hill crest and the home. Orephes's niece. Gargarus lifted her as she approached and gave her a kiss on the head.

"Have you come to fight?" Gargarus asked, trying to stay light-hearted. His daughter, typically amused by her father's wit, looked at him with the red, puffy eyes of a child who had been crying.

"Will they kill us?"

Shaken at the question, Gargarus smiled at his daughter. A hollow smile that Orephes could see through, though his daughter in her youthful naïveté likely could not.

"They won't even get inside the walls."

"You will stop them, right, Father?"

"Of course." Orephes knew his brother enough to know he would have rather held his daughter through the entire battle than go stand at the wall. He was a fighter by necessity, not by nature. "You should go find your mother. She will not want you out of the house." He put his daughter down and she ran off toward the house where her mother was inside waiting. Several soldiers rode past on horseback toward the wall, two of them breaking off from the pack—Eschelus, and their father, Tiberius Chalcedon, patron of the estate.

"I would say we have ten minutes before they are close enough that our archers can get some shots in," Eschelus stated calmly. "Gargarus, I could use you on the wall."

"I will be there."

"Orephes, take that armor off," his father said sternly.

Orephes couldn't help but notice how old his father looked upon that horse. His hands were skeletal and frail, eyes were sunken in. Even through the helmet, his white hair appeared thin and greasy.

"If you fight, I will fight," Orephes shot back. The inverse of his brother, Orephes was forced to remain on the sidelines despite itching to be at the forefront of the battle.

"You will not fight. That is an order," Eschelus added, backing up Tiberius.

"Why can I not fight? This isn't like the other raids. You need every man you can get. What purpose was my training if it will never be put to use?"

"I don't need you to explain the battle to me." His father suddenly sat straight in his horse, and color returned to his face, coming to life as the Tiberius of twenty years ago. "You will not fight and that is the end of the discussion. Get inside. Now!"

Orephes threw his sword to the ground and tore off his armor piece by piece where they stood, the small fragments of metal that adorned the chest and shoulders clanging as they hit the ground. He stormed off back toward the home, hearing the conversation continue behind him.

"Gargarus, you know better than that."

"He has to learn to fight, Father," Gargarus pleaded. "He may look young, but he is a trained knight, and he is damn well a man. And he's right—we need every man we have. I don't understand why you shelter him."

A horn blew in the distance.

"Sounds like they want to talk," Eschelus stated.

Orephes stalled as his hand reached the door of his home, and noticed Eschelus and Tiberius ride to the wall and make their way atop the main gate, where the bulk of the barbarian forces were approaching from. He knew what Father had asked of him, but he needed to know what was happening. Whatever Father was trying to protect him from was irrelevant if they made it through the walls.

He quietly made his way to the base of the wall, to a small crack in the stone and wood, where he could see out to the approaching army. Above him, unbeknown to his father, he could see the discussions with the defending soldiers.

"I will talk to them," he heard Eschelus say from the top of the wall. Tiberius grabbed his shoulder.

"No. This is my home. It has to be me." Tiberius made his way to the top of the gate just as three barbarians on horses approached, having broken off from the main pack. The rider in the middle wore an animal-hide cape adorned with ornate patterns that hung over the back of his horse. A Gothic general. He was tall, dark-haired with dark skin. He looked up at the comparatively pale Tiberius and bowed his head.

"Lord Tiberius of the County of Chalcedon," the general started in broken Latin. "I come with an offer from the great Euric, King of Spain and Gaul."

Orephes couldn't hear much else of what was said. What he could make out sounded like gibberish—talks of kings and courts instead of magistrates and emperors. He couldn't make out what his father was shouting, but he heard his voice booming back overhead in reply.

While the commander was midsentence, arrows flew from the top of the wall, knocking each of the Gothic commanders off their horses. The previously stoic horses ran, some dragging their former riders with them. A loud horn sounded, and the barbarian army began to run forward. Orephes backed away from the hole in the wall, ready to run into the comforting elegance of the estate's villa that he called home. He had wanted to fight, but now, with the battle underway, he felt unprepared.

On Eschelus's command, a spray of arrows flew from the top of the wall to the approaching barbarians, killing a good number of the first in line. Eschelus turned instead to face his men and lifted his sword.

"With every home that falls, we lose another piece of our civilization. Let no more of Rome fall today!" he shouted proudly.

"Let no more of Rome fall today!" his soldiers answered in unison.

Their chant was broken by a loud clank in the distance, and moments later an enormous stone came crashing to the walls of the villa. Finally heeding his father, Orephes headed back to his home, joining a stream of others who were pouring through the front door.

Orephes could see the villa inhabitants taking care to look away from him hurriedly as he made his way to a large table in the sprawling dining hall. As he sat, he took note that the only others relegated to remain inside were women, children, and the elderly. Most of the children were crying, held by their mothers, who were trying desperately to comfort them. He, instead, was a man of fighting age—indeed, a man trained to fight—sitting inside instead of fighting out there. They couldn't know his father had commanded him not to fight. For all they knew, he was simply a coward.

Paul, an elderly man whom his father had introduced him to, was sitting across from him. Like many of the others, he had been watching him since he sat down. Eschelus and his father had always told him that Paul was sick, not just of the body but of the mind, though he hadn't always been. He was forgetful, and his memories faded frequently. Orephes had never spoken to him at length before. Before he grew sick, he was one of Eschelus's feared knights. He had seen and done things Orephes could only dream of.

Orephes noticed the glasses on the table shake in unison with the shelves as the home shook beneath his feet. A few of the inhabitants fled to the cellar.

"Orephes, right?" Paul asked calmly.

Orephes was surprised he even remembered his name.

"Yes."

"Your father wouldn't let you fight?"

"No."

Paul laughed.

"Does that make you angry?"

"It does."

"Your father has his reasons," Paul assured him, "but if the fight comes to you, you aren't going to have a choice. Are you not trained as a knight? Do you know how to use a sword?"

"Of course."

"A bow?"

"Not as well."

Paul grunted.

"Hmm. It's something."

A scream rose from outside. Paul and Orephes shot up immediately. A few more families fled from the table to the cellar.

"Take this." Paul slid a sword across the table and grabbed another from an abandoned sheath on the table.

"If my father sees—"

"Your father isn't here. The enemy is."

The two of them stood—Paul with some trouble—and headed toward the scream. Outside, on the wall opposite the main battle, a few Goths had scaled the wall and entered the estate. None of Eschelus's soldiers were around, but there were women and children who were fleeing the area.

The Goths were led by two soldiers in black armor, who reminded Orephes more of Roman centurions than barbarians. They held long, pristine swords at their sides and their chest plates were emblazoned with large gold crosses that Orephes recognized as the Christian symbol. Their faces were covered entirely by helmets, masking their identity.

"Orephes, get ready," Paul said. His stature had changed when he saw the soldiers in black. Orephes couldn't tell if he was angry or afraid.

"We need to get the soldiers," Orephes replied.

"Look around. We are the soldiers here," Paul chided. "As much as your father does not want it to be so, you are a knight. It is time to fight. Draw your sword."

The Goths came running toward the pair, past the armored soldiers who stood eerily still. Orephes lifted his sword. He had trained with Eschelus's knights, but he had never actually had to use the training before. This was his moment. He had clamored to fight for so long, and now was his chance.

Mars, protect me, he thought as the first Goth took a swing at him. Orephes parried. It repeated. And again.

Eventually, Orephes gained the upper hand. He dug his sword into his opponent's arm. The Goth recoiled, letting out a painful yell. Paul appeared behind him and finished the job, either robbing him of the kill or sparing him from it, depending on your perspective.

Paul had taken out five. Orephes barely managed to defeat one.

"You all right?"

Orephes didn't have time to respond—a few dozen more Goth troops were pouring over the wall. The Goths already numbered at least twenty, with more climbing down the wall.

Orephes looked to Paul for guidance, but all he got back was a worried glance.

"What do we do?"

"Get back inside, boy," Paul grunted again. "Now!"

The Goths sprinted at them before Orephes could get away. Paul dove in front of the incoming men and took out a few who attempted to reach Orephes.

Orephes felt a forceful tug on his shoulder as he was thrown backward on top of a soldier. He drove his sword backward, stabbing him in the abdomen. The soldier collapsed backward. Orephes felt his lips go numb as his mind raced. Was it adrenaline, or his mind registering the fact that he had just taken a life? He didn't have time to dwell on it; he had to keep running.

He heard a shout and turned. Paul had been stabbed through the heart, his sword still in his hand. That quickly, Orephes was alone. No fanfare. No time to breathe or think.

As he neared the home, he tripped on a raised stone. His sword flew forward, out of his reach. He rolled over onto his back as the Goth forces closed in on him. Everyone else was across the villa.

Mars, protect me, he thought as he closed his eyes. Suddenly, he heard the hooves of a horse. Then another.

He opened his eyes and saw Eschelus and his father plowing through the soldiers on horseback. Eschelus hopped off and finished off the remaining men on foot. A few more soldiers emerged from the house as reinforcements.

"Orephes," his father shouted over the battle, "get inside! Now!"

This time, Orephes knew better than to disobey. He attempted to stand, but his ankle shot pain through his leg.

"Orephes, go!" his father boomed.

"My leg," he shouted back.

Tiberius hopped off his horse and ran toward his son.

As if they had been waiting, the black-clad soldiers finally started pacing forward. They were heading toward his father.

"Come on," Tiberius said, trying to lift his son by his arms. "You can't stay out here. Damn it, Orephes, I told you to stay inside!"

A soldier came over to help.

"I can take him sir," he said, taking Orephes from his father.

Tiberius released him and grabbed his sword from its sheath. He turned to face the two incoming black-armored soldiers, who were slowly approaching. Behind them, in the distance, a new figure had appeared. A hooded man was standing, staring at Orephes and his father. Orephes felt the hair on his neck stand straight forward. Something about him was disheartening. He remembered the stories that the Christian children told, of the hooded demon who hunted followers of the Old Gods. Hunted people like him and his father. Old wives' tales meant to instill fear.

"Orephes, I need you to–" his father started, but never finished. An arrowhead emerged through his abdomen, coated in blood.

The soldier holding Orephes shouted something about archers as he threw him to the floor.

"Father!" Orephes shouted, ignoring the soldier. Tiberius collapsed to his knees, gasping for breath. Orephes noticed one of the armored soldiers running at Tiberius with his sword drawn. He was going to finish him off.

"I have to get you inside," the soldier next to him stated forcefully, grabbing his arm. Orephes didn't even need to put up a fight. A second arrow did the work for him, right through the soldier's head. Orephes grabbed the dropped sword and stood up, noticing that he was barely able to feel the once overbearing pain in his ankle.

He noticed the sound of the surrounding battle fade to his ears. His periphery blurred. The motions around him seemed to slow. He could have dismissed it as adrenaline, but it felt like something else. Something more, like a breeze coming from within.

The numbness he felt in his ankle extended to his mind as he darted forward to his father. The soldier went to swipe, but Orephes parried his blow and kicked him backward. Orephes went on the offensive in an uncharacteristically aggressive manner, delivering swipe after swipe to the parrying soldier. His anger was transferring right to the sword he was wielding through his movements, drawing strength from someplace inside him he hadn't even known existed.

Eventually, the soldier's sword was knocked from his hands by a powerful blow. Orephes had already armed another swipe without thinking. He couldn't stop himself.

It came down into the soldier's neck. The blood gurgled and spilled over the blade as he attempted to shout in pain. As though released from a trance, Orephes panicked and released the sword. He hadn't been ready to kill like that.

He walked backward slowly, nearly stumbling over his own feet. His opponent dropped to the ground in a pool of his own blood, freeing the sword from his neck as he hit the floor. The second armored soldier retreated. Orephes looked up, and noticed the hooded figure still standing, unmoved. His attention was directly on Orephes, despite the chaos around them. The same feeling that had a moment ago given Orephes strength returned, but this time, it seemed to be streaming out of him. Pulling from him.

Behind the hooded figure, he saw the Goths pulling back. He smelled smoke and saw it rising far across the wall where the Goth army had once been. The hooded figure was gone in the instant he had looked away. Had he merely imagined him in the heat of the moment?

Remembering his father, he walked over to where he was laying, and pulled him into the home. He called for Gargarus. He was unable to escape the thought that had he just stayed inside, had he just listened, his father would not be bleeding out in front of him.

II

The dim light of the candle barely lit the small bedroom. The yellow glow seemed to hover over the blood pooling through the sheets covering his father's wound. Orephes held his father's cold hand, the grip weak, barely hinting of life. Now that he had lost so much blood, his skin felt thin and vulnerable, like a candle's wax. As if a strong pull would rip the skin right off. His father hadn't spoken since the arrow struck him, but he was alive.

Orephes heard more than saw Gargarus enter the room, his armor clinking with each step.

"Orephes, you need to get some rest," Gargarus said quietly.

Orephes stared at him dully, part of him noting how some of the blood had been washed from his armor. A spot had been missed near his elbow. Another behind his calf. Behind him Orephes could see the arrow that had been lodged within his father only a few hours ago, haphazardly tossed on the ground in a pool of blood near the door. Around them, the decorations that adorned his father's bedroom—pictures, gold and silver vases, and trinkets collected over a lifetime— seemed foreboding. Early commemorations to adorn his tomb.

"He could die at any moment," Orephes said. "I will be here for it."

Gargarus sat down next to his brother and placed his hand on his father's head. He sat for a few minutes before standing again, his movements restless.

"I can't bear to see him like this." Orephes followed him.

"It is better than not seeing him at all." Orephes placed his hand on his brother's shoulder, who turned back toward him. It was clear that Gargarus had been crying now that he had a closer view of his eyes. It wasn't like him to cry—a firm believer in stoicism as he ostensibly had been.

"Orephes," a faint voice whispered behind them. The two brothers quickly sat back and faced their father, who had awoken and was facing them. His eyes looked drained and lifeless.

"Father," Gargarus started, holding both of his father's hands. "Don't speak—you are too weak."

"Gargarus, my son," he said weakly, managing a smile. "You worry either too much or too little, never in between."

"Do you need anything? Water? Food?" Tiberius chuckled.

"I need skin made of stone." His jokes belied the nature of his wounds. Neither of the brothers knew what else to say, but neither of them wanted to leave his side. He seemed to fade in and out of consciousness but always returned to his glance at the brothers. "Gargarus," he finally spoke again, "I must speak alone with Orephes."

"Whatever you need," Gargarus answered, releasing his father's hands, and stepping out of the room.

Orephes and his father sat quietly for a few moments as Tiberius seemed to gather his strength to continue speaking.

"Orephes," he started finally. "You have grown to be such a fine young man."

"Thank you, Father," Orephes replied. He was holding back tears. This was likely the last conversation with his father.

"There is something I need to tell you that I don't want anyone to hear. Even your brother."

Orephes's head cocked slightly, betraying his attempt to conceal his surprise. It was unlike his father to keep things from Gargarus.

"What about, Father?" Tiberius let out a few coughs, the last one sending a few spurts of blood into the air. Orephes wiped his mouth clean with a nearby cloth.

"I wanted to tell you a story."

"A *story?*" Orephes asked in disbelief. The man was lying on his deathbed. Had he already lost his mind?

"Yes. Your story. From twenty-five years ago." Twenty-five years ago. When Orephes was born.

"My story?"

"I've raised you to be a good believer in the Old Gods your entire life, even as my faith has waned in my old age. But when I was a younger man, my faith was strong. Even as Christianity grew. I believed in the pantheon of Gods. I believed that praying to them would grant us prosperity."

Orephes thought only of how he spoke of his belief in past tense, as something no longer there. What did he mean? Did he no longer believe in prayer and the Old Gods? Why did he raise him for years to believe so?

"You never mentioned your faith waning to me," Orephes said. "Why didn't you tell me?"

"Because how could I raise you as a child of the faith if you didn't even believe that I had faith?"

"If it wasn't true, why did you bother?"

"I never said it wasn't true," Tiberius corrected. "I said I didn't have faith." Orephes didn't understand the distinction. Tiberius let out another cough before continuing, "I must finish. Twenty-five years ago, our world was in upheaval. Christianity hadn't eliminated the followers of the Old Gods, but it had certainly forced us underground. Many of my friends and allies simply pretended to be Christian even if they had not a single belief in that God. It was easier than the alternative."

"Which was?" Orephes interrupted.

"Death. Or at the very least imprisonment. I lost many good friends and family back then. But once the emperors had turned, there was nothing we could do. There was a time when followers of the Old Gods had killed Christians. They didn't forget.

"My wife had just passed away and I had to sneak the burning of her body. I couldn't risk one of the nearby villas noticing and warning the magistrate. As her flames dimmed, Gargarus and I were alone. The hour was late. We said our final prayer and headed back. Then, just as we stepped inside, there was a knock at our door. It was a gentle but persistent knock. Someone with a purpose.

"I opened the door and standing before me was a ragtag group of travelers in the night wind. At first, I thought them barbarian based on their haphazard attire. But they were old and seemingly sick. The one in front had a long white beard, hunched over with a cane. Next to him was a woman in a flowing blue robe, clutching something in her arms.

"I demanded to know who they were. What they wanted. At first, they stood silently, simply staring at me. Eventually, the old man in front spoke.

'Tiberius Chalcedon,' he said to me. He wasn't asking—he knew who I was. The next words he said to me changed my life." His father grabbed Orephes's hands. They were colder now than they had been before. "He told me I was a man of the faith. He told me that there weren't many left. Then, the woman beside him held out a child.

"He asked me to take the child. That it was his son and that he would be safe with me. He told me that he was dying, and he couldn't keep the child with him. This boy was his last child—his last chance at keeping his family alive. I made him a promise that night that I would raise that child to be a man of the faith." Orephes began to realize what was happening.

"Father, I–"

"Orephes," Tiberius cut him off. "That child was you. That man was your father."

He knew it was coming but hearing it out loud nearly knocked the wind out of him. "I am not your son?" Orephes asked grimly.

"You will always be my son," Tiberius continued. "But you are not my child."

Orephes sat staring at his incapacitated father, trying to find the words he wanted to say. Tiberius tried to push himself up.

"Father, no," Orephes chided, "you will hurt yourself."

"Damn it, Orephes, enough with the worry," he said, setting himself upright. He let out a pained sigh. "I am as fine as a dying man can be."

"This man, my father, who was he?"

Tiberius looked Orephes straight in the eyes, as though he was trying to decide whether to answer the question.

"He has gone by many names in our history. The Romans know him as Jupiter. The Egyptians called him Amun-Ra. He goes by another name in the Far East. He prefers the name the Greeks gave to him—Zeus."

Orephes stood silently, his mind blank from trying to comprehend the news. Then he started laughing. "Father, you can't be serious."

"This is the *truth*, Orephes," Tiberius nearly shouted. "On that night, I was handed the son of Zeus and a human mother. I was tasked with raising this child as my own. I saw the Gods, Orephes, and they were dying. This is why I say I believed, but my faith is gone. They existed once. I saw them with my own eyes. But now they are gone. We prayed not to hear an answer from the Gods. We prayed because *you* are the answer."

Orephes felt his father's head. He was feverish. This tale must have been a delusion. A fever dream.

"Father, please," Orephes pleaded, "this isn't how our last conversation should end. Come back to reason."

"Orephes," Tiberius pleaded, growing weak again, "you are their last living descendent. Their story will die with *you*. You must believe."

"Why should I believe that, Father? It sounds mad!" Orephes was angry at him, despite his father's condition.

"Because if you do not"—Tiberius looked weakly into his son's eyes—"then I have failed."

Orephes looked down. He was upset at his father's crazed insistence but couldn't show it. He was embarrassed that even as he watched his father dying before him, his first inclination was to call for him—as though he would be in the other room waiting to solve this matter as he had so often in his life. Dealing with death was foreign to Orephes, having been shielded from battle—or, truly, any sort of difficulty—for so long, even as the world was filled to the brim with it.

"I don't know how to handle this, Father," Orephes said. His father would certainly believe he meant the story he had told, but Orephes had meant prying the old man's mind back from the brink. He fought back tears. This was it. This would be how his final conversation with his once illustrious father ended. Rambling on from fever-induced delusions.

"You don't believe me," Tiberius said. "This is much for you all at once, I understand. War, death—it came to you all at once after years of me trying to keep it from you."

"Why did you keep me from it?" Orephes asked, as if by impulse. It was a question he had asked for so many years, only to be ignored. It rested always on the tip of his tongue. Now, more than ever, the question made sense. "If what you say is true, why would you not have me fight to defend our home?"

Tiberius closed his eyes momentarily, as if resting his mind. Preparing himself to finally give an answer his son had sought for so long.

"I thought I was protecting you. Keeping you hidden. Now I realize, I may have done more harm than good." Tiberius struggled to finish his sentences as his coughing increased.

"Hidden from who?" Orephes thought about the dark-clad soldiers at the villa. The legends of the demon. His father's coughing continued. Blood dribbled down the sides of his mouth, which Orephes moved quickly to wipe away with a cloth from the foot of the bed.

"There isn't any more time," Tiberius said as he finally collected his breath. He weakly lifted his hand and pointed to a shelf in the back of the room where there were several statues of the Old Gods that had been there for as long as Orephes could remember, after the two of them had worked together to carve them when he was a young child. "Grab Jupiter. Bring him here."

Orephes stepped away from his father and reached above to grab the statue of Jupiter. He took a moment to admire the detail that he and his father had carved into the small marble figure. The hair, the facial features, all painstakingly designed to match a description. What description was it, exactly? Nobody had met the Gods, except, apparently, his father—possibly in his delusions. The Christians would have you believe they are all a myth, and they are clearly winning the argument. If the Gods were real, why didn't they stop Christianity from conquering Rome?

Looking at Jupiter, or Zeus, or whatever the people had wanted to call him, all he could see now was the specter of death coming for his father. The image would forever be seared in his mind. A timeless reminder of when his father lost his mind in his last minutes.

Before he reached his father, he noticed for the first time that the statue was hollow. Surprised, he lifted it to glance inside. He noticed a small bundle of cloth tucked away, covered in dust.

He reached in and took it out. There was something hard inside—something that felt like stone. He sat back next to his father and held it out.

"Is this what you wanted me to see?"

"Open it," Tiberius said.

He started to unwrap whatever it was, but it finished the job for him, as the cloth nearly disintegrated as he pulled it apart. A small sphere made of stone and iron attached to a metal chain fell to the ground. The stone and iron were interwoven to make a pattern. This had taken time to make. Artistry.

He leaned forward and placed his hand on the exposed sphere to pick it up. The moment his skin made contact, he felt a strange sensation. A mix of déjà vu and unease. Then, for a few blinks of an eye, everything became dark. Flickering before his eyes was the image of his father being handed a small child in the rain. Nearly as quickly as it had come, it was gone. He looked around, noticing that nothing had changed. He picked up the object off the ground and twisted it around in his hand, expecting something to happen again. Nothing did. Had he simply imagined it?

He was left holding the only other content of the package—a small scroll. It was older parchment; he could tell by the quality. Today, good paper was increasingly hard to come by.

This particular piece looked incomplete, as though it was ripped from someplace else. There was only one written line. It was his father's handwriting.

So, I promised to raise him by the teachings of the Gods, so that he would be raised by the lessons of his family. The amulet will be his when he is ready.

The note was from years ago, written far before he could call his father mad or dying. He could no longer convince himself that it was all the figment of his father's feverish imagination. This simple note, dusty and torn, and metal sphere, spoke to the very thing he most feared: that his father wasn't lying.

He dropped the scroll and looked at the statue it had been enclosed within. Zeus's face stared back, emotionless and still. It was the face of a God. Was it also the face of his family? The true patriarch for his blood?

"This was hidden away at the same time you were given to me," Tiberius said. "It is yours now. It will help you. You must take this east, to Mount Olympus. There, you can find the truth about what happened to the Gods. You can reclaim your birthright."

Orephes had a dozen questions, but his thoughts were interrupted by more coughs by his father, followed by a soft moan.

"Orephes, quickly, get your brother," Tiberius said between coughs. "Before I die. I must speak with him, as well."

Orephes let go of his father's hand and prepared to leave his father's side for the first time in what felt like hours.

"Father," he started softly, "I love you."

"I love you, too, my son."

III

Roman Village, Northern Italy

The crowd was unusually silent for an execution. Typically, they were raucous, looking for blood. Shouting obscenities at the accused, perhaps taking early passes at tossing items at them. Not this time. The crowd stood silently, some looking away, otherers unable to, hands over their mouths in disbelief. The silence was broken only by the occasional crack of rocks slamming against rocks as guards dropped large stones into a pile already formed beneath the poor man strung up in the village center.

A hooded man stood arms-crossed among the crowd rather than with the guards he had arrived with in the center, watching intently as though supervising the scene in front of him. His wardrobe was unlike the townsfolk or even the armored guards. The long, hanging robes hearkened back to a different time in the empire. His sandals, the straps wrapped around his calves to above his shins, seemed unfitting for the cold, harsh climate of the town. The hood over his head did little to conceal his face, instead casting an eerie sort of shadow below his green eyes.

The man strung up finally woke. His eyes were bloodied and bruised, one barely able to open, and he spit blood from his mouth before he looked around to see his arms and legs tied to a stake, body stripped naked with nothing but a small bit of cloth keeping him from being entirely exposed. He was missing several teeth, and a few others were hanging by a thread of his gums in his mouth.

"What is this?" he asked. "Where am I?" He began to struggle, attempting to break free.

"Be still, Peter," answered the soothing voice of the archbishop from behind him. "You have suffered enough." He stepped forward, his armor clanking with each step. As he came before Peter, his ornate white armor and attached robes seemed out of place for such a humble village. The large golden cross emblazoned across his chest plate belied the bloody scene before him.

"Archbishop Martel?" Peter asked. "What is all of this?"

Martel touched his hand to Peter's face. "Clearly, they had their way with you. Do you remember anything about this evening, Peter?"

Peter shook his head, trying to remember. "I remember being in my home. I remember...I remember—you. You coming to visit!" Peter said, finally coming to. "You said you had come with a message. That's all I remember."

"A divine message, Peter," Martel answered with a gentle smile. "A message of salvation."

"Salvation, sir?" As Peter spoke, more blood spit from his mouth through the gaps in his teeth.

"Do you know what this is, Peter?" Martel held out a wooden staff about the length of his arm. The top had an ornate design of interwoven wood and iron. The end had a sharp tip, worn from years of use.

Peter's expression quickly changed, fear apparent on his swollen face.

"A prayer staff," he said quietly.

"*Your* prayer staff," Martel corrected. "We found this in your home." He took a moment to admire the design on top. "Beautiful piece, I must say. Christians have no need for such antiquated items, Peter. Which of course begged the question: Why did you have one? So, after the guards had momentarily incapacitated you, we took a look around your home." Martel finally looked back at Peter. "We found further incriminating evidence. You believe in the Old Gods."

"They are just family heirlooms, sir," Peter shot back. "They have been in my family for generations."

"Unfortunately, we both know that isn't true. But there is hope for you, Peter, in the next life."

One of Martel's guards stepped up next to him, audibly clearing his throat.

"Sir, when do we start putting down wood beneath him?"

Martel took note of the large pile of rocks beneath Peter, so high they were nearly touching his feet.

"No wood," the hooded man, unengaged as he had been before, finally spoke. "Only stones."

"Saint Volusian," the guard stammered, bowing, "I didn't realize you would be here."

"I go where the good Lord needs me," Volusian answered, stepping gently forward next to Martel.

Another one of Martel's men, a young man named Gaius whom Volusian considered a foolish sycophant, stepped beside the archbishop as Volusian approached. Volusian noted Gaius's relative lack of armor compared to the others. Unlike the guards, Gaius saw himself, as endeared to the archbishop as he was, above the petty fighting that often accompanied these excursions. He was the heir apparent to the Archbishop, relegated indefinitely to teat-sucking until Martel either passed away or passed the torch.

"Interesting strategy to burn a man at the stake with merely stones," Gaius said sarcastically. "Archbishop, you can't truly believe this will work, do you?"

"The point of a miracle, Gaius," Martel replied, "is precisely that it is unbelievable."

"Your men should not have wounded this man so severely," Volusian said as he examined Peter's beaten body. "The offering is not as strong. These people will feel compassion for him."

"This is ridiculous," Gaius barked. "I should have slit his heretical throat and been done with this."

"You are a man of the cloth now, Gaius," Martel said. "Have a little faith."

Gaius laughed. "I have no faith in magic tricks."

"Please, my lord, have mercy," Peter was shouting in the background. He'd been shouting for a while, but only now in the silence did they hear his words. Martel grasped the prayer staff before slamming it on the ground beneath Peter, snapping it in half.

Martel stood so that he faced the crowd, positioning himself next to Peter.

"Peter, you stand accused of sinful beliefs and heresy. How do you plead?"

Peter looked around at the townspeople. Many were crying, a few still unable to look. He saw a few children among them, who would grow up in an era where the Old Gods were all but forgotten. He looked down at the broken prayer staff, the legacy that had lived for centuries in his family, and found his resolve. He had heard of Martel and his men. He knew there would be no mercy. His plea mattered little.

"I hope that you burn in the hell that you have created for yourself," Peter shouted, spitting toward Martel.

"Guilty it is, then. You are hereby sentenced to—"

Martel was interrupted by several horses appearing through the crowd. On the first horse sat the Roman magistrate of this village, installed by the final Western emperor before the fall. He was accompanied by several guards and a woman that Martel and Volusian recognized as Peter's wife.

"What is going on here?" the magistrate demanded loudly. "What is this?"

Peter's wife leaped off her horse, climbing the pile of stones to grasp her bloody husband. The magistrate stared at Volusian, clearly unnerved by his demeanor and attire.

"What did they do to you?" Peter's wife whispered, holding his face.

One of Martel's guards attempted to pull her off the stone pile, prompting one of the magistrate's men to hop off his horse and stand in front of her for protection.

"This man stands accused of worshipping the Old Gods," Martel answered.

"I don't care what he was accused of," the magistrate shot back angrily. "There are courts for this. I have seen no testament against this man!"

"Courts?" Martel asked dismissively. "When was the last time anyone used courts for anything outside of Rome? Thirty years ago? No, Magistrate, the sword has replaced the courts, and I will not stand idly by while sinners spread their filth among what is left of our society."

"As long as I have anything to say about it, standing idly by is exactly what you will do."

"You are speaking to a man of God," Gaius shouted, pointing his finger at the magistrate. "Have some respect!"

"Is this what your God wants for this world?" the magistrate shouted back, pointing at Peter from his horse.

"*Our* God?" Martel asked.

The magistrate stirred in his seat before relaxing and sitting back on his horse. Volusian recognized in the magistrate's deflated demeanor that he knew his error. That was not a sentence spoken by someone who was a Christian.

"Untie this man," the magistrate ordered his guards. They attempted to reach Peter, but Martel's men raised their swords and blocked the way. "I can have you arrested, Archbishop! Do not try me!"

"Being a heretic is not only a sin, Magistrate," Martel started, grabbing the hilt of his sword. "It is a crime. A position of power can't hide the truth from the eyes of God." Martel had exposed him. The magistrate hurriedly drew his sword as his eyes widened.

"Guards, arrest this man!"

Martel's guards quickly and efficiently took down the Romans who had dared to cross them. Martel had drawn his sword, but the magistrate was shot from his horse by an arrow long before he had to swing. Martel turned to his guards as Peter's wife screamed in the background, struggling to untie her husband.

"Inquisitors," he said calmly, extending his arms, "let us pray for those who have sinned and perished. May they find peace in heaven."

In unison, his men replied. All except Volusian, who stood silently. "Amen."

Martel turned his attention to Peter's screaming wife, who hadn't been able to untie her husband before he reached them.

"You bastard!" she screamed, slamming her fists into his chest plate.

She continued to kick and scream as he grabbed her, ignoring her tirades. He motioned to his guards, who took her by the arms and legs and strung her up next to her husband above the pile of stones.

"Two for one," Martel, said, looking at Volusian, "is that better?"

It was the first and only time Volusian had managed to smile since the scene began.

With a hand motion by Volusian so subtle as to nearly be imperceptible, the stones beneath the screaming husband and wife erupted into flames, catching fire like wood in a heated oven. The townspeople murmured and whispered among themselves as the pair screamed and struggled futilely, the flames painfully licking their legs until they had become engulfed. Many of the townsfolk began departing, heads shaking or down to avoid continued witness to the gruesome sight.

Volusian noticed Martel studying him, ignoring the fiery scene he had helped to create in front of them.

"Is something troubling you, Volusian?" Martel asked. They had worked together long enough that they could read the subtleties in each other's behaviors. "You have seem…off since you accompanied my men on that raid in Gaul."

Volusian did not look back at Martel, instead seemed to stare blankly, emotionlessly at the bodies writhing in pain as they burned in front of him. He considered not responding to the Archbishop. This was the third—perhaps fourth, truthfully he had lost count—of these men of the cloth that he had the "pleasure" of serving alongside. He owed Martel nothing, least of which was any insight into his thinking. His concerns, however, did relate directly to their joint mission. Only because it might become useful, Volusian decided to share.

"At the Chalcedon Estate, there was a particular young man," Volusian said. "He seemed to be family with Tiberius."

"We had record of one son," Martel answered confidently. "Entirely unsurprising that he would be there."

"It wasn't him," Volusian shot back, finally turning to Martel. He was tempted to chide the archbishop for belittling his concerns, given who he was. However, after centuries he had learned to control his temper. He remembered another archbishop who had not fared as well in challenging him when he was younger and less level-headed. He calmed himself and turned back to the burning bodies in front of him. A slight breeze had picked up, and the smoke and ashes had started to blow toward them. "The son, Gargarus, was fighting at the wall. Some of the Goth soldiers recognized him. Yet Tiberius made it a point to try to save this other young man himself. They seemed close. More importantly, I felt something from him."

"Felt something?" Martel asked. He raised his hand to cover his eyes from the smoke blowing toward them. Volusian seemed unaffected, almost relishing the smoke as it broke around him. "Felt what?"

"I don't know. It could have been nothing. A whisper in the heat of battle. Nonetheless, it was something I haven't noticed in a very long time."

There was momentary silence as Martel walked back from the stake, coughing from the ceaseless flames and soot. A few of his men broke off from the others to follow him. Before leaving Volusian's earshot, he turned back.

"Gaul has been culled ceaselessly, Volusian. I trust you will determine whether your 'feeling' is anything other than, as you say, a 'whisper.'"

IV

Orephes stood in the temple quietly. It was dark this time—he hadn't lit the candles—and was dimly lit by only the setting sun on the horizon peering through the two small windows. He was looking at a few of the miniature statues of the pantheon of the Gods—an empty spot in the middle, the rest flanking outward—and holding Jupiter in his hands.

Holding it felt different this time. If his father was telling the truth, this was an image of a *real* father he would never get to know. A real father who abandoned not only him, but the world he was supposed to be watching over. He had prayed to these figurines his entire life, always hoping for an answer that never came. Except, according to his father, *he* was the answer. What that meant, of course, he couldn't yet know, but he felt the burden nonetheless.

He thought again about his father and the arrow that had ended him. Tiberius admitted that he had kept Orephes from fighting in the very army that could have protected them to keep him hidden and safe. Who had his father been keeping him hidden from? He had the blood of a God in his veins. Would he not have been more of an asset in the field all this time? He felt his arm tense as he remembered the countless arguments between him and his father about fighting. His father's insistence with barely an explanation that he could not join the other knights in the field.

Almost out of reflex, he threw the statue to the floor, shattering it to pieces. The rest of the pantheon sat idly by, seemingly judging him with their expressionless faces. Swinging his arm, he knocked them all off their positions, each shattering atop the other as they hit the floor.

He fell to his knees and wept into his hands. His father was gone, and he couldn't bring him back. These statues couldn't bring him back. They were tainted now, a reminder of that battle and his father's demise. A reminder that the very figures these statues represented had failed them.

Leaving the shattered mess behind, Orephes gradually departed the temple as he recomposed himself. He locked the door and tossed the key into the tall grass outside, expecting never to see it again.

Outside, the villa's citizens had all gathered in the fields in a large circle. In the center stood Eschelus, towering over the battle's deceased who lay, arms crossed, in a line in the center of the crowd. He was joined by Gargarus and his family, who seemed in particularly low spirits.

In the center of the deceased lay his father, Tiberius Chalcedon, skin pale and drained of blood. He was dressed in fine robes that were a stark contrast to the armor worn by the soldiers beside him. In front of the dead was a line of holes where they were to be buried in a matter of moments.

"These men fought bravely to defend this estate," Eschelus was saying as Orephes approached, "and they died so that we may live. Each of these men took with them a piece of Rome that may never return." Eschelus dipped his head in prayer momentarily. "Let no more of Rome fall today."

"Let no more of Rome fall today," the crowd replied in unison.

"Wait," Orephes said, emerging from the crowd. Eschelus and Gargarus looked over, almost surprised to see him. "My father would have wanted to be cremated."

"Cremation is against the word of God," Eschelus replied matter-of-factly.

"Not the ones he believed in," Orephes shot back.

Eschelus nodded and signaled for two of the men to take Tiberius's body. The remaining bodies were placed into their burial grounds, and some nearby soldiers began to cover them with dirt.

Eschelus held a torch over Tiberius's body, who was laid upon a table haphazardly created from wood. The rest of the villa stood at the base of the hill, looking up at their now deceased patron. Eschelus stopped short before placing the torch down onto the body.

"Orephes." Eschelus turned toward him and held out the torch. "It should be you."

Orephes took the torch and took one last look at his father. Gargarus gave him a nod, and he brought the torch down on the wood beside his father. After a few brief moments, his body was engulfed in a powerful flame that would erase any trace of his existence.

Immediately, Eschelus handed Gargarus the scrolle containing their father's title and said that he was now owner of the estate. According to the barbarians, Gargarus would now be lord of this land.

"Orephes," Gargarus said, as he approached after the brief ceremony, "how are you doing?" Orephes didn't answer, so Gargarus placed his hand on his shoulder. "The pain will subside soon. I remember it all too well from when my mother died."

My mother, Orephes thought. Not ours. How many times had this slip happened before and he hadn't noticed, subconsciously replacing *my* with *our* dutifully? He hadn't mentioned to Gargarus or anyone else what his father had said to him. Partly out of embarrassment and partly out of wanting to preserve his father's dignity. As the heat from the fire struck his face, and he watched his father disappear from existence, he felt himself begin to question his own reaction to his father's revelation. Perhaps he had been going mad, but what if he truly was not his son?

"Gargarus, what did Father say to you?"

"What do you mean?"

"After I left the room, and he asked for you. What did he say to you?"

"He told me that this estate was to be mine," he said calmly. "He told me to take care of its inhabitants. And you."

"Did he seem in his right mind?"

"Yes," Gargarus stated, suddenly concerned. "Did he not seem in his right mind to you?"

"Something he said to me. When I was alone with him…" Orephes hesitated for a moment, trying to decide whether telling his brother was the best thing to do. Gargarus stood there, listening intently. "He told me that I was not his son. That I was given to him by a group of travelers twenty-five years ago."

Gargarus looked uncomfortable for a moment, then sighed and crossed his arms. "So, he did tell you after all. I wasn't sure since I heard no mention from you."

"You knew?" Orephes asked.

"Of course, I knew. I was there."

"Do you know who it was that left me here?"

"Father never told me, but I always wondered. I know they looked old. There were quite a few of them. I simply assumed they were refugees from a nearby city. Barbarian raids had just started back then." Damn. He wouldn't get an answer from Gargarus. "Why, did he tell you?"

Orephes thought for a moment about telling his brother, if for no other reason than to share the burden of wondering about his father's sanity at the end. However, it was important for the villa residents to believe that his father had been in his right mind when granting Gargarus the title. Their claim to this land was already tenuous given the local king's insistence that the land would cede to him upon Tiberius's death. If the raids, ostensibly against the will of the king, were bad enough, a full invasion with his blessing would be far worse. The last thing they needed was some of his father's old trusted advisors and friends, some of whom were still alive, thinking they could do a better job running their homestead. The understanding that Tiberius granted the land to Gargarus in his right state of mind was of utmost importance for the coming negotiations.

"No," Orephes replied. "He wouldn't tell me who they were. He said it didn't matter."

"Well, that is one secret that died with him," Gargarus said sadly, looking back at his father's nearly completely burnt corpse. The flames from his father seemed to energize Orephes as they finished their burn, the mental and physical wear of the past few days seemed to disappear.

Suddenly, he remembered the temple and the key he had tossed away. Despite what his father said, he wouldn't have wanted the temple to simply fall into disrepair. They had built it together. It was one last memory he had of him. It didn't have to be a negative one if he didn't let it be.

After the final flames had died, Orephes returned to the temple. He searched the ground, and luckily found the key right where he had dropped it. Unlocking the door, he walked back inside and placed the key on the mantel where it would remain.

V

In the days after his father passed, Gargarus and Eschelus made plans to continue to build their army. Before he had arrived, Eschelus had gathered forces from all across occupied Gaul. Anyone loyal to Rome with the ability to fight joined him. Most came with him to the Chalcedon Estate, but some had stayed out in Gaul to protect their families and cities, pledging to fight alongside him when the end came.

"The end." That is what Eschelus always called it. That was when he was planning on taking his forces south and reclaiming Rome for the Imperial citizens. What Eschelus didn't realize—or perhaps he did and simply ignored—was that with every passing year, with every day that barbarian kings maintained control over what he considered Roman provinces, that term *citizen* meant less and less. There would come a time when his forces would no longer be seen as liberators but as conquerors to a people who had never lived in a Roman empire nor wanted to.

Then there was the question of the black-armored soldiers with the golden crosses on their chests. He wasn't sure anyone else at the villa had seen them, let alone the hooded figure at the wall that seemed to draw him in. Surely someone had seen the one he had killed. Why had nobody mentioned them? Who were they? Why did they stay so still, except in the presence of his father? He knew the cross was the symbol of Christianity but they certainly weren't priests. It nagged at him every single day. Was that who his father had been afraid of?

Eschelus's constant callings to "the end" served as a reminder to the villa residents that his soldiers and the protection they give this estate is and always would be temporary. Soon, they would be alone. Just as they had been before.

The first time Eschelus had come, he didn't stay. He merely brought a warning that his father didn't heed, and in hindsight Eschelus was lucky that his father had been so stubborn. The day would have been an easy one to recall in any case; it had been the day after the last Roman Emperor in the West had fallen. Now, having stayed for so long, he was another source of structure for the villa residents.

Eschelus was sitting across from him at the table. Gargarus was seated to the right, his hand tapping nervously on the edge as he looked on.

"Do you know why I called you here, Orephes?" Eschelus asked. Still dirty from working the fields, Orephes shook his head.

"No idea."

"I will be blunt," he continued without emotion. "It is time for you to earn your place alongside my knights." His knights. The fearsome fighting force known throughout the civilized (and feared throughout the uncivilized) world. Besides Orephes, there were four: Bracchus, their commander, Michael, Antonius, and the fourth they simply called "Roman". They were his most elite and experienced men who had been with him since Rome fell nineteen years ago. If anyone could do a special task, it was them. At the time that Orephes had been asked to join them, he had been honored. His father's insistence on being trained and yet not fighting had served as a constant embarrassment for him. This was his chance to change his image.

Yet his father had given him a task, and it did not seem to align with Eschelus's "end." All he had ever wanted to do was fight and be respected alongside the other knights. Even in his demise, his father had thrown those plans awry.

"I appreciate the training more than you know," Orephes replied. "But I have not fought since then. I fear I will not be useful to you."

"You can train someone to fight," Eschelus replied confidently, "but you can't train them to be Roman. You can't train them to have heart. *You* have heart. I saw it when you were fighting to defend your father."

"Why now?"

"Gargarus believes you are ready."

Orephes looked at his brother and shook his head, a wry smirk briefly appearing. "Father would kill you if he was still alive."

"He might still be alive if you knew how to fight then," Gargarus shot back almost rabidly, as though he had been holding it back for a while. Orephes nodded and sat back in his chair. The tone was unlike Gargarus. Orephes had not expected the conversation to take this turn.

"So, it is my fault that Father died, is it?"

"I didn't say that," Gargarus said, pulling back and calming down. Running the villa was taking its toll on his brother, and he knew it. It had been only a few weeks, but Gargarus had grown irritable and unhappy. It didn't help that Eschelus was constantly pushing him in a direction that he knew their father wouldn't like. His father was very adamant that the villa would never become a military base, even if it became a temporary home for Eschelus's soldiers. Gargarus seemed to be changing that by the day.

"Gargarus, that one battle shouldn't change what Father wanted our land to be," Orephes continued. "This was to be a place of refuge and peace for fleeing Romans, not a fort." Gargarus's eyes seemed to widen and the muscles in his face became less tense. He was getting through to him.

"There is no such thing anymore," Eschelus chimed in from across the table. The pair of brothers had nearly forgotten him at the head of the table. Gargarus immediately snapped back into war mode. "Your father died because he didn't let us defend ourselves properly. Anywhere that still claims to be Roman is at war. We didn't choose that, but it is the truth."

"He's right, Orephes," Gargarus added. "We can't hide behind a facade of peace when war is tearing down our walls."

Orephes could tell he was losing this argument. Frankly, a few days ago, this conversation would have been all he had ever wanted. Eschelus's knights struck fear in the barbarian world and the Roman. The four-man group did more to instill fear in an already scared world than an army one hundred times its size. Being at their side would have been a dream come true, if only his father had ever let him join them.

Why? Because he thought I was some demigod? Orephes pondered. Maybe this would be good for him after all. To clear his mind of such nonsense. Of his father's end-of-day feverish dreams. His father's aimless mission for him to travel halfway across the world was not reality. This war was.

"I am ready," Orephes finally let out.

"Excellent," Eschelus said with a smile.

"I will go make the preparations for your materials," Gargarus said, standing from the table. "Orephes, I'm proud of you." He patted his brother's shoulder and walked out of the room. Orephes looked at Eschelus and shook his head.

"I won't be any good compared to the others. This last battle was my first time lifting a sword that wasn't training."

"Every single one of those knights had to train to get where they are. Hell, even I started as something I never thought I could be." It was then Orephes realized he never knew much about Eschelus. He knew his title, of course, and his beliefs in a new Rome. He knew he was brave, somewhat callous, yet noble. But he didn't know his past.

"What did you start as?" Orephes asked curiously. "I mean, before you got here."

The corner of Eschelus's lip curled as if to form a nostalgic smile. "A soldier," Eschelus began. "A member of the scholae."

"You were on the Imperial guard?" Orephes asked excitedly.

"Back when there was an emperor to guard, yes. Your father did teach you well." Eschelus sat back, crossing his arms. "I'm impressed."

"How long ago was that?"

"Seventeen years ago," Eschelus answered, falling deep in thought. "When the last Emperor in the West fell."

"You were there?"

"I spilled blood on the very wall that   breached," Eschelus said, reminiscing. "I still remember it so clearly. I think about it every time I draw my sword. I feel it every time I kill."

*　　*　　*

Ravenna, Western Roman Imperial Capital, Seventeen Years Prior
September 2, 476 A.D.

Crunch.

That was it. The sound of his first kill. It was the only thing he could hear besides his own heartbeat.

There was no scream. No struggle. Just a sword piercing a chest as though it were air. Pulling the sword out was more difficult. He hadn't trained for that part. He struggled and tugged, eventually breaking his weapon free from the chest cavity he had lodged it in.

The entrails that spilled out across his feet barely distracted him from his lifeless opponent who fell to the ground, his eyes now empty and hollow.

The sounds around him began to refocus, Eschelus took a good look at the poor soul who had come between him and survival. That stare into the sky, as though longing for one more opportunity to kiss his parents goodbye, was a great equalizer. In our last moments, we all want one thing: life.

"Sir," Eschelus heard a guard next to him shout. The voice sounded muted, as though behind a shroud. "Sir, the gate!" Eschelus snapped back into reality, remembering where he was. His small company was scrambling. The gate was flung open, and barbarians were pouring in.

"Legions, the gate!" Eschelus's fellow Roman guards had been awaiting his orders. They hurried over with their large shields, blocking the path as best they could. On his way to the gate himself, Eschelus nearly tripped over his commanding officer. He hadn't been much older than Eschelus. He fell not even ten minutes earlier, a stray arrow having caught him in the head. His death within moments of the battle's onset promoted Eschelus, without fanfare, to tribuni scholae—the commander of the last vestiges of the emperor's cavalry escort that had once been the vanguard of Rome.

"Sir," he heard another soldier yell, "the Imperial Palace!"

They seemed to be pouring in from every side. He saw another group of soldiers—*limitanei*, the second-tier soldiers of the army—running toward the palace while a few more waited for his orders. Behind him, the gate continued to fall.

"Get to the gate," he shouted, withdrawing his sword. "Go!"

Eschelus ran toward the Imperial Palace to join his comrades. He stuck his sword into the rear chest cavity of a barbarian that happened to cross his path—the second kill was much easier than the first. He ran quickly past the contingent of men outside the palace gates into the walls of the complex, where a small group of soldiers—likely new recruits for the scholae—were standing at attention. They were all young boys—half of them didn't even look Roman, and even fewer had proper armor. This is what had become of the once mighty legions.

Eschelus took the reprieve to sit, his head still spinning from the blood on his sword. It wasn't as red as he expected, but it was certainly thicker. It was heavy, syrup-like, and it added a small yet noticeable weight to the sword he needed to swing. He sat for only a few minutes attempting to clean his sword and boots before he couldn't help but to vomit against the formerly pristine walls of the complex.

He wasn't sure if it was the anxiety or the blood, but it didn't matter. He hadn't experienced either of them before. After a few moments he stood, legs shaking and body sweating, and approached the group of young men standing at attention away from the battle in defense of the "emperor" cowering inside. All he could think about was that they could be out helping defend the wall.

"What is your regiment? Who is your commanding officer?" Eschelus asked. One of the boys replied in an accent he could barely understand. They were mercenaries.

The marching and shouting of soldiers overtook the usual noises of traders and carriages lining the streets of Ravenna as the standard ambient noise inside the Imperial complex. A disguised Senator Severus Verengi hurried to meet with Eschelus, who was standing at the head of a small regiment as the sound of swords crashing echoed over the walls.

Severus looked past Eschelus to the dozen or so soldiers behind him, waiting for their chance to defend their emperor. They looked fierce, fearless even, but like Eschelus he knew what he considered the truth: too many of these soldiers were not loyal; too many of them were not Roman. He knew they wouldn't defend this city as true Romans would. They didn't fully grasp what it was they were fighting for. They didn't understand that they weren't just defending a city. They were defending a way of life.

"Eschelus," Severus shouted loudly. The tribuni hurried over to the senator, sword clenched in his hand.

"Senator," he shouted over more shouting, "you shouldn't be out here. The city's defenses—"

"The city is going to fall, Eschelus," Severus said somberly. "The emperor is going to fall with it. Let us not deceive ourselves." Eschelus said nothing, his silence being all Severus needed to hear. "There isn't much time. There are many friends of the Senate that must be warned of what is coming."

"What is coming, Senator?"

"If this barbarian *magister militum* takes the city, there is no guarantee that Romans outside of the city will be safe. I have many friends and family who need to be warned."

"Sir, with all due respect, to abandon the emperor is treason."

"The emperor? Which one? Romulus Augustulus here in Ravenna? Or Juilus Nepos in exile in Dalmatia?"

Eschelus sat silently again as Severus struck a chord. It was an unspoken elephant in the room—the emperor was considered by many to be a usurper. Another royal overthrow in a long line of overthrows that had brought the empire to ruin.

"We have a chance to help some good people, Eschelus. If we are to preserve our way of life, we need to save those who make it possible. Not those who have helped take it away."

Eschelus stood uncomfortably, hand still on his sheathed sword, as he looked back at the mercenary soldiers behind him.

"Look at them, Severus," he said, shaking his head, "Avars, Slavs, some Alemanni. Not a single one of them is Roman. They fight against an enemy made up of soldiers who also are not Roman. Yet all of them, our allies and our enemies alike, call themselves Roman."

"It speaks to how powerful this way of life we have created is, that these barbarian hordes sought to become more like us," Severus replied, extending his arm with a small satchel of monetary compensation. "For your troubles. There is some extra for any men you choose to accompany you. There is a list inside—get the message to all of them."

"Right away, Senator." Eschelus hurried away as Severus attempted to hurry back toward the Curia.

There was a loud crash followed by muted screams in the distance.

"The walls have been breached!" a soldier shouted in the distance.

"There goes the neighborhood," Severus muttered under his breath as he returned to his chambers, the sounds of pillage ringing throughout the hallways as he sealed the door.

Back outside the Imperial Palace, Eschelus saw barbarians pouring over the walls, slaughtering the Roman soldiers who dared remain fighting. The soldiers who stood firm at the gate began to crack, several of them fleeing to save their own lives. Eschelus had to act now; there wasn't much time left.

He approached two of the remaining scholae, killing another barbarian on his way. That made three.

"Your orders, sir?" a young boy, no older than ten, asked as he approached from within the city. He was followed by a small force of young boys all around that age, all looking just as scared and ill-equipped as the one in front of him. These boys, these *children*, were the reinforcements to hold the wall. He couldn't bear to tell them their sacrifices would all be in vain.

"Go home to your parents," Eschelus said quietly as he turned away.

"My parents are dead, sir," the boy replied. Eschelus turned back, having run out of orders to give. "I want to help save the city." Eschelus couldn't bear to tell him that the city was already as dead as they were.

"Follow me." Eschelus sheathed his sword as he turned back to the soldiers at the wall. "You two, come with me!" Eschelus shouted. "That is an order!" The soldiers hesitated before they dropped their shields and obliged, the remaining soldiers giving up hope as they witnessed their commanding officer fleeing away into the innards of the city. The final few soldiers fled or were slaughtered as the Western Roman Empire came crashing to an end around them.

Eschelus led his group out of a back entrance to the city on horseback, and stopped at a hill shortly outside the city limits. They turned to see the great capital of the *Imperium Romanum* lit like a candle, her buildings burning and smoking like a bonfire. Though they were far from the city's walls, Eschelus swore he could hear still hear the screaming of its people.

"God has forsaken us," one of his soldiers said in a loud whisper.

"Where are we running to now?" another asked. "We have abandoned our city and emperor. We should have died with honor!"

"Our deaths will come," Eschelus said solemnly. "But our duty to Rome is not yet complete."

"Rome?" One of the scholae walked his horse over to Eschelus aggressively. "What Rome? Do you see that smoke? That is Rome, returning to our God in Heaven as we speak." The soldier pulled closer to Eschelus, his demeanor becoming calmer. "Sir, Rome is dead."

"No. Rome lives in us. Rome lives in all of us, and all who still call themselves Roman." The scholae looked at each other, a few putting their heads down in thought. "Rome will survive as long as we do. And I plan on surviving." He pulled out the satchel that he had on his hip. Reading the list of names, they were spread out across different provinces. The journey would be a long one. "We go to the Seven Provinces, and then to northern Gaul."

"Northern Gaul?" one of the scholae interrupted again. "Sir, northern Gaul is a wasteland."

"Apparently Senator Verengi doesn't believe so. I have my orders, now you have yours."

*　　*　　*

"I failed Rome that day," Eschelus finished, lifting his head as though returning to reality. "But together we can avenge it. This is why I need you fighting now. I need someone with your heart on my team. What makes my knights so powerful isn't merely their skills, but the heart and minds that drive them to use those skills for what is right. The time is right to strike at Odoacer, and strike we shall."

"You didn't fail Rome," Orephes replied. "Ravenna would have fallen anyway. If it wasn't for you, thousands more Romans would have perished in Gaul."

Eschelus scratched his beard where a scar had developed before letting out a dull laugh. The young man's knowledge of history was serving him well.

"Tell that to the emperor I was supposed to be protecting."

"You protected our villa."

Eschelus nodded and smiled. "That, there. That's the heart I am talking about. Go, get some rest. We begin gathering the forces tomorrow."

VI

Orephes was panting, his body coated in sweat and dirt. He made it to the top of the hill within the villa's boundaries and took a moment to peer at the surroundings like he used to.

Six months, he thought. *Six months of this training to become a knight only to let it all atrophy away.*

The six months had been absolutely brutal, and at first, he had much to show for it. His arms were firmer. His physique more overpowering. His skills with the sword vastly improved. Then years passed, and to call himself a knight became a stretch. He would need to work to regain what he had lost.

As he caught his breath, he began to head back toward the home. In the corner of his eye, he caught glimpse of a small marble building shimmering in the dusk sun. It was the temple he and his father had built. He hadn't been inside since his father's funeral.

His father. He sometimes was able to clear his mind of his father's passing, but he could never truly forget. There was a void there, filled now with swords and shields. What would his father think of him abandoning it like that? Regardless of the building as a symbol, it was a product of their labor together.

He considered turning back toward the house and ignoring the temple, just as he had done when he passed this route every day for the past six months. But something, perhaps the way the light reflected through the windows perfectly, was drawing him toward it today.

The stones surrounding the entryway looked just like they had. A few more months and nature would begin to reclaim the entirety of the structure for herself. He gently pressed into the door, sending dust and light swirling into the interior.

The statues were still broken on the ground, exactly where he had left them. A reminder of what had brought him to that point—his father's maddening admission, or tall tale—at the end of his life.

Standing among the shattered statues that pockmarked the stone flooring, he felt a weight in his pocket. The strange stone and steel amulet his father had given him was resting in there, as it had been since it had been handed to him. Something about being in the temple made it feel heavier, as though it was tugging at his pocket. He pulled it free and examined it, holding it in front of him as though the figurines around him might explain it to him further. He was answered only by the wind, which picked up through the open door and blew some of the smaller pieces around on the floor.

Something about the amulet in that moment—like a faint whisper in his mind—made Orephes realized that the idea of finally fighting with the knights had been a good distraction, but he wasn't happy. He hadn't been since his father passed away. Some of it was sorrow, yes, but some of it was the mystery behind who he really was. He was happy to put it to the back of his mind when he considered there were far more important tasks at hand for Rome. Something about this amulet, this place, made him consider that perhaps there was nothing more important than what his father had told him. His service to Rome could not be in Eschelus's army. At least, not yet.

"What are you doing in here?" Antonius's voice boomed from behind him. The fellow knight stepped into the temple, looking around at the meticulousness inside. Orephes realized that Antonius had never been inside here. Nobody had, except for him and his father. Occasionally, Gargarus had been curious enough to peek inside.

Antonius had his shirt off, the sweat causing the dirt to cake on his toned figure. His curly dark hair, shimmering from the exercise, was sticking to his forehead. His blue eyes seemed energetic, like they always did after a run. Of all the fellow knights, Antonius had always caught the attention and admiration of Orephes. Despite being older than Orephes, he was still younger than the others by a significant margin. When the others had lost patience with him during his training, and even at times since, Antonius had always taken pains to keep helping.

"Nothing," Orephes quickly answered, hiding the amulet back in his pocket. "Thinking of old memories."

Antonius moved closer, and Orephes could smell the sweat on him. Antonius moved the shards of statue around on the ground with his foot. He rested his hand on Orephes's shoulder, giving him a momentary, rare smile.

"Your father would be proud of you," Antonius tried to assure his brother-in-arms. Orephes didn't have the heart to remind him how opposed his father had been to him fighting. He enjoyed watching Antonius attempt to make him feel better.

"Thank you."

"I was running past and saw this door open, which it never is. I wanted to be sure everything was OK."

"It is."

Antonius nodded and curled his lips. He didn't believe that nothing had happened in the temple, but he wasn't going to press the point.

"Well, all right, then. I'll see you back at the villa."

Antonius went to continue his run, and Orephes held the amulet in front of him again. He resigned himself to figure out if his father was telling the truth. To find out the truth about his family.

He went back to his home and made his way to a back room where the shrine dedicated to his great-great-grandfather stood. He had been a consul, back when that meant something. His family's wealth was built from the man's work.

In the center of the shrine was his ancestor's armor. It was very different even from the best you could find now. It was ornate yet functional. Decorative yet inspiring. Next to the armor sat his sword, held up by a metal frame. *This armor,* Orephes thought, *represented a Rome that no longer existed.* It also represented a family lineage that may similarly no longer exist.

At this moment, staring at the shrine of a man he had worshiped for years, blindly assuming he was family, Orephes realized that he would never forgive himself if he died in this villa and without ever knowing his true lineage. He may not truly be descended from the Gods, but he certainly wasn't descended from his father.

He pulled the armor off its holders and placed it on his body quickly. He ripped the old sword from its metal holder and sheathed it in his great-great-grandfather's hilt.

Making his way toward Eschelus's chambers, he drew stares from the villa residents who couldn't believe the armor he was wearing. For some of the older ones, it was likely as though they were looking at a ghost of a different time. For the younger ones, an armor like this was something they had only seen in history books.

Eschelus was looking over some scrolls as Orephes stepped in. Noticing the knight's armor, he placed the scroll in his hands down and sat back in his seat.

"I haven't seen armor like that in years," Eschelus started.

"You won't see it again for a while."

"Oh?"

"I am leaving the villa."

Eschelus sat forward. "Leaving the villa? To go where?"

"East. To Greece."

"Why?"

"On his deathbed, my father said something to me. Something that I must find out for myself if it is true."

"What did he tell you?"

Orephes briefly considered mentioning the whole story to Eschelus, whom he was sure would be more inclined to believe than even someone like his brother. However, he thought it best to keep Eschelus, like everyone else in his life, in the dark about why he would truly be leaving.

"He told me that I am not his son. He told me that I must travel east, to Greece. That my true family left something for me there that I must reclaim." Not *entirely* a lie.

Eschelus seemed to be a bit confused by the news, but continued on nonetheless. "Orephes, I have invested years of training into you and have been unable to use you that entire time. You are just now going to find yourself helping to lead our army. For you to just depart now—"

"I have waited this long. What is a few more months?" Orephes shot back.

"You wouldn't have even dreamed of leaving these walls six months ago. You being given free rein to join us has built your confidence, I understand that. But you know what is waiting for you out there. I wouldn't even take the journey alone myself."

"Eschelus, I am grateful for the training. This is no reflection on the mission you seek to undertake or your abilities in teaching me. This is something I must do for my own sake—and for Rome's. Something tells me that if what my father told me is true, it will have implications far beyond this home."

Eschelus sat running his hand on his scarred chin, as he often did when he was thinking. He appeared emotionless, other than a slight raise of an eyebrow when Orephes mentioned far-reaching implications. And then, it was only for a moment.

"Okay." He sat forward, his hands crossing on the desk. "You are your own man, and it is your right to leave here as you see fit."

Though Orephes wanted to show excitement, he instead stood calmly slightly bowing his head. "I appreciate your understanding."

"Before you go, I want to give you something."

Orephes was surprised. He had been expecting more resistance and certainly hadn't been expecting anything as far as gifts. Eschelus reached into his pocket and pulled out a small coin that he placed on the table. It seemed crude and makeshift, as though this coin had formerly been something else and had been melted down again. On the top face, beneath the image of an eagle, Orephes could make out four letters: *S.P.Q.R.*

"What is this?"

"It is a coin that serves as a symbol to yourself and to the world that you are one of my knights."

It took a moment before Orephes realized what he meant. "I haven't fought with the rest of you. I can't accept this."

"You have six months of brutal combat training, and enough heart to compensate for the rest," Eschelus said. "This coin was Paul's before he passed. Given that you and he fought alongside each other, even if briefly, I thought it right for you to have it."

Orephes lifted the coin and twisted it in his hands. On the opposite side of the coin, there was only one word, sloppily engraved by hand: *Invicta.*

"Keep this safe. Friends of our cause will know this coin," Eschelus continued. "It will get you far when you are in need."

"I will." Orephes placed the coin into his small satchel.

"So, Greece, then? How were you planning on getting there?"

"Horse," Orephes replied matter-of-factly.

Eschelus let out a laugh under his breath. "You plan on traveling across hundreds of miles of disputed territory by horse?"

"Do you have a better idea?"

"I have traveled that many miles and more into the heart of barbarian territory and back," Eschelus hissed out, seeming aggravated. "I have seen things you could not possibly imagine." Eschelus seemed to disappear into thought for a moment. Orephes noticed his hand shaking before he took a moment to catch his breath. "The world outside these walls is something that I would never wish to see again if I didn't have to." Eschelus looked up at Orephes, and through merely glancing at his eyes Orephes could see the toll that whatever he had seen had done to him. "Traveling east by land will break you. If you aren't killed, your mind will be. You have heart. I don't want to see you lose it."

"Well, I do not have a boat, or else I would say I could travel by sea."

Eschelus quickly wrote a name on a scroll and handed it to Orephes.

"Travel south, to Rome. I have heard from scouts that the path is much less treacherous. Meet with Senator Severus Verengi. He is an old friend. He will find someone to take you by sea. It is faster, and this way you might be able to make it back for some of the fun."

"I don't know how to thank you."

"I look out for my knights." Eschelus stood. "Thank me by bringing yourself back in one piece. Have you told your brother?"

Orephes stopped for a moment, having nearly forgotten about Gargarus. "No. It is better if he doesn't hear it from me. Tell him after I have left."

After a brief pause, Eschelus nodded with acknowledgement, but Orephes could sense his disapproval.

"Hurry back. I would hate to take back Rome without you."

The two men shared a quick embrace before Orephes finally departed the room, not taking a moment to look back for fear of Eschelus changing his mind.

Eschelus sat staring at the word on his own coin moments after giving Orephes his. His hand was shaking as he recalled one of the many memories that he wished he could forget. *Invicta.* The scene that had inspired him to place this on the very item that would come to define his knights, his movement, was bloody. It was the type of thing that soldiers fear. They don't fear battle. They don't fear death. They fear seeing the people they love having to suffer.

He could only pray that Orephes would fare better on his journey. The world had changed much in seventeen years. But none of it was good.

VII

Worn, battered, and hungry, Eschelus and his scholae had driven deep into Gaul. Eschelus remembered a time not too long before when the very roads they were riding on had been maintained in meticulous condition, facilitating trade and helping soldiers move quickly. Today, as they gently galloped down the stone walkways of their ancestors, clear overgrowth and stone displacement had begun to erode the very foundations of the prosperity these channels of commerce had been built on.

"Sir," one of the scholae said quietly, picking up speed to be alongside him. It was Paul, a gentle older man who had initially offered a bit of resistance when departing the capital. His short graying beard—product of a few days growth, no doubt—was beginning to show through his Roman helmet. His wise brown eyes, drained as they were, still exerted such compassion and care that it was hard to ignore him. "We have to break for the sake of our younger troops. They aren't used to marching like this. We've been at it for days after leaving that last villa."

On the limited journey so far, Eschelus had gotten to know Paul very well. He was a former merchant from Italy, though he hadn't mentioned where exactly from. In the late 460s nearly his entire merchant fleet had been destroyed by a Vandal raiding party off the coast of Sicily. He sold the remaining ships and joined the scholae, pledging to fight the barbarian plague wherever its flame still flickered. His resolve had been weakened, but not broken, by Odoacer's sack. He had made it very clear to Eschelus that he believed that Roman culture could never fall, even if its emperor had. That is what he was fighting for. Nominally, Eschelus was his commanding officer, but he was his equal in all but name.

"Were they not trained for this?" Eschelus asked, slowing his horse. He looked at his younger troops—the children he had encouraged to leave the capital alongside him—and saw that they could barely sit up on their horses. He had forgotten just how young they were.

"To be trained is not to be tested," Paul replied with a tinge of condescension, "you of all people should know that." Paul was, of course, referring to Eschelus's haphazard promotion to tribuni upon the death of the former. Sure, Eschelus had trained for the remote possibility. That didn't mean he had been ready. Not when it happened.

"You are right," Eschelus admitted upon seeing the poor state of his younger soldiers. "We need to rest." He took in his surroundings; it was evening and the sun was preparing to set, but he could still make out where they were. "If I am not mistaken, there is a *mansio* nearby used for the *cursus publicus* and other official business. We don't have official papers but given the situation I think we qualify. We can stop there for the night, changes horses if need be, and get a good meal."

"I've never gotten a good meal at one of those, but it is better than nothing," Paul answered jokingly. "How do you know? Have you been keeping track of our pacing?"

"No, I used to work for the *cursus publicus* delivering important correspondence for Italian nobles to Gallic aristocrats. I recognize this area well. It isn't far ahead. A good friend of mine helped finance it."

"From postman to tribuni," Paul joked, "quite a career. In all seriousness, we can't even be sure that the *cursus publicus* still exists."

"It was still functioning eleven months ago. I was still receiving correspondence, then."

"A lot has changed in eleven months."

"Indeed it has, but there is only one way to find out. It is either that or we continue marching."

"I agree." Paul stopped his horse and signaled for the men following to hold.

"If there is any civilization left in this prefect, it will be there," Eschelus said quietly, more to comfort himself than Paul, who had fallen just out of earshot.

"All hold!" Paul shouted loudly.

Eschelus stepped forward to speak to the group. "We will be stopping at a *mansio* up ahead," he shouted to his men. "We will rest there for the night."

"How much farther? We are losing daylight," another soldier asked, stepping forward. Eschelus had gotten to know this one, too. His name was Michael, as blue-blooded as they came. A soldier in a long line of soldiers from a patrician family, he was brazen, aggressive, and had a tendency to question everything Eschelus said. In the current Roman army, filled to the brim with barbarians and mercenaries, pedigree soldiers like Michael were hard to come by. He was, in his mind, far more qualified to be tribuni than the man who unfortunately held the title now.

Michael had been the most upset about abandoning the capital given the circumstances. He felt they hadn't just abandoned the emperor, they had abandoned their people. But he was a damn good soldier, and Eschelus needed those skills if this ragtag group was going to make it through this.

"Just up the road," Eschelus replied dismissively. "You can make it out from here if you look to the northwest."

"Well, at least we know there is still a building there," Michael retorted, heading back to his place in the pack. On his way, he tapped the shoulder of one of the younger soldiers, Antonius, as though comforting him. "We are almost there, hold together," he said quietly. Eschelus took note. There was a soft side to the man after all.

Antonius was the oldest of the young soldiers at about sixteen, which is likely why he was given the command of his small cohort of men. Eschelus had spoken to him briefly during the ensuing travels. He had lost his father and brothers in some of the final fighting of the empire. He couldn't be sure in which exact battle they had perished, but he knew they never came home to the capital after they left months ago.

The rest of Antonius's group, dubbed the "boy army" by the older men, were still nameless to Eschelus, who hadn't had the time to acquaint himself with all of them. Nonetheless he felt a responsibility to them. They chose to follow him, on his orders, at the capital. These children were his responsibility now.

The group slowly pattered their way to the outside of the *mansio,* a walled villa estate sitting among several other buildings at a fork in the road.

Eschelus knew immediately something was wrong. He expected there to be little signs of life on the journey here. Most knew it was unsafe to travel on the roads alone by this point. But here, near a *mansio,* he expected to see someone. Anyone. Yet the closer they headed toward the entrance to their lodging, the more he realized that there was nobody around for miles.

The buildings they passed were empty and barren, hollow husks of a former community. Along the side of the road were carriages and containers, still intact and some perfectly aligned, abandoned where they stood.

Michael approached a set of containers still sitting perfectly organized within a shipping carriage. Dismounting, he took the lid off one of them and inserted his hand, withdrawing his red-stained palm and licking his finger.

"Wine," he said as he wiped his hand. "Old, sour, but all here. No sign of theft. Hell, no sign of anything."

"There are no signs of battle," Paul noted.

Eschelus shared his concerns. There were no overturned carriages, no pillaging, hell there wasn't even any spilled wine. Everyone had left here, but they had left on their own.

"If they left," Eschelus noted, "they left in a hurry. They didn't even bother to take their wine."

"Or their food," Antonius shouted from across the road. He and his men were digging through a carriage filled with cheeses and some meats, all of which were rotted and smelled to high hell.

"Stay away from that," Paul shouted, "you'll get yourself ill and then nobody will be taking care of you."

"Something tells me that *mansio* is going to be very empty," Michael said as he remounted.

"Or filled with rotted cheese," Paul joked.

"We have no choice but to try," Eschelus commanded. "The boys need a place to rest, and the next *mansio* isn't for miles."

"I agree," Michael nodded in agreement.

"Then it's settled. Maybe everyone in this surrounding village ran to the villa for safety behind the walls."

"Possible, but unlikely," Paul retorted. "Not without their wine and food like that. These people left as fast as they could."

The small cohort of men approached the front gate of the walls to the villa, where Paul, Eschelus, and Michael took up positions immediately in front. Eschelus was not surprised to see nobody manning the gates, either inside or out. If they were going to get in, they would have to get in of their own accord.

Eschelus dismounted, followed by Michael and Paul, all of whom approached the bars.

"Can you see anything?" Eschelus asked.

"Looks just as abandoned as the rest," Michael said. "There's nothing here."

Eschelus grabbed the gate and pushed but was met with nothing more than the sound of shaking rusted metal.

"Odd," he said. "These gates are never locked."

"Not by Romans, anyway," Paul whispered quietly.

Eschelus peeked at the center of the gate and saw a rope interwoven as a makeshift lock. The rope was tied very tightly and extensively, to the point where he was surprised he hadn't noticed it on the first approach to the gate. It was tied specifically so that nobody could untie it with their hands—that much was clear.

"Someone is trying to keep someone else out of here," Eschelus noted.

"Not anyone with a sword," Michael said abruptly as he stepped forward. With a strong swipe, he cut the rope blocking the gate in two and it swung open, as though it had been held in an uncomfortable position and was now returning to where it felt best.

The group poured into the gate one by one, with Eschelus taking count. Eventually they made it to the front of the actual *mansio* itself—a large, expansive villa, just as beautiful now as it was when it was occupied. Eschelus had stayed here many times in his past; this was the first time he had seen it so empty.

"Come, if there is anyone here, they would be through the main entrance," Eschelus assured them, dismounting again and leading his team toward the main entry. "Antonius, you and the boys stay here so that we can make sure it is safe for you. Michael and Paul, come with me. Remaining scholae remain here with the boys."

Eschelus, Paul, and Michael walked up to the main entrance, where they were yet again met by silence.

"I think it is clear nobody is here, Eschelus," Michael said, getting frustrated. "You know how these worked. Someone would have been there to greet us on the damn road if this was still up and running."

"If people are hiding, they wouldn't be out greeting others, would they?" Eschelus shot back. Pushing the front door aside, they entered the dark villa to another serene, picturesque scene of utter abandonment. The villa, at least from what they could see, was empty, yet all its elegant and expensive furniture remained in place.

"Couldn't be looters," Paul said grimly, "this would all be gone."

Michael walked ahead to investigate other rooms, while Paul and Eschelus continued to try to determine what may have happened to the caretakers.

"There is no way the Senate would have allowed this *mansio* to simply degrade," Eschelus said quietly. "This was on a vital route to the north."

"Eschelus," Paul said calmly, resting his hand on his superior's shoulder. "I know it is hard for all of us understand, but the Senate, the emperor…these terms may not mean anything here anymore. Likely haven't for years. The only question left to answer, is if this will." Paul tapped the sack of coins that Senator Verengi had given to Eschelus when leaving Ravenna.

"Eschelus," Michael said in a hurried tone as he reappeared from deep in the villa. He looked pale and distraught. He had seen something. "You should follow me."

Paul and Eschelus obliged, following Michael deeper into the villa. He stopped outside the main living quarters where he slowly opened the door.

The first thing Eschelus noticed was the rancid smell. For a split second it almost smelled sweet before devolving into a malodorous cacophony in his nostrils. It was the sort of stench that had a veritable weight to it, making the air feel thick and sticky.

When he finally could focus, he saw the bodies. There were dozens of them, stacked and sprawled across the room. The floor hissed beneath him as he stepped through the thick, old blood coating it, nearly drowned out from the sound of the flies that bounced back and forth at eye level. The bodies were pale and bloodless—they had been here a while—yet their robes were entirely intact. There were men, women, and children strewn about like wine bottles after a circus.

"Roman. All of them," Michael said solemnly. "And look up." Eschelus peered up to the ceiling, where blood was smeared in a pattern. At first, he wasn't sure what he was looking at, but then he realized they were letters.

"*Roma invicta*," Eschelus said out loud as he read it. *Unconquerable Rome.*

"They were probably killed for being loyal to Rome," Paul said calmly. "Poor bastards."

"What the hell happened here?" Michael asked grimly. "Who did this?"

Suddenly, the trio heard a shout from outside. Followed by another and then a few more. They looked at each other momentarily before hurrying out the way they came. Stepping back out into the courtyard, they saw their cohort surrounded by a group of men—barbarians from the looks of their animal skins and makeshift armors. A few of the horses had been killed, and it was clear at least some of the men were wounded. They were standing, swords drawn, in typical defensive formation. They had learned well. Eschelus, Paul, and Michael drew their swords and ran forward.

Before they could make it to the rest of the group, Eschelus felt his feet fly out from under him as he saw Paul and Michael fall, as well. After a brief moment of being unaware, he managed to flip over to see his feet bound with rope and steel balls. He tried to reach for his sword but within seconds his hands had been grabbed by two large barbarian men who tried to lift him to his feet. A third had his sword in hand, charging at him.

His arms still being held by the two men, Eschelus kicked his feet into the air as the third barbarian slashed, cutting a gash into his leg but also cutting the ropes binding them. His legs now freed, he managed to force his way out of the arms of the men holding him, kicking one to the ground and head-butting the other with his armored head. He quickly grabbed his sword off the ground, taking out the two barbarians closest to him and blocking a strike from the third.

After finishing off his foes, Eschelus quickly ran and helped Paul and Michael similarly out of their traps. The three of them began to run forward again before a group of barbarians on horseback strode into the walls of the villa.

"Defensive formation!" Eschelus yelled as the mounted men surrounded the three of them. He could see the bulk of his men continuing to fight a few feet away; they hadn't given up yet.

"Stop!" a new barbarian shouted in Latin as he strode in on horseback. Unlike the others, this barbarian wore a somewhat respectable-looking armor, at the very least influenced by Roman garb, if not modified from it. Slowly the barbarians all backed away, giving the Romans a reprieve, and, more importantly, a chance to regroup. Eschelus and his trio took the opportunity to return to the bulk of his men, where he could see one of Antonius's boys was severely hurt. Unfortunately, he would have to tend to him later.

The armored barbarian dismounted and walked toward the group. He was bearded and unkempt, with hair down to his neck. He smelled nearly as bad as the rotting cheeses and meats from earlier, as did his entire company.

"Who is the commanding officer?" His Latin was broken and accented, but it was at least an attempt. The other barbarians were speaking a Germanic tongue; Eschelus had no idea what they were saying.

"I am," Eschelus said, stepping forward. He knew full well this could mean his death, but he wasn't a coward. "My name is Eschelus, tribuni scholae. On authority of the emperor and the Senate you are under arrest for raiding and pillaging."

Laughter erupted from the barbarians.

"My name is Athaulf, servant of King Gundobad of the Burgundians," the barbarian replied proudly and dismissively. He took a moment to observe the Roman soldiers in formation before him. "There haven't been Roman soldiers in this province in almost fifteen years. The only reason I bothered to hold off on killing you is to understand what exactly you are doing here." Gundobad. Eschelus knew that name. Before Odoacer, Gundobad had been in negotiations with the emperor. He was an ally to the Romans.

"This is Roman territory," Eschelus replied indignantly. "That we are here or not is irrelevant to you."

A few of the barbarians snickered.

"Yes, of course, Roman territory," Athaulf replied snidely. "I'm sure you found your fellow citizens safe in the villa?"

"Cheeky cunt," Paul muttered under his breath.

"Am I to assume you are responsible for that massacre?" Eschelus accused.

"Me? Why, of course not. I would never do such a thing. This is, after all, Roman territory," Athaulf replied in a mocking tone. "I will ask again. Why are you here?"

"I was looking to stay in this villa as it is part of the *cursus publicus* and I am on official Imperial business. I'm sure I needn't warn you the penalty for interfering with Imperial business."

"Surely, you must be joking, or deluded," Athaulf replied with a laugh. "Warn me of the penalties? Tribuni, this is King Gundobad's territory. Any who choose to oppose his rule or his code are to be put to death."

"We are allies with King Gundobad," Eschelus reassured him, changing his tone. "We mean no harm to his reign or his people. We merely desire safe passage through territory that is rightly ours. Surely, King Gundobad would understand."

"Aye, King Gundobad is your ally and he may," Athaulf said, the smile running from his face. "But you aren't allied with me." Athaulf stepped closer to Eschelus, where his height in comparison to the Romans was stark. He was much taller than any of them, but Romans were used to the barbarian height difference by now.

Eschelus moved closer to Athaulf.

"It is clear you haven't seen Romans in many years, barbarian," Eschelus said calmly and dismissively. "If you had, your uncultured mind might just achieve sentience enough to understand your folly." Still calm, Eschelus walked right up to Athaulf's unrelentingly malodorous face. "By allowing your enemy the time to regroup, you have given them the opportunity to plot out the best strategy to defeat your larger but woefully underequipped group of simpletons. Not to mention your enemies happen to be Roman scholae known widely for their defensive stance but considering your level of intellect and learning I wouldn't expect you to have been able to read enough military history to understand."

"Are you mocking me, Roman?" Athaulf growled.

Eschelus smirked. "Good, you aren't a complete fool. I won't feel as bad killing you. Allow me to present you the exact train of events as they are going to unfold. I will be killing you—how I haven't quite decided yet. Then, my men will make quick work of your remaining mounted soldiers there"—Eschelus pointed at one of the mounted men—"and there," he continued, pointing at the other. "Then, your foolish horde will charge our outnumbered group that has already entered defensive formation. This will give my men the perfect striking opportunity at two of the body's most vulnerable points. Here and here"—he pointed at Athaulf's lower rib cages on either side.

Athaulf looked sternly at Eschelus before quickly masking a smirk. A few of the barbarians were muttering.

"Only God knows the future," Athaulf muttered confidently.

"You can ask him if he knew yours when you see him."

Eschelus quickly drew his sword and sliced Athaulf's throat before kicking him back into two of his men. Instantly, two scholae fired arrows at the remaining barbarians on horseback, knocking them from their rides. The surrounding barbarians drew their swords.

Eschelus waited for their charge, but it never came. Instead, they started to back slowly away and head out of the gates of the complex the way they had entered. A few dropped their swords as they left, sprinting out of fear of what they had just seen.

"Nice work," Paul said, impressed.

"They will be back," Eschelus replied. He sheathed his sword and turned to his men who were coming out of formation. "We can't stay here."

"Seems to me like you scared the pants off them," Antonius said excitedly.

"All it will take is one more charismatic fool like Athaulf to change that. We can't risk remaining here through dusk."

"He's right," Michael admitted. "We will have to keep moving."

Eschelus remembered the wounded soldier, and quickly headed to where he had been placed on the ground by some of his friends. He had a gash across his chest and a stab wound under his rib cage. He was coughing up blood and unable to stand.

Eschelus knelt over him, feeling his head as he examined his wounds. Michael joined him, kneeling over the boy on the opposite side.

"Gash, piercing"—Michael rubbed around and felt near the sword wound—"severe swelling." Michael stood up and motioned for Eschelus to join him a few steps away. "We can't do anything for him," Michael said grimly. "We have nothing to treat him with. That is a fatal wound."

"We won't lose a man here. Not like this," Eschelus dismissed.

"He is already gone, Eschelus," Michael pleaded. "There is nothing we can do for the boy. The only question now is whether we allow him to die slowly or end it quickly."

Eschelus ran his hand through his hair and stared at the ground. "I can't kill one of my own men," Eschelus sighed.

"You are their tribuni, Eschelus. This is your role. His life is over. You can ensure that his remaining hours aren't spent in misery." Michael grew forceful. He came from a long line of soldiers; he knew what had to be done. Eschelus was merely having trouble accepting it.

They could hear the young man coughing blood and inhaling as much air as he could a few steps away. The two men returned to his side, and Eschelus placed his hand on the boy's head. Eschelus lowered his head and closed his eyes, praying for the soul of the poor boy whose misery he was about to end.

"What is your name, scholae?"

"Oedinus," the boy gurgled out over the blood in his mouth.

"Oedinus, there is nothing that we can do for you here. I pray that your soul finds peace in the presence of our Lord."

Oedinus closed his eyes, trying his hardest to weep, but his wounds prevented him from doing anything but cough and gasp.

Eschelus drew his sword and gently placed it over the boy's chest.

"Amen."

He plunged the sword through Oedinus's heart, the boy letting out one final gasp before his already pale face turned lifeless. As the sword entered, Eschelus felt a chill, as though one more segment of his soul had simply evaporated from the surface of his flesh. He felt his hand shaking as he withdrew it, adrenaline coursing through his veins and his breathing becoming heavy.

He stood, feeling his throat beginning to ball up. He couldn't show weakness. Not in front of his men. He dropped his bloodied sword, partly out of a sudden weakness in his hand and partly out of anger.

"We lost a young soldier today," Eschelus said to his remaining men. His voice cracked faintly at his first word as he struggled to regain composure. He took a deep breath and brought his mindset back to where it needed to be. "Every one of us that goes down is one more piece of civilization destroyed. May this be the last piece of Rome that falls today." He picked up and sheathed his sword. "Grab what you can from the abandoned villas and homes. We must keep moving before they return."

VIII

Orephes finished loading his horse in the back of the villa. He had believed that nobody had seen him leaving. He was surprised to hear footsteps approaching as he went to mount.

He turned around quickly to see Antonius running past him on the next hill, leaves crunching beneath his feet. He was looking around, as though looking for someone. Orephes quickly ran to hide behind the nearest tree, but the sound of the armor he was wearing gave him away. Antonius stopped short and looked over, seeing him sticking out next to his horse.

"Orephes?" Antonius hurried over, examining the scene. He looked at the satchels on the horse and realized the imminent departure of his fellow knight. "So, it is true. You are leaving."

"Who told you?"

"There are hundreds of people stuck together in this villa. Rumors spread quickly. Where are you going?"

"East." Orephes threw his last satchel over his horse and mounted it. "I have to find out the truth about my family."

There were a few precious moments of silence when Orephes believed that Antonius would just nod and walk away. When he could leave as he wanted. In peace, with no goodbyes.

"You didn't tell me," Antonius finally said. The disappointment in his voice stung. He didn't need to say the second part of that sentence: *after everything.* They were both already thinking it.

Orephes thought of the right words to say. "I will be back."

"You know how dangerous it is."

"I do."

Antonius shook his head and sighed. "Then I am coming with you."

"No," Orephes said firmly. "Eschelus needs you. The war is yet to come."

"You are not doing this alone. You are just as much a knight as I am. And we stick together." Antonius did not take no for an answer, fetching his horse, and joining Orephes a few minutes later over the protests of his friend.

"Don't say anything," Antonius interrupted as Orephes went to speak. "Just ride."

The two rode south in near silence, the pair only checking on each other to make sure they were well enough to continue on. The journey south to Rome was not longer than half a day if the horses were fast and the track maintained. Luckily, the roads were in much better service outside the villa than they had expected after the stories they had heard. They got even better the deeper into Italy they headed. Soon, they were surrounded by others atop horses and carriages, heading in either direction on the road to Rome.

The silence was punctuated by their very different upbringings. They had learned much about each other during Orephes's training. Orephes was a child of rural Gaul, of estates and villas. A farmer's life. Antonius was born in Rome during a period of upheaval and uncertainty. He was a child of an urban culture that was, at one point and time, the life of the wealthy. Now, they were simply used to sieges and drafts. Of missing parents and dead families. Antonius was a living, breathing example of how the mighty had fallen.

"I can't believe Eschelus allowed you to leave," Antonius started, breaking the silence.

"I didn't realize that I needed his permission to leave my home," Orephes replied.

"You are a knight now. You surrendered your life to the cause of Rome." Orephes smirked and shook his head. *The cause of Rome,* he thought. *What a joke that was.*

"What about you?" Orephes poked back.

As he spoke, the two had arrived at the outskirts of Rome. The conversation ended abruptly as they saw walls and marble buildings unlike anything out near the villa. The gate before them stood open into a different world, its portcullis drawn into the ceiling. Antonius saw that Orephes was standing awestruck and grabbed his shoulder.

"You have never been, have you?"

"To Rome?" Orephes seemed to snap out of a trance. "No. Never."

"It was beautiful once."

"It still looks beautiful," Orephes assured him. A distant smile swept across Antonius's face.

"In some ways."

The two entered through the main gates, which were guarded by what looked like standard Roman soldiers atop a watchtower on each side. The pair had expected the city to be guarded by barbarians after Odoacer's conquest. Their curiosity was stopped short as they entered through the gates, surrounded by trade caravans and merchants, and were met by the beautiful cacophony of city life.

Antonius hopped off his horse and took a deep breath. He seemed right at home.

"It has been a very long time."

"Is it different now?" Orephes asked.

"The people change. But Rome always stays the same."

To Orephes, the entire thing was a marvelous spectacle. Everything, from the merchants selling their wares at the bottom of the insulae, to the innumerable buildings lining the streets, to the stores and fountains and obelisks—everything here seemed to be simply glowing with life. This certainly didn't look like a captive city, let alone one that was conquered and oppressed.

He couldn't help but think about the stark difference between the city and the countryside in Gaul. It reminded him of something his father used to say: *If Rome was swallowed by the Earth, their circuses would carry on and cause earthquakes to tear the rest of us down.* It made sense. The city that had conquered the world seemed to move on untouched. The lands they had conquered centuries past...*those* would suffer instead.

Orephes showed Antonius where they could find Senator Verengi, as described by Eschelus. Apparently, it was his old neighborhood. He directed them down several city blocks in what seemed like an endless, repetitive walk, until Antonius started to slow and look around. His head was looking left and right as though something didn't seem right. Eventually, he stopped in the middle of a block.

"What's wrong?" Orephes asked. He looked around trying to figure out what was irking Antonius. The buildings here looked similar to the ones in the rest of the city they had passed through, but they were missing a few stones from their walls. Orephes hadn't noticed at first, but it was much less populated here than it had been a few blocks back. The people here seemed different, too. Most of them weren't wearing Roman robes, instead covered in animal hides and furs. A few men walked past them with stares like daggers, tall and muscular, and much darker in skin tone than either of the knights.

"This was my home," Antonius said, nodding toward the insula to their left. "I lived on the very top floor with my parents. We had one small window that my mother used to try to decorate with small fabric she scrounged up the money for." Antonius could see Orephes's disinterest. After all, he was simply describing a place he used to know. "Look at it now."

"It seems we found the barbarians we were looking for," Orephes added.

"Of all the neighborhoods in the city they could have taken, they took mine. To destroy not only my physical presence here, but also my memory of it." Antonius continued to stare longingly at the insula beside him. Orephes peered into the lowest level of the building, which in the more populated areas of the city were dedicated to shops, and saw entire families in them living in relative filth. "And what the hell is that sound?"

Orephes again had barely noticed in the background a high-pitched banging sound, as though two stones were being rubbed together. The pair looked around briefly before noticing a small child chipping away at the stones of one of the insula near them, putting the stones that came off into a satchel. Antonius angrily drew his sword.

"Hey!" he shouted, marching toward the child.

Orephes hopped off his horse and chased after him. "Antonius, what are you doing?"

A few of the barbarian men in the vicinity lifted their heads at the noise.

"Get away from there!" Antonius grabbed the child's satchel and tossed it aside, the stones tumbling out. "It took someone years to build that."

Suddenly, a barbarian man emerged from behind the corner of the building, a satchel filled with stones off the same insula. The child ran behind the man's legs.

"Is there a problem?" he asked in a very crude, vulgar-sounding Latin.

Orephes grabbed Antonius's arm and shook his head. A few more barbarian men were listening closely from nearby windows and doors.

"None," Orephes responded. "I am sorry for my friend's behavior." Antonius looked around and placed his sword back in his sheath. They hopped back on their horses and slowly rode down the block as the child put the stones he had lost back into his bag.

"What the hell were you thinking?" Orephes pried.

"Where are the guards? Is there no rule of law here anymore?" Antonius lamented. "These used to be respected homes, built by Romans for Romans."

"These barbarians are making their home here just as you did," Orephes replied. Antonius looked his fellow knight in the eyes, as though he snapped back from a distant reality. He pulled his shoulder forcefully away from Orephes's grasp.

They continued on past the next few blocks of barbarian-filled insulae until they reached a walled and gated home in the middle of the block. To Orephes, it seemed bizarrely out of place, as though someone had decided to build a villa like his own back home in the middle of the city. Unlike the apartment buildings surrounding it, this building seemed to exude wealth, not the least of which was due to the guards standing outside. The first Romans for several blocks.

"We are here."

The two approached the gates, but the guards immediately drew their swords.

"Stop," one shouted. "State your business."

"We are here to see Senator Verengi."

"He isn't taking visitors," the guards replied forcefully. "Move along."

Orephes looked at Antonius, who drew his knight's coin from his satchel.

"I come on important Imperial business," he stated, holding the coin up for the guards to see. The guards examined the coin and sheathed their swords. The word *Invicta* shone in the sun as it was held.

"I will let the senator know you are here," the guard said with a slight bow. "Welcome to Rome."

Orephes kept silent, but it was clear that this was a very useful little coin. Eschelus had been right about it being able to get him access when he needed it. It made him remember how new he was to this whole "knight" business. Eschelus had been working behind the scenes and in the open for years. He had just joined in at the end. He almost felt like he didn't deserve to have one of these coins, but he was happy to have one.

As they stepped inside, they bypassed a few small statues and a garden where they left their horses before being invited into the home proper. The insides of the senator's domus was opulent and expansive, much like the villa they had come from. It was smaller than what you would find up in Gaul, certainly, but it was respectable nonetheless. Particularly for being in the city.

A few servants brought out wine and cheese while they waited in a living area, decorated with murals and curtains.

"This home is beautiful," Orephes commented.

"I would expect nothing less in a senator's home," Antonius responded dismissively. At times, the knight seemed annoyed by Orephes's perceived innocence. It was obvious that he had never left the walls of his villa before, and to Antonius, it certainly wasn't his responsibility to teach the younger man all there was to know about Rome.

Eventually, an old man in robes emerged from the next room. He was hunched over slightly and moving very slowly, almost shuffling to where the men were seated. His hands were clasped together in front of his body, as though he was holding his chest back from falling any more forward. His face was old and wrinkled yet warm at the same time. The bangs of his white hair covered most of his forehead. He smiled when he saw the two knights in armor. Orephes noted how full of life his smile seemed to be, even while the rest of his body seemed to be collapsing in attempting to hold it up.

"You two," the senator started, "you come from Gaul? From Eschelus?"

"Yes, sir," Antonius said, standing and bowing. Orephes followed, as he assumed Antonius knew the protocol for meeting a senator.

The senator's smile grew even wider. "I haven't heard from him in so long I had feared the worst. Please, sit." The trio sat as the guards continued to bring them all wine. Severus signaled to the servants that he wanted to be bypassed. "I can't drink that stuff anymore. Poisoning what little life I have left doesn't seem very prudent."

"Sir"—Antonius pulled a small scroll out from his satchel—"this was to be delivered to you directly on General Eschelus's orders." Orephes hadn't been aware of any note. The senator took it into his hands but didn't open it. Instead, he was fixated on Orephes, reading his expression.

"You look uncomfortable," Severus started, placing the scroll down beside him. "You didn't know he had a scroll, did you?"

Orephes looked even more confused now. *How did he know?*

"No, sir, I didn't," Orephes answered.

Severus laughed. "I've been around long enough to know when someone has that look of being left in the dark. Particularly as a senator. Keeping people in the dark is what we do best." Severus let out a few heaving coughs into the sleeve of his robe. "What is your name?"

"Orephes," he answered. "From the Chalcedon Estate in Gaul."

"The Chalcedon Estate?" Severus's head perked up. "Of Tiberius Chalcedon?"

"You knew my father?" Orephes asked, surprised, though he quickly remembered that Tiberius wasn't truly his father anymore.

"You are Tiberius's son?" Severus asked excitedly. "My God, of course! Orephes. I knew the name was familiar. My goodness, the last time I saw you..." Severus seemed to be trailing off, trying to remember. "It must have been when you were just born. Your mother had just recently passed away. I traveled north to give your father my condolences." Severus's smile was still plastered on his face. "There weren't many Romans who didn't know your father once upon a time. He was very well-known. An excellent writer, an even better fighter. How is he?"

"He is dead."

Severus's smile faded into a confused stare. He likely had expected more than a cold, distant one line to describe his friend's death.

"I see. How did it happen?"

"In battle. Against the Goths."

Severus nodded. "A fitting death for a Roman of his stature." Severus extended his hand and grabbed Orephes's. "He was a great man. He will be remembered fondly."

"Thank you, Senator. You are very kind."

"And look at you—he would have been so proud to see you in that armor. I am glad to see you are following in his footsteps. I have heard many stories of my other Gallic friends losing their children to the barbarian kings. If not by the sword, by the mind. Romans are a hot commodity to have in a court. They know that we have more going on here"—he pointed to his temple—"than most of their uneducated 'advisors,' if you can call them that."

"No true Roman would ever join the court of a barbarian king," Antonius said sharply. "They are cowards."

Severus turned to Antonius with a sly smirk. "Of course."

Orephes could tell that was a hollow reply. Severus simply didn't want to debate with Antonius on the matter, but he clearly knew things that the two knights didn't. "So, what else can I do for the two of you? I don't suppose Eschelus sent the two of you all the way here simply to hand me this small letter."

"We are looking for a way to travel to Greece," Orephes answered. "Eschelus mentioned that you might have a ship that we can use for the journey."

Severus sat back. "I haven't had a ship in years. Sold most of them off to pay for added soldiers around my home. I am not sure if you realized, but this neighborhood isn't exactly what it used to be. A product of me not being friends with Odoacer's appointed consul…" Severus seemed to be trailing off again before remembering the topic at hand. "Unfortunately, I can't help you there. Even if I had a ship, it wouldn't be the kind that could get you far. Not in these waters anymore. Vandal raiding ships have infested nearly the entire sea."

Knowing that they had no other connections in Rome, suddenly Orephes's journey seemed much more difficult. He was sure they didn't have enough money to pay for travel, and their little knight coin could likely get them only so far. Perhaps he had been foolish for expecting that his trip would go much farther than Rome itself. Perhaps Eschelus had known this already, and simply sent him off to help Antonius deliver the letter.

"Thank you for all of your help, Senator," Antonius said, standing up and placing his hand on Orephes's shoulder. It was his cue to stand and begin to depart, as well. Severus was looking right at Orephes, as though he was reading his face again.

"What is in Greece?" he asked curiously. "Another mission for Eschelus?"

"No," Orephes replied. "This one had been for me."

"That is a far journey. And a dangerous one. People don't travel that far for just any purpose. Not in these days."

Orephes saw Antonius was eager to leave but instead turned back to face the senator. Antonius had lied to him. He could wait. He hesitated for a moment in telling the truth, but something about the senator in that moment made him decide to explain himself.

"My father, on his deathbed, told me that I wasn't his son. That I had been left at his home by a group of travelers."

Severus sat forward, visibly interested. "My," Severus said after a moment. "That is certainly news."

"I am traveling east to find my true family. My ancestors. To understand where I come from."

"You may not be your father's son," Severus said with a laugh, "but you certainly sound like him with all this ancestor talk. And those crazy myth stories he loved to tell about the Old Gods. Do you believe in those things, too?" Orephes stood silently. His father has always taught him to deny. It was safer for them in a world of Christianity to pretend they believed in the one true God. Severus smiled and nodded at the silence. "Smart boy. So, tell me, why do you think your family is in the east?"

"My father mentioned that is where the travelers came from. That is all I know about them."

"People traveling west back then were either criminals or barbarians. It is likely whoever you are looking for is already gone."

"I still have to try. Everything I believe is based on where I came from. Who my ancestors were."

"I can't help you." Severus looked at Antonius for a moment, as though he knew that what he was about to say was going to upset him. "But I know someone who can."

IX

The senator saw the two young soldiers off, explaining that the planned route by sea to Constantinople, then northwards towards Greece, would be far safer than attempting to dock in Greece or traveling by land the same distance. As the two young men departed his home, Severus took another moment to look at the state of the city surrounding him. The decay, morally and intellectually, that was plaguing this new world reached far and wide. Yet here he lived in the center of it.

Of course, the announcement to house the Heruli tribe in his area of the city didn't come as a surprise. Senators were always playing politics, and when his top rival for influence became consul, he knew he was likely to find himself in several unfavorable situations. He was lucky that his home itself wasn't given away as part of the peace package.

Once he was back inside, he took a look at the scroll Antonius had given him, though he already knew what it was going to say. There it was, spelled out in black and white, that Eschelus was coming for Rome. To "reclaim" it, as it were, from the barbarian invaders.

The senators had different names for Eschelus. Some called him the Emperor in the North. Others called him the usurper. However, they were all in agreement on one major aspect—the fact that none of them knew if they wanted him to come or not.

He only needed to look at the stack of coins on the desk near him to understand why. Engraved at the bottom of each gold coin were the words *senatus consultum,* something that hadn't been printed on a Roman coin since the Republic era hundreds of years prior. The fact was that the Senate today was in a better position than it had been under the emperors of twenty years ago. Whether the barbarian king Odoacer wanted to admit it or not, he needed them to both keep control of and manage his territory. He was a man of conquest, not of governance.

Antonius's thoughts on Romans becoming advisors to barbarians amused Severus, if only for the fact that the entire Roman Senate had, in all technicality, been reduced to this very thing. Yet in that state, they had more power than they had had for centuries.

There was one senator, however, who was benefitting the most from this arrangement. He needed only to remember the fateful aftermath of the last siege of Rome to understand why.

*   *   *

476 A.D., Seventeen Years Prior
Rome

The senators stood nervously in the chambers, trying hard to conceal their anxiety. They were entirely aware of the situation at hand and their power—indeed, Roman power—hung in the balance. Severus had been a few minutes late, as he had been taking care of some business and ensuring that those he held dear were informed about what had transpired in the capital.

"We must find someone, anyone, who can rid us of this barbarian plague!" shouted a senator from across the hall. Several shouted back inaudibly over some applause.

"There is nobody. We have no armies, no gold. Would you like to fight yourself?" another shouted as the furor died down, reigniting the feud.

"Come now, you can't be so shortsighted," said a man calmly from the entrance of the hall. It was Caecina Basilius, senator and esteemed member of the Decii family. He and Severus had never gotten along, primarily due to competing interests, but considering the circumstances, there was no sense to bringing in feuds that were out of place. "How many emperors and usurpers have come through those very doors before today? Dare I say dozens? What they have all had in common is an insatiable hunger for power that is quenched by their ascension to the emperorship."

"You are suggesting we should allow a *barbarian* with neither Roman blood nor claim to become our emperor, Caecina?" another senator asked in outrage.

"I am suggesting that we preserve our influence," Caecina continued. "If this barbarian soldier bounds in here and declares himself king, throwing off all vestiges of Roman authority, where does that leave our power? Where does that leave our wealth, and our families?" The room of boisterous senators fell silent. Even Severus himself listened intently to what Caecina had to say. "We will announce our intentions to make him emperor when he arrives, just as we have done in the past. He will accept, as they all do, and we will retain our authority through this…emperor. He is more Roman than barbarian in all but blood. Had he not been a faithful servant as *magister militum* for years? This is a unique opportunity. He will easily fall beneath our tutelage. This isn't about throwing Rome away, gentlemen, it is about preserving it. Preserving our way of life."

"Always the pragmatist, Caecina," Severus replied. "And suppose he walks into the chambers swords drawn, and decides to slaughter us all?"

The other senators were silent, clearly not having wanted to think—let alone discuss—that scenario.

"Then God help us all," Caecina replied.

A eunuch in typical senatorial robes stepped into the Senate chambers, hurrying to the center as the senators stopped their debate.

"He's here," the eunuch said calmly, before bowing and heading back out toward the door. He didn't make it back through the arches before several soldiers, some in Roman armor, marched into the chambers, blocking his exit. A decorated soldier stepped through the door last.

Odoacer, the infamous barbarian *magister militum*—commander-in-chief of the mercenary Roman army—who also happened to be chieftain of the Heruli barbarian horde.

Some of them had met the man in the past. That he had been such a high-ranking Roman soldier lent itself to several senatorial invitations. They knew him to be crass but shrewd, a spectacular general and man of the people, even if he could come off as rude and brazen to the typical Roman. They weren't surprised—he was, after all, a barbarian.

He stepped into the chambers quickly, without paying homage to the senators surrounding him as was tradition. His magnificent armor—Roman and Praetorian-like—seemed out of place compared to the ragtag soldiers surrounding him. It clanked as he stepped into the center of the senatorial chambers, his left arm resting on his sword and his right scratching his beard.

"Well, look at you robed bastards," Odoacer blurted out, seeming to be in high spirits. He glanced around and noticed, aside from the clanking of his soldiers, the utter silence. "Well, you all act like you have seen a ghost." His Latin was excellent given his background. Only a barely noticeable accent panged through certain words.

"Just a ghost of our great civilization," a senator shouted from the back. There were murmurs, but Severus sat nervously as so many armed soldiers stood only feet away. Upsetting Odoacer was not something he wanted to do. To his surprise, Odoacer just laughed.

"Cheeky," he said, his scruff voice echoing through the halls.

Severus couldn't figure out why Caecina hadn't yet mentioned his plan. His silence was deafening.

"Odoacer," another senator finally said, stepping up to the plate, "your armies are numerous and have conquered vast land. Having been the leader of our armies, you understand our system the same as any of our great emperors. We believe you can be a valuable leader in these dark times."

"Let's be frank, gentlemen, you don't have much of a choice," Odoacer said abruptly.

"You make it sound as though we have no say, Odoacer," Severus said, finally standing. "You do realize that we are the Roman Senate?"

Odoacer joined his soldiers in a laugh. "You barely had any power when your emperor was here," Odoacer blurted. "You have even less now."

"Power can sometimes be indirect. Subtle, not that you would know much about that. It would be in your best interest to work with us. Within the ranks of our Senate are the wealthiest families in Rome. Grain traders, property owners, weapons manufacturers."

"Enough money, debtors, and slaves combined to fund a small army for a very long time," another senator added.

While Verengi hadn't wanted to say it, he was happy another senator did. The Senate didn't have any real authority under the emperors. But in the face of a foreign usurper, the wealth that the senators could bring to the table could make or break Odoacer's reign—or any insurgency against it.

"The people of Rome and, indeed, the people of all of our lands could bow to you, Odoacer. But they will bow to you more easily, more safely, and wealthier, with our blessing. Emperors with the blessing of the Senate are believed to have the will of the people. Being blessed by the Senate gives you blessing by our Holy Father the Pope. You will not have just their respect—you will have their admiration. You will have their love."

Odoacer looked Severus in the eyes, the smile having run off his face. "You don't think I can gain the love and admiration of the people on my own, Senator?"

"You can," Severus continued. "Surely, you can. But why worry about earning it when you can get it granted to you in one vote?" Caecina, the mastermind of this plan, was still stunningly silent. "We, the Senate of Rome, would like to bestow upon you the honor of becoming the next emperor of Rome."

"You would make me emperor, though I have barbarian blood?" Odoacer asked, seeming surprised.

"Times have changed," Severus replied. He couldn't believe that Caecina had not taken this opportunity to ingratiate himself to who would soon be the new emperor. It wasn't like him to fade into the background; particularly not when there was favor to be gained.

"I have no desire to be your emperor," Odoacer said firmly, shattering the conversation with a surprising turn. Verengi hadn't been expecting this response. Most of the senators weren't.

"You overthrew Emperor Romulus with no wish to replace him? Why?" Verengi grew aggravated. "You brought this empire to its knees, and for what? For your own enjoyment?"

"I didn't bring your empire to its knees," Odoacer replied angrily. "Your empire was brought to its knees by greed, by weakness. You claim to fight the barbarian tribes yet you pay them to fight for you. Your emperors fight among themselves for power, each one killing the one before. Do you think I want to sit on that throne for a few months before some new Roman with a desire for standing before the people in a damn circus decides that it is time for my reign to come to an end? Or the next barbarian warlord decides that Rome hasn't paid its dues?"

"So then decline," Caecina finally chimed in. He stood and joined Verengi in front of Odoacer. "You can rule what you have gained without becoming emperor."

"Caecina, are you mad?" Verengi whispered, seeing Caecina's statement as not merely an admission of defeat, but a tacit acceptance of a collapse of their power.

"You marched your armies here not with the purpose of overthrowing anyone," Caecina continued. "You are not Roman by blood, but you are Roman by heart. You merely seek to live the life you see before you, something we can all relate to in these chambers. You were betrayed by a listless emperor and his father when all you wanted was what every other mercenary tribe that served Rome has received: a home. In the absence of an emperor, this body is willing to grant you that wish."

"What is your name, Senator," Odoacer asked, his interest piqued. Caecina replied proudly. "What are you offering?"

"You wanted a home for your people, and we, as the Senate of Rome, will grant you this just as the Goths have gained in Hispania and others elsewhere. You can rule over Italy as king of your people and the Romans, serving independently under our emperor. This land shall become yours. All we ask in return is to retain our influence as the Senate of Rome, representatives of the emperor and the people, to serve alongside you in ruling our people. Also, we ask that the Roman population be treated as well as your own."

"I like the way you think, Senator." Odoacer stroked his beard as he paced back and forth in the Senate chambers. After several moments, he stopped and looked at Caecina. "And what of the emperor in Constantinople? Will he not object?"

"If you do not claim to be his equal, he will not object. And the Senate? How do we vote?" Caecina asked.

"Aye," the body replied overwhelmingly. Severus stood silently and abstained, shocked at Caecina's cunning ability to wait until the proper moment to interject.

"Then it is settled," Odoacer said jubilantly. He turned to his soldiers who had been waiting patiently. "Our fighting has not been wasted, friends. We shall have a new rightful home and wealth here on Roman soil!"

His troops cheered and clanked their swords to their shield and armor. The Senate was visibly taken aback by the racket; they were used to the quiet bickering of politicians. Odoacer turned back to face the two senators, who had started to walk away.

"My first order is to send the Imperial seal to Constantinople and declare the dual emperorship at an end."

The Senate murmured, somewhat surprised by his decision. Declaring himself king was far different than ending the western emperorship entirely. Depending on the response from Emperor Zeno in the east, this could mean that Rome would once again be led by just one emperor, unified under the banner of the East. Had

Caecina planned this all along, and merely used asking Odoacer to be the emperor as a distraction? Severus continued back to his seat, recognizing that it was now Caecina's show to run.

"The emperor in Constantinople shall henceforth be the sole sovereign of this empire," Odoacer continued. "State in the message that I seek to rule Italy beneath his lordship. Your Roman subjects shall be treated fairly."

"Hail Odoacer, king of Italy!" a soldier shouted. His armies joined in the calls, shouting *Rex Italium* as Odoacerleft the senators to their business, not bothering to bow as he left.

As Odoacer left the chambers, the senators dissipated to discuss the events that had just transpired. Severus approached Caecina as he was leaving, forcefully grasping his shoulder.

"Caecina, do you have any idea what you have just done?" he asked.

"Certainly, Severus," Caecina smirked. "I just saved our legacy."

Severus left the Curia in a fit of fury. Caecina had played not only the Senate but also Odoacer and somehow come out ahead and in the new king's favor, even despite the fact that his little interjection had changed the face of the empire forever. Truthfully, his anger was less about honorable intentions and more about pure jealousy. That was favor he could have won.

X

Orephes and Antonius arrived at the location Severus had given them on the small parchment. It was in the middle of the great market, one of the most populated areas of the city. The building itself was run-down, and far from the opulence they were expecting of a ship owner. They heard laughing from inside. People were enjoying themselves in there. Antonius looked up at the sign above the door—Lupanar.

"It's a whorehouse," Antonius said, disgusted. "This can't be right."

"According to Severus, this is where he will be." Orephes spoke tersely to his friend. He felt betrayed. He had been used. He had known the entire time where Orephes was going—Eschelus had told him. He had sent him along only to send that stupid letter. He didn't deserve the courtesy of long responses anymore.

As they entered, they were surprised that the *lena*—the female head of the brothel—didn't seem to try to sell them on any of her wares. Instead, she just looked up from the parchment in front of her and rolled her eyes.

"Looking for Marius, I assume?" she asked. That was the name of their contact. She seemed annoyed.

"How did you know?" Orephes asked curiously.

"You are probably the fifth person who has come in here asking about him," she answered. "Besides, nobody comes in here dressed like they are preparing for war. People come in here to fuck." She signaled for the men to follow and they obliged. As they stepped deeper into that pit of fornication, the smell became increasingly heavy. The scent of the seed of hundreds of men and the sweat of sex lingered in the halls like the smoke of a fittingly malodorous candle, the product of a muted flame that ignites briefly between the whores and their clients before being abruptly put out by the sting of reality and money. The sounds grew equally thick, as the rooms, separated from each other and the hall merely with curtains, were live with customers.

"The poor bastard probably hasn't even gotten his cock wet yet with all these interruptions," the *lena* added crudely.

"I'm sure he will be back," Antonius replied. The three approached a curtained room where the sound of a man and woman laughing could be heard over the sound of what Orephes thought was a hand slapping another person's flesh.

"Some of the girls like to get spanked," the *lena* said. "They tend not to charge for that sort of thing. It makes it fun." The *lena* gave Antonius a smirk. "I give discounts for men in armor. Half price."

"No thank you," Antonius replied without even looking at her. The *lena* seemed disappointed.

"Hmm. Didn't seem like I was your type." She cast a glance at Orephes before looking back at Antonius. "Pity. You are handsome. I'd like to see if the flesh matches the bronze." She ran her finger along the sculpted abs of his bronze armor plate before finally stepping to the side. "He's in here."

Orephes peeled back the curtain to see Marius, still clothed, lying on a stone bed that had been covered in sheets. He was probably in his early forties, his hair slightly graying but worn well. He had a rugged demeanor but a charming smile that was plastered on his face as they walked in. The prostitute was straddling him, and his hands were planted firmly upon her behind. As the curtain flew open, neither Marius nor the prostitute moved, but both turned to look at the intrusion.

"I don't remember asking for company but the more the merrier," Marius joked.

"Joanna is one of our best," the *lena* said proudly. "They always keep coming back for her."

"Can I get two fucking minutes with my whore please, or do I need to pay extra for continuous time? Can't you screen my visitors or something?" Marius whined.

"I'll leave you all alone. I have customers to attend to," the *lena* said as she walked back to the front.

Then, there was silence. Until it was broken by Marius.

"Well, can I help you gentlemen? Or did you pay to watch me fuck this lovely woman?"

"My name is Orephes. Senator Severus Verengi told me that you could help us. He said you had a boat."

"And it required you interrupting *this*," Marius said angrily, eyeing Joanna up and down. He released the prostitute, who stood up and walked backward away from him. She ran her hair behind her ears and Orephes could see how beautiful she was. Her skin was dark, like the people from Anatolia. Her eyes seemed tired and worn. She smiled at the two men, but it was hollow. A projection of a smile that she once used to wear.

"We can pay you." Orephes tapped a satchel on his hip. There was a slight jingle. "Handsomely." His eyes lit up.

"Sorry, sweetie.. Business, and all," Marius said as he sat up. The prostitute stood but didn't leave, holding her hand out in front of him.

"Payment?" she asked politely.

"I don't pay you to keep me company. I pay you to fuck, and if my cock is any indication it appears that didn't happen," Marius answered, going to leave the room.

"That's not my fault," she said firmly, "you are the one who had all the visitors. I spent time on you that I could have been spending on other clients. You cost me money."

"Shouldn't you be enjoying the precious time we had not having sex?" Marius retorted. "Hell, you should be paying me. It was like a vacation for you."

"You're not leaving without payment," Joanna said, walking in front of Marius to block him.

"You don't want to try that. I am good with two things: my cock"—Marius pulled out a knife—"and my knives. And since the first one is clearly not getting used today I should be even better with the second."

Joanna quickly kicked Marius's knee, knocking him over and giving her the opportunity to grab his knife, which she quickly held up to his groin.

"You can either pay in gold or pay in testicles," she said. "Your choice."

"I like her," Antonius said with a smile.

"All right, all right. Gold it is," Marius said. "I don't have any on me. It's all on my ship. These gentlemen want to go there anyway. I will bring you some when I return."

"No," Joanna said, keeping the knife at his groin. "I'll come with you. Do you really think I trust you to come back?"

"I didn't even come this time," he whined back.

"I am coming with you to your boat, and I will leave with my money."

"Fine, fine," Marius said quickly. "Can you please remove that knife?"

Joanna dropped the knife on the ground and gave a much more genuine smile this time.

"Good."

The trio walked out past the *lena*, who was just seeing another customer out of the building.

"Joanna, where are you going?"

"To get my money," she answered firmly.

The *lena* gave Marius a resigned look.

"How many times before you learn your lesson? Eventually none of my girls will want to fuck you, no matter how much you claim you are willing to pay."

"There are plenty of whorehouses in Rome," Marius said, not even bothering to stop. As they stepped outside Orephes got a better look at Joanna. Her wrists were calloused and scarred, standing out among the soft beauty of the rest of her body.

"Where are you from, Joanna?" Orephes asked, breaking the awkward silence. She turned her head toward him with an eyebrow raised, as though it was strange for Orephes to ask such a thing. "What is it?"

"Why do you want to know?"

"I guess I don't," Orephes replied, continuing to walk stoically in silence.

After a few moments, Joanna broke. "I left home when I was very young to start a new life here in Rome. My family was from Greece. They were poor farmers. This was the city of opportunity."

"It still is, if you know where to look," Marius interjected. He continued to navigate them throughout the large streets and narrow alleys that was the city of Rome until they had reached the harbor. Antonius seemed unimpressed, but to Orephes, it was like seeing an entire world that he hadn't known before.

The ships seemed so elegant, and he envied those who got to ride on them across the sea to whatever awaited in Africa. He had learned some about how they worked from Tiberius. Seeing them up close was something entirely different.

The traders and merchants hustling about in the harbor felt so full of life. Back home, you could feel the weight of Rome's fall on your shoulders. Here, it was as though nothing had changed at all.

"There are so many," Orephes commented.

"You should have seen it twenty years ago," Marius said. For the first time since they had met him, Marius sounded something other than sarcastic or petulant. His voice carried a sort of lament as he described how many ships used to dock here, and how every year fewer and fewer docked.

"Well, it still looks impressive to me," Orephes responded.

"Where is yours?" Antonius asked impatiently.

"Patience is a virtue of every good Roman," Marius chided sarcastically. He brought them down to a dock near the end of the harbor. A small galley was tied to the end, bobbing back and forth. The sail was worn and torn, and the wood was splintering and rotting along the hull.

"There she is," Marius said proudly, placing his hands at his hips. "The *Nero*."

"I don't know much about boats," Antonius said, holding back a smile, "but that certainly looks like one that has seen better days."

"Nonsense. You won't find a better vessel in this harbor," Marius assured him. "This thing has traveled all around the Mediterranean and even to the east of Egypt and back. It even survived being caught between two warring triremes without a scratch."

"I would say it certainly has a few scratches," Joanna added snidely.

"Merely love marks is all." Marius excitedly made his way to the end of the dock, where he then hopped into the creaking boat. The wood seemed to bend under his feet as he took his first few steps, seeming to savor being back on board. He turned to face the remaining members of the group. "Well? What are you all waiting for?"

"Making sure the boat doesn't disintegrate before we hop on board," Joanna answered before hopping aboard herself.

Orephes was going to follow before he noticed Antonius seeming detached behind him. "Antonius, are you coming?"

"We can't go," he replied calmly. "We have to go back to the villa."

Orephes stopped in his tracks.

"What do you mean?" Orephes grew from surprised to angry. "What the hell do you mean? This is the entire reason we came here."

Antonius stood stoically, seemingly holding something back. "We have to go back. That is your home—do you not care?"

"You know as well as I do that the reason we are traveling east is precisely *because* that villa is no longer my home. What is all of this?"

Orephes stepped back from the edge of the boat and approached the silent Antonius. "Damn it, Antonius, answer me!"

"Eschelus never meant to allow you to actually head east, Orephes," Antonius finally blurted. "He wanted me to get to Rome and deliver the message to Senator Severus. Afterward, I was to bring you home."

"That can't be. You must have misheard the orders. He was the one who told me to ask Severus for transport," Orephes mentioned, stunned.

"Because he knew Severus had no ships," Antonius answered. "Finding this fool was never part of the plan."

"Did he just call me a fool?" Marius shouted from the boat.

The pair of soldiers ignored him. Orephes felt betrayed for a moment, but he wasn't surprised. Eschelus cared about one thing and one thing only: his planned "liberation" of Rome. Anything that stood in the way of that was deemed an inconvenience, or worse, a threat.

"I should have known he would never have invested months of training in me just to let me go," Orephes finally said, shaking his head. "And what if I refuse to go?"

Antonius hesitated for a brief moment. Though not as long as he should have given the answer. "Then you will be a deserter, and I am to bring your corpse back to the army for proper burial."

Orephes stood silently for a moment, staring his friend in the eyes. Antonius's hand was not on his sword. His face was stern but not aggressive. There was a small amount of sweat on his forehead. He wasn't going to kill him, no matter what the orders had been. He couldn't. And even if he had been planning to, Orephes wouldn't have exactly gone down without a fight.

"I am staying on this boat. You can either come with me or return to Eschelus empty-handed." Before he turned away, he saw the conflict on Antonius's face. His brow seemed to twitch between stern and confused. His eyes went wide. His mouth was slightly agape. He wasn't ready for this. He hadn't thought it would be necessary.

Orephes hopped onto the boat to find Marius coming up from belowdecks.

"What is he doing?" Marius asked, facing Antonius still on the dock.

"He is staying behind."

"It will still be the same price for just one of you."

"I don't care."

Marius smirked.

Orephes noticed for the first time he was holding a small box in his hands that he had brought from belowdecks. Joanna approached the pair as he opened it. Inside was plenty of gold. Likely enough to have bought a better ship if he had wanted.

"Thank God," Marius whispered as he took a look. He seemed excited to see it, as though he had half expected it not to be there.

"Thank God for what?" Joanna hissed, "You have the strength to open your own money box?"

"Marius!" a voice suddenly boomed from across the dock. "Marius, you cunt!"

"Fuck," Marius squeaked out worriedly. He quickly shut the box and placed it on the ground.

"Who is that?" Orephes asked.

"That's the owner of the boat."

"I thought this was your boat?"

"It was before that son of a bitch took it. We need to get out of here. He isn't going to be happy to see me."

A group of angry-looking Romans was quickly heading their way, swords drawn. They didn't look like they wanted to talk. Orephes was going to ask who they were and what they wanted, but frankly, in this moment it didn't matter. He would have to figure out what was going on later. The entire group was implicated now, and it didn't look like they were going to be willing to hear Orephes's explanation as to how they got there. Orephes saw Antonius on the dock, watching the incoming gang.

"Antonius, get over here! They will kill you."

Antonius drew his sword as the men moved closer but hesitated in moving toward the boat.

"Antonius!"

As the first few men reached the dock, Antonius came to his senses and made a mad dash for the boat. He leaped on board and cut the rope behind him, detaching the vessel from the harbor.

"We need to get moving," Antonius shouted as he landed on board. Marius had been at the sail and had finally got it ready. As it opened, the dozens of holes and tears in it became even more apparent. Marius stopped for a moment and stared at it angrily.

"That bastard added another hole!"

"Marius, we need to leave," Orephes said worriedly. The boat had moved a few feet from the dock, but some of the men were attempting to get on board from the water. Antonius had grabbed an oar and started whacking them as they emerged.

Marius grabbed the boom of the sail and turned it in the direction of the wind. Almost immediately, the boat started to move quickly away from the shore. Orephes was frankly surprised that the sail could even still pick up the wind with the amounts of holes in it.

A thud on the far side of the ship caught everyone's attention. One of them had made it on board, soaking wet with sword in hand. Marius turned his attention from the sail to the armed thug on his boat.

"Anthemius. Long time no see."

"Eudoc is going to kill you for this, Marius. You realize you can never show your face in Rome again? Stealing his ship? Have you gone mad?"

"Technically I am stealing *my* ship," Marius retorted.

Antonius and Orephes each drew their swords and approached him. Before they could make it, Joanna emerged seemingly from nowhere and shoved Anthemius off the boat. Orephes had forgotten she was still on board, and by Antonius's and Marius's surprised smiles, they apparently had, as well.

As the coast and the group of thugs disappeared into the distance, the four shipmates took a moment to have a good look at each other. It seemed all at once that they came to the realization that they were stuck together. Antonius wasted no time breaking the ice, changing the direction of his sword toward Marius.

"Your explanation better suffice," he hissed angrily.

Marius raised his hands slightly, attempting to show he meant no harm. "This was my ship. Had been for years. A few weeks ago, this son of a bitch took it from me."

"How exactly did he just *take* your ship?"

"Well, it is a bit complicated, but ultimately it was the result of a slight feud from some of the horse races in Constantinople—"

"So, you lost it in a bet, most likely fair and square," Antonius said cutting Marius off, "and then you used us to help you steal it back."

"I wouldn't exactly call a bet with the most powerful crime lord in the empire *fair*, particularly when he was already rather upset at me."

"Angry? At *you*? I can't imagine why." Antonius finally lowered his sword, but didn't look any less angry at the situation. "I'm not sure what you were looking to gain from all this. Yes, you got your atrocious ship back, but you can never go back to Rome again."

"I was planning on leaving for good anyway. In fact, this beautiful young woman was going to be my final pleasure in Rome before I departed." He motioned at Joanna, who rolled her eyes. "You gentlemen are lucky you found me when you did. A few more hours and I might have already been gone."

"Yes, well, this beautiful young woman wants her pay and wants to go home," Joanna added. "So never returning to Rome isn't exactly acceptable. Now that you have wasted even more of my time, I should be charging you even more."

"Next time we stop, you can take a boat right back to Rome. There are likely dozens of sailors willing to get you home. For a price."

Orephes had stopped paying any mind to the bickering. He briefly touched his satchel to ensure that the amulet was still inside. He felt its metal outline; it was there.

He was staring out over the bow of the ship toward the seemingly endless sea, the breeze blowing through his hair like a fine comb. The air was salty and unlike anything he had felt before. To the rest of them, who had seen this before, hundreds of times, this may have just been another boat ride. To him, this was the experience of a lifetime.

XI

Chalcedon Estate, Diocese of Gaul

Gargarus was at the end of the table leaning forward, his eyes fixated upon a crater in the marble rather than on his guests. The chatter of the people at the table around him all seemed to blend together into a mindless hum. His glass of wine was empty for the third time this sitting. Everyone else's was full—and had been all night.

"Gargarus, what are your thoughts on this?" he finally heard as he refocused.

"On what?" he asked, disinterested.

"Have you not been listening?" It was a woman's voice.

He looked up finally to see Almeida, the wife of a recently deceased friend, facing him as the rest of the table went silent. "Perhaps you should partake less in that awful wine and more in the affairs of your estate."

Gargarus laughed and shook his head. "You are free to leave this estate any time."

"Do you not care about anything, Gargarus? About the increasing frequency of the raids? About the fact that as soon as Eschelus leaves, as he promises he will, we will be defenseless?"

Gargarus looked her in the eyes. "Where is your son to help defend the villa, hmm? Where is he to help build the fortifications?"

"Don't you speak ill of my son," she shot back, shocked at the accusation.

"Speak ill?" Gargarus stood up and leaned forward toward her. "Your son is a traitor. Your son is a coward. He couldn't handle the fight so he decided to go be the barbarian king's bitch. In fact"—Gargarus looked around—"where are all of your children? Where have they gone? They became of age to fight and happened to disappear off the face of the Earth?"

"Our children did what they had to do to preserve our family legacies and survive," one man spoke up. "There is no shame in that."

"There is no shame in joining the court of a barbarian king? Perhaps we should just surrender and make it easy for all of us!"

There were a few moments of precious silence before Almeida spoke again. "Where is your brother, then?"

Gargarus smacked his glass off the table.

"Get out. All of you!"

Slowly everyone began to stand and depart the table, a few muttering to each other under their breath. Soon the room was empty except for one man standing up against the back wall.

"That means everyone," Gargarus repeated. He looked up and saw Eschelus leaning against the wall, his eyes beaming with displeasure. Gargarus sat back and relaxed. "I didn't realize it was you back there. I wasn't sure you were back yet."

"She's right, you know," Eschelus started, stepping forward toward his friend. "I will not be around much longer. We are almost finished gathering forces from around Gaul."

"I know. That is what scares me."

"I can leave a small contingent force, but it will only be enough to keep the peace around here. You will be defenseless."

"What exactly do you propose I do about it?" Gargarus stood, picking up his goblet off the ground to get more wine.

"You need to abandon this property, come with my army south to Italy, and carve out a new home for yourself there once we kick out those damned barbarians."

"I made a promise to my dying father that I would never abandon our home," Gargarus answered firmly. "I will die here."

"And you would doom these people to die with you?"

"They are free citizens. They can do as they please."

Eschelus grunted. "Free. What a silly word to use today. Those people respect you, Gargarus. Hell if I know why, but they will stay here if you do. And they will die."

Gargarus had filled his goblet with wine, but Eschelus took it from him before he could drink. Gargarus ran his hand through his hair, showing the faintest amounts of grays that had developed since he took over.

"Why did you let Orephes leave?" Gargarus asked quietly. "What good could possibly have come from that?"

"Antonius will bring him back, Gargarus," Eschelus assured him. "He has orders."

"Is that why you have been preparing to find two more knights? Because you are so confident they will return?"

"I have to plan for every scenario. I have a war to win. You should be doing the same thing." The two men stood silently until Gargarus finally started to leave the room.

"Was your most recent run successful?"

"No," Eschelus answered, following him out. "It is getting more and more difficult to find intact villages. The barbarians are getting more aggressive, and the native Roman populations are declining quickly. There isn't much time left."

"You have already gathered thousands. Surely you have enough?"

"You haven't seen the army that this Odoacer can gather. It won't be enough."

The two men continued their discussion as they walked with purpose throughout the property. Gargarus still couldn't believe it every time he looked out on the horizon and saw thousands of

Roman soldiers. He told himself that this is what it must have felt like to be alive centuries ago, at Rome's peak when armies were commonplace around Gaul.

They stopped as they reached Gargarus's wife and daughter, who were outside in the garden. His daughter was the first to notice him.

"Daddy!" she shouted, running at him and grabbing his legs.

"I'll leave you to your family," Eschelus said gently. "Let's discuss more later."

"Mara, sweetheart," Castella said softly, "leave your father be."

"It's fine," Gargarus replied, picking Mara up into his arms. "Eschelus was just heading back outside the walls to his camp."

Castella waited a few moments until Eschelus was out of earshot.

"Any word yet on when he is leaving?"

"Soon. That is all I know."

"I heard a few of the others walking back from your meeting. They said you weren't very happy."

"I don't remember the last time I truly was."

"You have Mara and me," Castella chided, holding her husband's face. "That is more than some have."

Gargarus held his wife back, running his hand through her hair. He stopped at the scar that went across the top of her head. The hair had grown in around it but never back on the wound itself. He knew how much it still hurt her, particularly in the cold weather. Castella pulled away from him.

"You know that I hate it when you touch that," she said angrily.

"Imperfections are what make us beautiful."

"Ah, then I have truly married the most beautiful man in Gaul," Castella replied with a smirk.

"Indeed."

"Every time I see or touch your scar, I hate myself for not killing that son of a bitch when I had the chance."

"He is surely dead by now," Castella assured him. "It doesn't matter, anyway. I am here now. With you." Castella kissed him and grabbed Mara from his arms. "Come, Mara. Let's go eat. You must be starving."

"I want to be a knight like Orephes!" Mara said to her father, swinging her arm around wildly as though she had a sword.

Gargarus laughed. "You may want to be a knight, but not like Orephes," he answered, rubbing her head.

"Is he coming back?" Castella asked worriedly.

"I don't know." Castella shook her head.

"He is such a fool for going out there alone." Castella carried Mara back into the home, leaving Gargarus alone with his thoughts.

Sometimes the scar on his wife's head made him wonder if he and Eschelus were truly on the right side. If the world that could damage something so beautiful—the world that labeled her as nothing more than a piece of property—was worth returning to.

Gargarus was angry at Orephes. Not just for leaving, but for leaving him alone. The burden of running this estate should have been theirs to share. Instead, it was his alone. It was a burden he hadn't been prepared for. Every day that passed was one day closer to the inevitable departure of the defending army at his doorstep, and one day closer to the Goths breaking down his walls. He wanted to prepare, but privately he knew there was truly nothing he could do.

They would come. When they did, they would destroy this villa. But he would die defending it.

XII

Chalcedon Estate, Diocese of Gaul

Eschelus and his knights were gathered in the dim candlelight, the moon's light creeping through the windows. They were alone. He had been sure to find an area where neither the soldiers nor Gargarus's residents frequented. It was a small marble building outside the walls, built as a small guardhouse in the centuries when Roman aristocrats had frequent guests and required such frivolity.

"What is this about?" Michael asked worriedly. "This is an odd time for a meeting."

"It is urgent," Eschelus answered curtly.

"It this about Antonius and Orephes?" Bracchus asked.

"Partly. There is something else." For the first time in years, Eschelus seemed uncomfortable around his comrades. They had been through everything together, but he wasn't sure he could prepare them for this. "Antonius and Orephes may return, but we do not have time to wait. We have exhausted all resources in finding fellow Romans across Gaul. Our army will not be growing any larger. The time has come to strike."

"We don't have nearly enough men to even think of taking Rome," Michael interjected worriedly. "What about up north? Soissons?"

"It fell years ago. We will have no armies from them."

"They were good Romans up there," Bracchus lamented. "We can't even think about heading south with an army this size. We won't make it halfway there."

"I know. Which is why I have made arrangements. I have been in contact with some allies from the east. If we are going to take back our city, we shall do it alongside their forces. It is the only way."

"Who are these allies?" Michael asked suspiciously.

"You will get to see for yourself. Tonight. We are going to ride to meet them. Just us four."

Roman, Michael, and Bracchus looked at each other before looking back at their leader.

"We trust you," Roman said finally, "but this doesn't seem right. Not to mention that traveling at night is near suicide."

"Some things are best kept among close friends. I trust that the four greatest knights that have ever lived can handle any raiding parties, don't you?"

The four knights boarded their horses that had been tethered out-side and headed out into the night road, torches in one hand and reins in the other. The sounds of the hooves striking the once magnificent roads interrupted the silent wall of darkness around them. The farther from the villa they went, the worse the roads seemed to become. Tree roots and broken stones replaced the solid, flat vein of commerce.

Finally, the knights saw a light beyond the trees in the distance. The amount of light was bright enough to be coming from the thou-sands of torches of an army. Eschelus began to slow down as they passed a single, dilapidated marble structure on their left.

"Almost there," he shouted.

The horses made it only a few more steps before several barbar-ian horses emerged from either side of the group, stopping them in their tracks. Immediately, almost as a reflex, the knights drew their swords and began entering formation.

"Stand down, knights!" Eschelus shouted, not having drawn his own sword.

"Sir, it is a raiding party!" Bracchus shot back.

"It's not a raiding party. It is a watch party monitoring their perimeter."

"Which means we are walking right into a barbarian army."

"Exactly."

The knights looked at each other before reluctantly sheathing their weapons.

"Eschelus," one of the barbarians said finally, "King Theodric has been expecting you."

"Take me to him."

The four knights were led by the perimeter force toward the torchlights in the distance.

"I don't like this," Michael whispered to Bracchus. "Keep your eyes open."

As they got past the tree line, the knights were led to a large village occupied by the barbarian army. It was alive with life, none of it Roman. Some of them in the village square were banging on drums while a few others danced around them. Women and children were with them as well, taking part in the festivities in the square. An old statue was still standing in the center, its head and arms removed and its body chipped and damaged. A barbarian soldier and his child were busily chipping away pieces of the feet.

One of the barbarian guardsmen, noting Michael's interest in the scene, slowed down to be next to him.

"For generations our people lived outside of a world where we could see marble and statues like this. Our people want to take pieces of it with them, as a piece of what their ancestors could never have."

Finally, they made it to King Theodric's "chambers," if they could be called that, where he and a few of his generals were sitting at a table that had a map displayed prominently at its head. Some of the generals hurriedly shut the map as the knights entered, standing abruptly at the intrusion. One or two were wearing Roman armor.

One in particular, who stayed seated as he eyed the knights up and down, looked particularly Roman.

"Ah, Eschelus," Theodric exclaimed, standing up and extending his arms. "Welcome. These must be your knights I have heard so much about."

"Theodric," Eschelus replied simply.

Theodric was tall, dark, and well put together. Unlike some of the other barbarian kings, he at the very least appeared clean. More importantly, particularly to Michael and Bracchus, he appeared earnest and trustworthy. His Latin was also near impeccable.

"I trust that you would like to take me up on the offer, then?"

"I think it would be prudent for us to combine our strength. We both want the same thing."

"That cunt Odoacer's head," Theodric muttered angrily.

"Returning Rome to its people," Eschelus corrected.

Theodric smiled. "Of course," he replied. "Emperor Zeno sent me west to reclaim Italy for the empire. You know this as well as I do."

"So far you have been unsuccessful."

"I underestimated Odoacer's strength. This is where your forces come into play. We are in a stalemate. The bastard wins a battle for every one he loses. Your forces can tip us over the edge."

"What do my forces and I get in return for helping your army complete its mission?"

"Rome back in the hands of the empire. Isn't that all you have ever wanted?"

"How will I know that it falling into your hands will be any different than Odoacer? He, after all, claims he is merely a governor."

Theodric approached the group of knights. "Let me be clear, Eschelus. I was sent directly by Emperor Zeno himself. Some of his very generals sit in this room beside me. This isn't some barbarian raiding force. I am acting on behalf of the emperor you so dearly claim to obey. There are no Roman armies that will come help. My army of Goths is what you have. If you are not my ally, you are nothing more than another usurper that Zeno will have me put down in due time."

"Zeno knows that I am no usurper."

"Does he? Then why has he not taken you to retake the capital? Why instead has he sent me, a measly barbarian king?"

As much as he hated to admit it, Eschelus was trapped. His end of the negotiation was limited at best. He didn't have an army large enough to take Odoacer alone, and even if he somehow managed, Theodric was waiting nearby to slip in to claim whatever was left. But the very fact that Theodric was willing to talk meant that Eschelus was not without his own bargaining chips.

"All right." Eschelus extended his hand. "Let us bring down this false king of Italy together. All I ask is that our armies be treated the same in the wake of the battle. That my men and their families get their rightful place back in Italy."

"Of course," Theodric replied. "Do you take me for a monster?" Theodric shook Eschelus's hand. "You have never been allied with a Goth before. We are brothers-in-arms now. All of us." He looked at the remaining knights behind Eschelus. "To my people, an alliance is not merely another treaty to be broken like it is to the Roman emperors. An alliance is how we grow our family."

"Well, that is reassuring," Michael murmured.

"Theodric," Eschelus started, "let us speak privately."

Theodric gave a slight nod and waved off his guards as he walked past the Roman knights.

The two men headed outside of the makeshift base alone. The two men were close in height, which was odd for a barbarian and Roman. Typically, Eschelus was far smaller than his beyond-the-walls counterparts. To him, it indicated that Theodric likely had some Roman in him, as well. How far back in his ancestry it went, he couldn't be sure. But it was there. He was sure of it.

"Let's take away all of the show for our men," Eschelus finally began as they were a few feet away from the camp. "What are you after in all of this?"

Theodric let out a wry smile and a knowing chuckle. "You are as savvy as my men had told me," he replied. "For a brief moment, I was worried that you bought into the servant of the emperor nonsense."

"I know better than that. Out here in the west, nobody is truly a servant of our emperor anymore."

"My men and I wanted nothing more than territory to settle in the east. Zeno, the stubborn bastard that he is, refused me despite me sending men to help him fight in several of his silly political squabbles. So, I threatened a few raids and he scrambled to find *something* to give me. He decided to give me the generous opportunity to take out another one of his uppity vassals in Italy. If I could take out Odoacer, I could have it."

"Pitting one troublesome barbarian vassal against another," Eschelus said, sounding impressed. "That is quite a plan. Even for an emperor."

"Odoacer is getting popular. Even among his court and the senate. He is desperate. Competition for the throne from a barbarian? What does that say of his reign? Luckily for him, I agreed. I knew what he was doing, but Odoacer's men are far less skilled and numerous than the legions in the east. If I was to claim territory by blood, it would be here."

"And if Zeno determines after you take Italy that you are a threat as well?"

"Then I figure that our two armies combined are more than enough to ward off an invasion."

Eschelus paused for a moment. "What are you suggesting?"

"Once Odoacer is gone, we will rule the West together as co-emperors. You as a Roman, I as a Goth. A symbol of a new era of Rome. One where barbarian and Roman no longer mean anything. We will all be citizens together and bring about a new Pax Romana."

Eschelus thought of the implications. It was a magnificent proposition, of course, but would ruling alongside a barbarian jeopardize his legitimacy in the East? With his own men?

"That is quite a dream," Eschelus replied. "However, you fail to acknowledge that the Roman Senate would prefer to be ruled by a Roman. They will side with my army, not yours."

"The Roman Senate already coexists peacefully with Odoacer. It is no longer new or unheard-of. We will rebuild Rome together."

Eschelus tried to maintain his stoic poker face. "What do you mean, coexist?"

"You haven't heard?" Theodric smiled again. "The Senate supports Odoacer. In fact, he named a senator as consul. Here"—Theodric flicked a coin at Eschelus, who caught it in midair—"take a look for yourself."

Eschelus looked closely at the inscription. *Senatus consultum* was engraved at the bottom—*by the consult of the Senate*. That hadn't been engraved on coins since the days of Augustus, long after the Senate ceased to have any real function.

Eschelus now started to run through possible scenarios in his mind. He had sent Orephes and Antonius south to Rome, anticipating that they would have allies there in the Senate. He hadn't yet heard back. He hadn't heard from Severus in months. Had he sent them to their deaths?

"The Senate that you had hoped would be backing you has abandoned you, Eschelus. If we are to defeat Odoacer, you have no choice but to work with me."

Unfortunately, without the backing of the Senate, it was true. Eschelus needed Theodric more than Theodric needed him. This hadn't been expected, and it certainly wasn't welcome.

Before Eschelus could answer, Theodric started up again. "A while back one of Odoacer's generals surrendered to me. He has been helping me as we have progressed southward. I already have other Roman generals at my disposal, so I would like to offer his services to you."

"I don't need it," Eschelus shot back, offended.

"You don't have a choice," Theodric admitted wryly. "It is part of my terms for us working together. You accept him and his escort, or you and your army can go at it alone." There were a few moments of silence. "You need him, Eschelus. He knows more about Odoacer's army than we can ever hope to know."

Eschelus wanted to scream at this upstart Goth, adding terms to the agreement and pressing his advantage. But truly, it wasn't anything that he wouldn't be doing in the same situation. Theodric may have been barbarian by blood, but he was certainly Roman in his negotiation style.

"Fine," Eschelus said begrudgingly. He extended his hand and Theodric shook it.

"Then it is settled. We are brothers-in-arms now. Together, we will defeat this Heruli bastard and send him back to the forests he came from." The irony seemed to be lost on him that they were the same forests that he had come from.

They returned inside and continued to put on the show for their men, giving another shake and discussing the terms they had spoken about privately. Then Eschelus and his knights departed back to the villa.

XIII

*O*rephes...

    The voice was distant. Detached.

Orephes.

It was louder the second time. It sounded like his father. At least, the man he used to call his father.

Orephes looked around, but all he could see was darkness. He couldn't even see the floor beneath his feet.

"Father?" he asked faintly. "Is that you? Where are you?"

At first, the voice started to say things Orephes had already heard his father say in the past. Things as mindless as "we need more for the harvest" all the way through him mentioning who his true parents supposedly were on his deathbed. Finally, after a short break, it spoke again. This time, it was different.

Orephes, can you hear me? Orephes!

"I can hear you, Father!" Orephes shouted, but it was in vain. He was shouting at nothing but blackness.

Orephes, you must go to the home of the Gods. It is the only way. It is our last hope.

"I am trying, father. I am headed there. Where are you?"

Orephes? He sounded worried. *Orephes!*

"Father!"

Orephes shot up, his head slamming into the wooden beam above where he had been sleeping. He looked to see if the noise had startled anyone else awake. It hadn't. The boat's rocking seemed to have died down a bit from the night.

It had been a dream, but it had felt so real. He didn't feel like he had woken up. Merely that he had opened his eyes. He still heard a faint sound—like an inaudible whisper—nagging at his ears. He wasn't sure why, but he knew to open his satchel and grab the amulet inside. As soon as he held it, the sound seemed to dissipate, as though his hand had calmed something inside it.

He clenched the small metal and glass ball for a minute before placing it down. Whatever had just happened, it was over. He felt like he might have been going mad as he placed the amulet in his pocket.

He stood up to stretch his legs, walking over to Antonius and Joanna carefully so as to not to disturb them. It had been a long day—they deserved the rest.

He made it to a small room just above the storage area where the three had slept. There were some haphazard belongings, a small cot with tattered sheets, and glass bottles strewn about. Orephes noticed some crude engravings on the walls near the stairs for the first time. They seemed to be dates or numbers. He rubbed his hand on them. They were soft and didn't splinter. They were older.

"They are from me," Marius said, startling him. He had been peeking into the entry but made his way down the stairs when he saw Orephes was awake. "Here and here are just a few notes while I was building the thing, and here"—Marius pointed to a more ornate carving on another piece of wood—"is my signature."

"You built this boat?"

"Helped to," he replied proudly. "I was a shipbuilder. Thought I was going places. This was the only ship I ever finished. I used my entire stock of gold that I had earned building it to buy it."

"You aren't still a shipbuilder?" Orephes asked.

Marius laughed. "Sure, if someone wants to pay me to build one. Unfortunately, there need to be some people with money around to do that."

The two of them went back on deck and peered out at the sea.

"It usually takes people a bit to get their sea legs," Marius noted. "You haven't been sick at all. I am impressed."

"So, you make no money from your ships. How do you survive?"

"Not easily."

"Well, what do you do?"

Marius glanced at Orephes and shook his head. "Did nobody ever teach you to mind your own business?"

"There are four of us alone on this ship," Orephes shot back. "I don't find it odd to want to know who we are sharing close quarters with."

"Have you ever heard of Eudoc?"

"The man whose boat you stole?"

"Re-requisitioned is more like it. He is a master of the under-arts, if you will."

"A crime lord?"

"I work for him. I did, anyway."

"So what are you considered?"

"A faithful servant." Marius stood to walk away, fiddling with the sail.

"Have you ever killed anyone?"

Marius continued to manipulate the rope with his hands while staring intently at Orephes. "Have *you*?"

Orephes had almost forgotten about the soldiers he had killed that day at the villa.

"I have. To defend myself."

Marius let out a slight smile. "Yeah. Me, too."

Marius continued talking, but Orephes wasn't really listening. Instead, his eyes were fixated on a small boat in the distance. It was the only thing visible for miles.

"Did you notice that boat out there?"

Orephes was surprised when Marius shot toward him, peering out at the ship in the distance. He pulled out a small bottle from a bag on the floor of the ship and peered through it with one eye toward the ship.

"Damn it," Marius whispered worryingly.

"What?" Orephes asked. "Eudoc's men?"

"Worse," Marius answered solemnly. "Vandals."

Orephes had heard of Vandals before, of course. They were the infamous barbarian tribe that had sacked Rome for the first time in hundreds of years back in the late 300s. Then they had gone south and seized the empire's breadbasket—North Africa—where they established a kingdom their own. It didn't take long before the bread and circuses that had kept the empire running for hundreds of years started to unravel when the poor were going hungry. It was said that the damage they did to Rome was unprecedented. It had never fully recovered.

"What are they doing out there?"

"Likely making their way over here." Marius began shifting the sail to head the opposite direction.

"Here?" Orephes asked worriedly. "Why?"

"Haven't you ever heard of a Vandal raiding party?" Marius barely could respond with how quickly he was moving.

The boat shook as it abruptly shifted direction. As the boat turned, the pair took a good look into the distance again—there was another boat that had appeared in the horizon.

"That can't be good," Orephes said.

Marius licked his finger and put it into the air for a few moments.

"Wind is blowing toward the east. I have a plan." He tugged at the line and the sail shrank down immediately.

"Does that plan include stranding us here to be captured?" Marius glared at Orephes.

"Have you captained a boat before?"

Antonius and Joanna finally made their way to the deck, looking around in a panic.

"What the hell is going on?" Joanna shouted.

"Vandals."

"Then why are we just sitting here?" Joanna shouted even louder.

"I have a plan," Marius reiterated.

"So, we are all going to die, then," Antonius muttered, drawing his sword.

The boats were getting closer as the *Nero* sat still in the sea, bobbing back and forth. They started to make out a few outlines of a crew on the ships as they got closer. They were definitely bigger than the *Nero*, with larger sails and reinforced hulls.

Eventually, the two boats were parallel to the *Nero*, straddling it on each side. Marius stood firm with one hand on a rope near him.

"Hello, there!" one of the Vandals shouted from their ship. Their clothing seemed well made, yet worn and sun-bleached. They had spent far too much time on those ships. "Having some sail issues?"

"Unfortunately," Marius answered calmly. There was a brief moment of pause before a few pirates from the second ship leaped over. They were all women.

"Gento!" one of the women pirates shouted. She appeared run-down and ragged, but she was beautiful. Her skin was darker even than Joanna's, certainly darker than Orephes had ever seen before. Her skin looked worn and dirty, like the shells she had laced around her neck. Her sword was curved and marred with imperfections along the edges, caused by too much fighting and too little mainte-nance. "This is *my conquest!*"

"You have been following my ship around for weeks, Callista!" another shouted back feverishly. "Are you a pirate or a scavenger, looking to pick up after my meals?"

Gento from the opposite boat and a few of his men leaped aboard the *Nero*, drawing their swords toward the four seemingly defenseless crew members.

"Perhaps it is you who have been following me? I believe you protest a bit too much."

The pirates continued to argue on either side of the *Nero* crew, shouting over them as though they didn't even exist. Marius was looking back and forth from crew to crew quickly, as though scanning them for something.

"Well?" Joanna pressed. "What is your big plan?"

Marius looked at her and pressed his finger to his lips.

"Patience," he whispered back to her eye roll.

"Orephes and I can probably take the lot of them," Antonius said proudly. "I don't understand why we are sitting here."

"There are dozens more pirates on that boat," Marius whispered back angrily. "If you want to try to fight every single one of them, be my guest!"

The pirates' shouting got louder, and they began to wave their swords around wildly at each other as they spoke.

"Pardon me for interrupting," Marius finally shouted over the two groups. Callista and Gento were so taken aback they immediately ceased their threats to each other and stared at the *Nero* crew. "You are all being awfully rude, thought I shouldn't expect much more from Vandals."

Joanna punched Marius in the arm and he let out a slight grunt of pain.

"A light punch would have worked!" he said to her quietly.

"That *was* a light punch."

Callista laughed and pointed her sword at Joanna.

"I like her. Who is the captain here?"

"That would be me," Marius answered proudly, standing to face Callista.

"You? That is disappointing." She laughed in disbelief. Marius scrunched his eyebrows, mouth somewhat agape, as she walked past him dismissively. "You three men have two choices. You can die here in the sea, or come with us as prisoners. You will be either kept aboard as slaves or sold to slavery in Egypt. You, woman"—she pointed to Joanna with her sword—"I will offer you the one chance I give every other woman to join my crew. Otherwise, you can join your friends."

"Working as a slave aboard an all-woman pirate crew," Marius considered out loud. He bobbed his head left and right, pondering. "I can certainly think of *worse* fates."

"Pardon," Gento finally shouted after having guffawed a few times from afar, "have we forgotten that this is *my* ship? They will be *my* slaves!"

"That being one of them," Marius pointed out.

"I tire of this," Callista said dismissively. "Take our prisoners and let us go from here."

Gento's men drew their swords and surrounded the *Nero* crew.

"They are not yours to take!" Gento reiterated.

Marius let a sly smile slip onto his face. He leaned in close to the other crew members.

"On my signal, we toss these bastards closest to us overboard. Then we take care of the rest."

Before Marius could do anything, Callista unleashed her women at Gento's men. Marius shot up quickly and grabbed the closest of Gento's men, shoving him overboard with all his strength.

"I guess that was the signal," Antonius shouted, grabbing the pirate closest to him and following suit.

Orephes did the same but was immediately surrounded by several of Callista's female fighters. He parried a few of their blows, but they were fast and light in comparison to his bulking sword.

Suddenly, he felt a strange sensation, as though a breeze had blown through the inside of his body. It was followed by a strange sound, like a gentle whisper in the distance behind his mind.

He wasn't sure why but in the next instant he lowered his sword and instead raised his outstretched hand. Instantly, each of Callista's pirates were thrown off the edge of the boat, flying backward as though a tremendous wind had lifted them off their feet.

Orephes continued to hold his hand in the air, turning it around to see if anything had changed. What in the world had just happened? He was excited, but more than that, he was scared. Whatever that was that had thrown those pirates of the boat, it wasn't him. And he certainly didn't control it, and that chilled him to his bones.

Almost out of reflex again, he clenched his satchel and pulled out the amulet sitting inside. The seemingly innocuous ball of glass, metal, and stone seemed to pull at him, even as he couldn't bring it any closer. Whatever had just happened, it must have been tied to it somehow.

He put it away and turned to see the rest of the boat crew staring at him intently.

"What the hell was that?" Marius finally asked.

"I don't know." It was the honest answer.

Marius was distracted by the sound of Callista impaling Gento behind him.

"No time now, stick to the plan!" Marius drew his two knives and started up against another one of Gento's pirates.

"We don't even know what the plan is!" Joanna shouted back, as she was attacked by two of Gento's men. Her sword had been knocked out of her hand, so she was fighting with a plank of wood.

"Just get them all off the boat," he answered, running to help her. He dug one knife into the first pirate, who had just gone to grab her, and kicked the other unsuspecting pirate backward off the boat. Joanna nearly fell forward off the boat from the force of the dead pirate on top of her, but Marius grabbed her by the waist and spun her around, keeping her on board.

"I was fine," Joanna assured him angrily.

"I just saved your life!" Marius shouted in disbelief.

"I can handle myself."

"You were about to be carried away as a slave."

"Wouldn't have been the first time. I've always done all right."

"Marius," Antonius shouted from the opposite side of the boat, "they are all off. If you are going to do something, do it now!"

"Right!" Marius shot over to the sail and cut two ropes quickly with his knife. The sail almost instantly unfolded in all its torn glory, sending the *Nero* flying across the sea away from the pirate triremes that had been straddling it a moment before. A few of the pirates on each ship took notice, but they were too consumed with fighting each other to care. Callista had just killed Gento, and his crew was certainly not going to let her or her crew get away with that.

Once it was clear the *Nero* was safely out of harm's way, Marius moved away from the sail and back toward the other members of his haphazard crew.

"See. All under control."

XIV

Bracchus and Michael were watching their new barbarian broth-er-in-arms train from right outside the villa. Michael was lean-ing against the wall, but Bracchus paced, seemingly uncomfortable.

His name was Torix. It even sounded foreign, and Bracchus hissed at the end of the name each time, as though it pained him to say it.

"It isn't right," Bracchus said, shaking his head. "It is bad enough to have these barbarians on our side at all, but to make one of them a *knight*?"

"Get over it, Bracchus," Michael answered dismissively. "We were down two knights and the kid was good with a sword. Your general has made the decision. He has never led us astray in the past."

Bracchus grunted. "Things can change."

"They already have. You just need to catch up." Michael moved away from the wall and grabbed Bracchus's shoulder. "The world stopped making sense years ago, my friend. We can salvage parts of what we had, but not all of it. I believe the general's decision was wise, though I wish he had told us about his plan in advance."

"He knew I wouldn't agree," Bracchus continued.

"I suspect that is exactly why he kept it quiet."

The two headed over to the training grounds, where Torix and Roman were parrying as Bracchus reflected on the decision. He was trying to comfort himself with the success of Eschelus's previous calls, but truly he wasn't sure he ever would. Michael was of a different breed. He was from a long line of Roman soldiers and had grown up in a traditional Roman family in Italy. Bracchus respected him, but in many ways, he considered him spoiled.

Gaul's rapid collapse had hardened the men and women who had withstood it. Michael hadn't been there. He just got to tour the aftermath.

*　　*　　*

Somewhere in Central Gaul, Seventeen Years Ago

"There's bread in this one here," Paul shouted from an abandoned home. "Not much, but it can feed a few."

"Ration it," Eschelus ordered. "Get food to as many people as possible."

Eschelus walked his horse gently up to the side of one of the buildings where he saw some graffiti etched in. He ran his hand over it, taking some of the dust off.

Paulina hic—Paulina was here. She certainly wasn't there anymore, whoever she was. Nobody was. This was the third village they had found, and the third in which they had come up empty-handed.

"Eschelus," Michael said, pulling up in his horse behind him, "this is the third village we have passed on this route. They have all been empty. Either everyone fled, or everyone was killed. Either way, there is nothing for us up here. Why do we continue?"

"Because we were given a mission by the Senate of Rome, scholae," Eschelus replied tersely. "Do not forget your duty."

"How can we even be sure the Roman Senate exists anymore?" Michael pressed. "We have no idea what happened after we fled."

"Then there is just as much north as there is to the south," Eschelus answered. "We press on. There have to be people alive out here in this forsaken diocese."

"Sir," one of the soldiers shouted, "come look at this!"

Michael and Eschelus made their way to the large building painted with black graffiti across the primary wall that faced the street.

Roma Mortus

"Rome is dead," Paul said under his breath. Written in the wall nearby were a few other texts, most of which read "Rome, Save Us."

"When the legions left there was nobody to save these people," Michael explained. "There is no way they survived. If they did, they are likely back in Rome where we should be."

Suddenly, the group heard a crash from one of the buildings.

"Do we have anyone in there?" Eschelus asked quickly.

"No," Paul replied.

They drew their swords and quickly surrounded the building.

"I will go in first. Michael, you follow."

Michael nodded and hopped off his horse.

The building was large and ornate, likely a place of exquisite wealth, none of which remained.

"Who is in there?" Eschelus shouted, sword drawn as he pushed the broken wooden door to the side. He looked and saw a broken vase on the ground, wine spilling out of it like blood from a skull.

"That must have been the noise," Michael said confidently.

"See anything?" Paul shouted from outside.

"No," Eschelus replied, "but that doesn't mean there isn't anything here."

No sooner had Eschelus finished talking than Michael stopped moving, drawing everyone's attention toward his line of sight.

"I know that furniture has feet," he started with a grin, "but I don't think it looks like that." He pointed his sword to a human foot just barely hanging out from beneath a bed.

Eschelus let out a muted laugh and signaled Michael to pull him out. Michael obliged.

He grabbed the foot and tugged, dragging a young boy, about the age of Antonius's boys, out from beneath the once elegant bed.

He was a skinny, starved-looking young man, unarmed and wearing torn Roman robes. He was filthy, and struggling in Michael's arms.

"Calm the hell down," Michael said pinning him down again. Eschelus knelt over next to the now incapacitated young Roman as a few other soldiers ran into the room.

"We heard the commotion," one of them said, "Are you guys all right?"

"We finally found some signs of life in this godforsaken place," Michael answered.

"Who are you?" Eschelus said gently.

The young man had finally calmed down a bit. "Roman," the young man shot back.

"We can see that, but what is your name?"

"That is my name," he answered.

"What are you talking about? Your name is Roman? What did your parents name you?" Eschelus asked, not understanding.

"I don't know. My parents were taken when I was very young. So, I just call myself Roman. There aren't many left here in case you haven't noticed."

"My name is Eschelus. Do you know what happened here?"

"I'm not sure if they were men or demons," he started, clearly shaken, "but whoever they were, they came and took everything. The people. The food."

"How did you survive?"

"I hid." His eyes started to water. "I hid while they ravaged the women. While they decapitated the men. I hid while they brought my brothers and sisters one by one to be their slaves."

"You survived," Michael said, attempting to justify Roman's actions.

"I survived because I am a coward," he retorted angrily. "What world do we live in now where cowards outlive the brave?"

"The world is turned on its head," Eschelus answered. "But you are safe now. We are scholae from Rome itself. Unfortunately, we don't need cowards." He tossed Roman a sword. "We need men." Roman backed away from the sword.

"I can't possibly, I am so weak I can barely stand," he replied, looking to Michael and Eschelus hoping for some sort of compassion in return.

"We will get you fed, and then you will fight." Eschelus helped to pick Roman up so that he could stand. His legs were small and frail, like twigs holding a tree. "Though it might be longer than we might like. The other alternative is to remain here to die."

"This was my home," Roman said weakly as they began to step out.

"No," Eschelus stopped Roman and looked him in the eyes. "This *is* your home. You will return to it, and you will make it yours just as your father had done before you. You departing with us is not surrender. It is your opportunity to fight to defend this place." Roman tried to eke out a smile, but his hollow eyes allowed only the faint whisper of joy to creep across his face.

"Those are some mighty words," Michael whispered quietly. "When are you going to tell him that was all bullshit?"

"When he doesn't need that bullshit to have a will to survive," Eschelus retorted abruptly.

"Eschelus." If it was possible, Roman managed to look even more despondent, his sunken eyes growing with a rooted despair. "Why didn't Rome send the legions? Why were we forsaken? We had paid our taxes, done all we had needed. Why were we left to die?"

"We were all left to die," Eschelus replied grimly. "That doesn't mean we have to."

The small troop left the village only to end up at another and another, all in similar states as the last. Disrepair and abandonment plagued their journey farther north. Increasingly, the road itself became even more treacherous, with the stones that had once lined the magnificent roadway becoming jagged obstacles to both man and horse. To Eschelus, this was a sign more so even than the abandoned villages. Rome had paid good money to ensure that these roads were traversable for their legions. Clearly, they had no intention of ever sending legions here again. Not even to save their people.

"Tribuni," Paul started, interrupting Eschelus's thoughts. "Look ahead."

Finally, some signs of life. There was a small military outpost ahead, with lights shining out from the tower. It was stationed on top of a small but formidable wall. He just needed to know if they were keeping something out, or keeping something in. This tower was many miles from the most recent village, and farther even from the most recent villa they had encountered.

"Looks Roman," Eschelus said, pointing out the marble textures and Roman flag showing proudly above it.

"Well, I'll be damned," Michael said happily. "Someone is alive out here."

The group hurried over to the outpost, where they were greeted by the scent of wine, oil, and roasting food.

"Someone is very alive in there," Paul exclaimed happily.

"You there!" a guard shouted from a small tower nearest the main facility. "What is your business?"

Eschelus's heart nearly skipped a beat. These guards were Roman.

"My name is Eschelus, tribuni scholae. We have journeyed from Rome to bring you news from the capital."

"Well, aren't you a sight for sore eyes," the guard shot back. "We haven't seen another Roman troop out here since...hell, I can't even remember the last time. I'll announce your arrival."

The gate that was blocking the entrance into the Roman facility opened slowly, revealing a few Roman cavalry on horseback, and a few dozen *limitanei* soldiers, all eagerly awaiting the arrival of Eschelus's ragtag group.

Eschelus rode up to the first man on horseback. He was wearing tribuni armor like himself. He couldn't be more than forty, with dark brown eyes and brown hair peppered with gray peeking out from beneath his helmet.

"Are you in command here?" Eschelus asked.

"Aye. My name is Bracchus, I am commander of this barbarian outpost. Boy, am I happy to see you folks. And you command these men?"

"Yes. I am Eschelus, tribuni scholae. These are my men, as well as a few we picked up along the way."

"I count roughly twenty men," one of Bracchus's cavalry started. "Nineteen, if you don't count the dying one."

"Twenty men," Bracchus said nervously. "I'm not sure our rations can accommodate. What word have you from Rome? Have you brought our payment?"

Eschelus looked at Paul, who shook his head gently. Eschelus dismounted, and all the mounted men on both sides followed suit.

"Bracchus, when was the last you heard from Rome?"

"Over a year ago now," Bracchus replied somberly. "If you are asking when the last time Rome sent anyone here, then I can't remember the last time. We had been sending contingents south to Rome to pick up our payment after they stopped coming."

"They had stopped sending you payment?" Michael asked abruptly. "Then why did you stay?"

"Because it is my duty," Bracchus replied defiantly. "I have not been discharged, nor have my men."

"But you weren't being paid," Michael pleaded.

"We were. I was making sure of it. The first year that Rome stopped coming, we sent men there instead. They returned with our full year's payment."

"So, they paid you only if you sent your men to get it," Paul muttered. "Sounds like a raw deal to me."

"Rome told us that it was no longer worth the investment to send a battalion here to pay us or reinforce us. The troops were being diverted to Italy. They were more than happy to continue our service as long as we sought payment ourselves."

"I'm guessing your most recent contingent to Rome hasn't returned yet?" Eschelus asked worriedly.

"It has been months longer than it should," Bracchus replied. "I fear they have been lost. These roads have been getting more and more dangerous every day. Every month. I'm not sure what Rome is waiting for. Without reinforcements all of Gaul will be lost."

"Bracchus"—Eschelus pulled him to the side—"Rome has fallen."

Bracchus looked at him momentarily before beginning to laugh.

"Surely, you are joking," Bracchus began, almost frustrated. "You journeyed all the way here to tell me that Rome has fallen? To whom?"

"A barbarian *magister militum*. The emperor has been deposed."

Bracchus shook his head and looked around. A few of his men had heard the conversation.

"Listen to me," Bracchus said, pointing his finger at Eschelus's chest. "These men here have been starving and dying for that godforsaken city. You will not tell them that it has all been in vain. Do you understand me?"

"Just because the emperor has fallen does not mean their work has been in vain, Bracchus. You were not defending the emperor. You were protecting Roman interests here in Gaul."

"Well, one hell of a job we have done there, haven't we?" Bracchus shot back furiously. "Have you seen out there? What the world is like when you leave this camp?"

"Bracchus, I…"

"Gaul is gone, Eschelus, tribuni scholae, and Rome did nothing to save it. We were outnumbered so we did nothing but wait, and do you want to know the one thing that has kept us going? The hope that once Rome had its shit sorted out, that once someone down there remembered us, that they would come back. Now here you are, a genuine Roman legion, here to tell me that it was all for shit? That we need to pack up and go home?" Bracchus put his helmet back on his head. "Rome may be full of quitters, but here in Gaul we finish what we started."

"These barbarians that you are watching over," Eschelus started as Bracchus turned away, "what will you do when they discover the truth? That there will be no more legions to keep them in their place once they storm this outpost?"

Bracchus stopped walking and turned to face Eschelus. "Then they can join with the rest of them running wild in Gaul and nothing will have changed," he replied tersely. "Until then, this is one small island of sanity and safety left in this place. I will not see it destroyed as long as I live." Bracchus turned back to his men. "Give these troops some rations for their journey. They will not be resting here with us."

Paul and Michael, whom had remained near the main gate, saw what was transpiring. However, what caught their eye more than the fighting commanding officers was a small boy peering at them through a small crack in a wooden portion of the wall, who then ran off when he was seen.

Bracchus remembered what happened next as if it was still yesterday. It ended with years of his life burned to the ground as he and his men and their families fled with Eschelus even farther north. As he watched Torix gently clash swords with one of his best friends, those same feelings came back to him. He didn't consider himself old-fashioned, but he certainly considered himself a pragmatist. Romans training alongside barbarians had failed time and time again. In fact, it was the very thing that had ended up driving the last Emperor in the West into exile.

"Good!" Roman shouted, pulling his sword away from Torix. The two shared a momentary smile before they noticed Michael and Bracchus watching them. "He is good. He will learn in no time," he said to his fellow knights.

"Good," Michael answered. "We will need the help."

Torix noticed Bracchus standing silently, his expression emotionless.

"Bracchus, right?" he asked in his Gothic-accented Latin.

"Yes," Bracchus answered quickly.

"I realize that I am not like the rest of you," Torix continued, "and that you don't trust me. I'm sure none of you do yet. I will work to gain that trust. We are brothers now."

"What do you know about trust?" Bracchus shot back. "The only thing that can be trusted about your people is that you will always find new ways to bring destruction where you go."

"Trust is very important to my people," Torix replied helpfully. "Romans have always had wealth, food, circuses. All we have had for generations was trust."

"Our emperor trusted your people. It got him exiled."

"My people trusted your emperors over and over again, only to be betrayed. Broken promises for decades."

Bracchus was going to continue, but Michael grabbed his shoulder, cutting him off.

"That is all in the past. Now, we move forward together. To a better future for both of our people." He stared at Bracchus, using his eyes to tell him what he wouldn't say out loud.

Bracchus backed down. It wasn't the time to fight, and even Roman seemed uncomfortable.

"You are right about one thing, our new young friend," Bracchus started up again, "you will have to work to gain that trust. I will work hard to give it."

XV

Joanna made her way onto the deck, rubbing her arms as the cool air lifted her hair from her face. She sat down next to the mast, looking toward the faint glow of city lights to the east. It was Constantinople. They were close now. It would only be a matter of a day or so.

"It is always prettier at night," Marius said from the other end of the ship. Joanna hadn't noticed him on her way up, but she turned to see him sitting down, arms crossed, right up against the front wall of the boat.

She thought for a fleeting moment about the real reason she was on this boat. About how easy it would be to accomplish it right now. But she saw Marius's smile, and she hesitated.

His voice had startled her. There hadn't been much said by the passengers on the *Nero* after their escape. Aside from a bit of obnoxious bragging by Marius in the immediate aftermath, barely more than a word or two had been spoken by anyone. They had continued to rotate their shifts of sleeping and manning the deck, avoiding a few other Vandal triremes on their journey.

"From afar," Joanna corrected. "The city is never nicer at night when you are in it yourself."

"That depends on what you are looking for," Marius answered. He stood up and reached into a barrel near him. Inside was a cloth, made from some type of animal hide. It looked barbarian. He came over next to Joanna and held it out.

"Here, this will keep you warm," he said. "You look like you are freezing."

She was surprised by the kind gesture but accepted it. She *was* freezing.

"What is that?" she asked, running her fingers over one side. It was softer than it looked.

"It is a barbarian coat. They use them up north. Don't really need them around here. Try one. They are pretty nice once you get past the fact that you are wearing a dead animal."

Joanna grabbed it from him and put it around her. Almost immediately she felt warmer, her skin rubbing against the animal hide giving her an odd sense of comfort.

"Thank you."

"Did it help?"

"It's OK."

"Just OK?"

"Smells a bit."

Marius crossed his arms. "Forgive me for not having a proper way to scent the barbarian clothing we have on board, YourHhighness," Marius said.

"Your Highness?" Joanna hissed back.

"Oh, pardon me, I figured I was in the presence of royalty with all that entitlement."

Joanna sat silently for a few moments, staring out into the distance before Marius decided to speak again.

"This is quite a long way just to get a bit of money from me," he started.

Joanna heard the words but couldn't turn to look at him. She knew what her sticking around was really about. She just didn't want him to know.

"I take getting paid very seriously."

"Nobody takes getting paid as seriously as yours truly," Marius shot back, "and there is no way in hell I would journey from Rome to Constantinople to get mine. You could have hopped off this boat as soon as I told you I didn't have the money. Those goons back at the harbor in Rome wouldn't have hurt you if you had just told them you were a whore looking for your pay. What is this really about?" Marius waited a bit for an answer that never came. Eventually, he nodded and started to walk away.

"I am tired of the secrets."

Orephes had just made his way up from the bottom of the boat, taking a moment to admire Constantinople lit like a candle in the distance.

"Just the man I want to see," Marius said, pointing to a seat on the deck. Orephes obliged and sat down.

"Is everything all right? I noticed we haven't been moving for a bit." Orephes asked.

"You tell me, kid," Marius said, sitting next to him. "I've been all around the world, fought with and fought against hundreds of people. I've been to places few on this side of the world could even dream of visiting. I have never seen anything like that stunt you pulled back there against those Vandals."

"I don't know what you mean," Orephes answered nervously.

"Don't disrespect me on my own boat."

Orephes shifted in his seat, rubbing his legs and finally sitting back. "I don't know what it was. I felt something, as though something was telling me to lift my arm. Then that happened."

"Some young man shows up in a whorehouse wearing Roman armor that hasn't been seen in decades, asking for me to take him east, and while on my boat manages to throw pirates into the sea without lifting a finger. It doesn't add up. You haven't told me something."

"Technically," Orephes interjected with a grin, "I lifted all five of my fingers to make it happen."

Marius cracked a small smile, that looked as though he was trying to hide it. "I like you, kid. But you need to be honest with me right now. Where are we really going?"

"To find my family."

"I don't believe you, and this boat isn't going any farther until you tell me the truth."

"I'm telling you the truth!"

"Then you are leaving something out."

Orephes gritted his teeth and shook his head. He hadn't told anyone else what his father had said to him. Not even his own brother. To tell, of all people, Marius, a bandit who he barely knew, felt wrong. It felt like a betrayal. But if he wanted to get answers, it seemed to be the only way ahead.

"The man that I believed was my father was a patrician in Gaul," Orephes started. "Villa, slaves, everything. I grew up there, but when he died, he told me that I was not really his son. He told me that I was left on his doorstep by a group of travelers." This was as far as he had gotten with anyone else telling the story. He considered ending it there, but he pressed on. It was like water was finally breaching the dam and ending up where it belonged. It felt good to tell someone.

"He told me that the travelers were not just some refugees from the north. He claimed that I was the last son of Zeus with a human woman, and that he and the Gods had brought me to him to protect."

Marius had been sitting forward intently, and he sat silently for a moment before breaking into laughter.

It wasn't the response Orephes had expected. Or wanted. After a few moments, Marius realized that Orephes was still sitting there with a confused look on his face.

"Wait, do you truly believe this?" Marius asked.

By this point, Joanna and Antonius had been watching the conversation, and walked over to join in.

"I didn't," Orephes answered, "how could it be real? It sounds mad. My father was dying. I had convinced myself that they were feverish rantings. Until he gave me this." Orephes reached into his pocket and held out the amulet, which shimmered in the dawn sky. "Whatever this is, this is what did what you saw before. It whispers to me in the night. It gives me visions of the man who raised me as my father. Dreams, but they feel real."

The other passengers took a good look at the amulet, taking turns feeling it curiously. Joanna held it the longest amount of time, staring at it longingly. As if she had seen a ghost.

"Did you know about this?" Marius asked Antonius.

"No," he answered quickly.

"Whatever that rock is, I have never seen anything like it before," Marius finally said, standing, "and you somehow shoved those pirates off this boat. I saw it with my own eyes. So, something is going on here. But there is only one God, kid, and he doesn't give people stones with magical powers."

"I want to know exactly what you want to know," Orephes replied. "The truth. I don't know whether anything my father said was true. But this amulet, and everything that has happened since…they mean something. I intend to find out what."

Marius, Joanna, and Antonius exchanged looks.

"Why didn't you tell me this?" Antonius asked.

"Why didn't you tell me about the letter for the senator?" Antonius huffed.

"That is different, Orephes," Antonius said softly.

"Would you or Eschelus have believed me if I told you?"

"We would have thought you were mad," Antonius admitted.

"I still might," Joanna interjected, still mesmerized by the amulet.

"I will get the boat moving," Marius said, walking away.

"So, you believe me?" Orephes asked.

"I believe that you believe that. It is good enough for me."

XVI

Bishop's Cathedral, Central Gaul

He had grown to hate the smell of incense. There could be none burning, but the scent would still seep through the cracks in the wall. The cathedral would never be free of the smell, short of it getting burned down. Even then, he thought, it would simply send the odor throughout the province and enslave the noses of hundreds of others.

The cardinal was sitting in front of him, glancing over several dozen parchments on the desk. His red robes stood in stark contrast to the nearly ubiquitous white, purple, and gold that adorned Martel's chambers; like a stain of blood on a stark white robe. Gaius and Volusian sat next to Martel on either side, across from their guest.

"There are still a few outlying villas that haven't been converted," the cardinal noted calmly, placing the parchments back on the table.

"These things take time," Martel replied sternly. "Finesse."

The cardinal tapped his finger on Martel's desk, listening to the gentle echoes from the hollow drawers inside. He barely took his eyes off Martel, except to occasionally glare at Volusian, seated next to him.

131

"His Holiness would like you to be present for the upcoming council in Ravenna. It would be optimal if this could all be complete by then."

"It will be."

It wouldn't be. Frankly, Martel didn't much care. He knew about the current church leadership's obsession with saving Roman culture by making its *boni*—the affectionate term that the wealthy upper class used for each other—into priests and bishops of the Christian church. It wasn't something Martel believed would work, nor was it something he much cared about even if it could. The wealthy had been saving the wealthy since humans built cities. Claiming it was benevolent didn't change anything.

"Good." The cardinal stood, a callous smile on his face. "What we are doing is for the good of Rome. We can't save the empire, but we can save its people. In the church."

"Of course."

The cardinal finally turned his attention to Volusian.

"Why is he still here, Martel?" the cardinal asked tersely.

"His mission is not yet complete."

"You and I both know that is a lie," the cardinal hissed, crossing his arms. He looked Volusian in the eyes. "The cult of the Old Gods will never truly be destroyed as long as you continue to *disgrace* this church with your presence."

Suddenly, the flames from the fireplace behind the cardinal leaped forward, igniting his robes. Gaius hurried to get a flask of water, which he threw on the cardinal to put out the flames as he stood in a panic. Martel looked angrily toward Volusian, who sat as motionless as he had the rest of the time.

"I want him gone," the cardinal pressed. "Or it will be your head."

The cardinal gave a slight bow, and Martel reciprocated. As he stepped out, Martel saw someone sitting in the hall waiting for him, two of his guards standing on either side.

"Sir," one of them said, "this barbarian has asked to see you. We have told her to leave, but she insisted."

"I have information for you!" the woman shrieked, the second guard keeping her seated. "I was told that you were looking for this kind of thing."

Martel looked at the barbarian woman. She was passionate and ragged. Whoever she was, she had traveled to get here to tell him this.

"Come." The guards released her and she slowly followed the archbishop into his quarters. She sat down and looked around at the high ceilings and marble stonework that outlined his existence in the cathedral. "Wine?" Martel outstretched his hand, grabbing a chalice.

"No."

Martel shrugged and sat back, folding his arms. "Vandal?"

"How did you know?" she asked, looking at her own attire as though she was accusing it of betraying her.

"You smell like salt and your skin is tan and broken. You have spent much time at sea. Rare to find a Goth who sails."

The Vandal looked untrustingly at Martel, who was holding back a smirk. Barbarians always did entertain him. Like an animal that has been released from a crate, free to explore the world around them.

"I was told you pay good money for certain types of…information," she pressed. "Stories about strange happenings."

"Who told you that?"

The Vandal smirked.

"Nobody. Is it true?"

"I am a man of God," Martel answered. "I don't deal in tales of superstition."

"This isn't superstition." The Vandal sat forward, her eyes opening wide. "I saw it with my own eyes."

"What did you see?" Martel asked, taking care to not appear too curious. He glanced at Volusian, who finally seemed interested.

"I saw my crewmates thrown off the side of a boat," she started. He noticed her wringing her hands on her legs. "The man who did it…he didn't even touch them. He just…lifted his hand."

"Impossible," Martel answered back quickly. "Things like that simply do not happen."

"I thought that I was going crazy," she continued, looking down. "So did a few others on the crew. But we know what we saw."

They sat silently for a few moments, their eyes meeting. Finally, Martel reached under his desk and pulled out a large satchel that let out a thud and a jingle as he dropped it down.

"You didn't see anything, and you certainly didn't come here to tell me. Do you understand?"

The Vandal women smirked, snatching the bag of gold on the desk quickly.

"Please," she shot back, "like I would talk to any of you Roman bastards again after this."

"My guards will see you out," Martel snapped, and the guards quickly threw the door open. "Take her outside please."

Martel waited until everyone was out of earshot before he turned to his wall, gently moving a small statue aside to reveal a tiny compartment in the marble. He pulled out several scrolls, dusting them gently before placing them on his desk. He locked the door in front of him quietly, and sat back down before unrolling each scroll separately side by side across his desk.

On the scrolls were hundreds of names, connected by lines and arrows in a haphazard manner. Most of the names had an X written above them in ink, while a few simply had a line through them.

He ran his finger along one of the pages, following the arrows from name to name in a pattern. He muttered incoherently to himself as his gaze traced the ink. Finally, he let out a sigh as he removed his hand from the parchment.

"How can it be? A sighting?" Martel asked gently, taking care to not speak so loudly that the guards outside could hear. "I supposed your instincts to spread the word about a reward for odd happenings has borne fruit. Another old worshipper?"

"No," Volusian answered. "What she described is not a power a simple worshipper can do."

"An augur?" Martel looked Volusian in the eyes.

"No. I sense…" Volusian's eyes darkened. Something changed in his expression. "That's impossible," Volusian shot out. "They are all dead. We made sure of it."

"I have been looking up and down the tree," Martel pressed. He pushed the parchment toward the end of the desk, implying that Volusian should come closer to see it. "How could we have missed one?"

"That young man from the Chalcedon Estate," Volusian remembered. He took time to look over the parchment himself before continuing his thoughts. "There was no record of him."

"What are the odds it was him, so far from the villa?"

Volusian didn't answer, instead closing his eyes. He took a few deep breaths before returning to the room, gently reopening his eyes. For the first time in a very long time, Martel could see a hint of surprise behind them.

"It can't be." Volusian's voice was a calm whisper.

"Did you feel something?" Martel asked curiously.

"Something. Faint but something."

"I don't understand. How were we so wrong?" Volusian grabbed Martel's parchment, looking it over one last time before ripping it apart. "This ink. These lines. They mislead us. The simple methods of man do nothing but block out the *very thing* that should have been leading us."

"You just destroyed years of work!" Martel said angrily. The family tree of every important old worshipper, and, more importantly, every child of the Gods sat tattered at his feet. Years of work across multiple bishops, from the start of the time of Christianity.

"I don't need that useless parchment."

Martel stepped out from behind his desk.

"You seem to forget that this isn't just about you, Volusian," Martel warned. "Years from now, when both of us are gone, our descendants will need it."

"You are wrong, Martel. If we do our job now, they needn't ever care about this again."

"Go and find this young man," Martel commanded. "If he is what you think he is—"

"He will be destroyed," Volusian interrupted, robbing Martel from giving him a command. "Just like all of the others."

"Thanks be to God."

Volusian offered no response, instead letting out a sneering hiss as he headed out of the room. Martel smirked. He knew that bringing up Christianity's God in such endearing means bothered him, not unlike a barbarian bringing up their king to a Roman and expecting some form of respect.

With Volusian's footsteps disappearing into the distance, Martel picked up the two halves of the ripped parchment, placing them back together and back hidden into their hole behind the statue.

XVII

Odoacer's Palace, Ad Laurentum, Ravenna

The dinner table was decorated as ornately as any good Roman's, with a wineglass at every seat. Odoacer had already taken his seat at the head of the table, patiently sipping his wine and stroking his beard. He hadn't yet touched his food, though a few of his soldiers surrounding him had begun digging into their hens.

Immediately at his right was the esteemed senator-turned-consul, Caecina. Like his king, he had not yet touched his hen. It was polite, after all, to wait for their visitor. Caecina was pleasantly surprised just how little the palace had changed after Odoacer supplanted the final emperor. Sure, there were more of his Heruli tribesmen around, but the decor and, more importantly, the *class* of the palace had not suffered in the least.

In some ways, it made Odoacer's entire reign feel transplanted. Even from emperor to emperor, there had always been a large transition, as each decorated every last Imperial holding with their flavor of desire. Odoacer seemed to have no interest in such things. The entire palace was exactly as the former emperor had left it, even including a few marble busts of his family, though one or two of them his tribesman had taken it upon themselves to "fix" with charcoal or wine, coloring in the lips and eyes.

One of the soldiers at the table caught Odoacer's eye as he began picking apart the hen with his hands. He allowed it to go on for several moments before slamming his fists on the table, immediately stopping any small conversations that had broken out. Everyone stopped and stared at the king, who was sitting staring at the lone soldier with a piece of white meat in his hands.

"Is there something wrong with that fork and knife?" Odoacer asked in an angry, low growl.

The soldier finished the piece of chicken in his hands before slowly grabbing the fork and knife.

"We didn't spend years trying to make our way into Roman society to keep acting like a bunch of damned animals," Odoacer continued. "Those utensils are there for a reason. Any of you cunts have any questions on how to use them?"

Before anyone could answer, the door to the dining room opened. A few guards escorted Senator Severus Verengi to his seat opposite Odoacer, at the other end of the table.

"Welcome, Senator," Odoacer said, raising his glass. "I was beginning to get worried you weren't going to show."

"I am a man of my word," Severus answered. He took a brief glance at Caecina, who was seated with his arms crossed. Odoacer was willing to entertain him, but Caecina was certainly not. Their rivalry had only gotten worse when Caecina became consul, and worse still when he put the Heruli relocation zone right in Severus's neighborhood.

A few servants promptly brought out Severus's food and poured his wine. He took a single sip, as to not be rude. He wasn't planning on having any more.

"I have been told you have some information for me," Odoacer started. "About the war."

"I came upon this information, and I simply couldn't allow it to transpire."

"Well, let's hear it, then. Every minute wasted here is a minute I could have been at the front beating that Goth bastard who thinks himself a servant of the emperor."

"Theodric has made an alliance," Severus said somberly, "nearly doubling the size of his army. They have kept it a secret so as to not give you wind of it. Together, they planned on breaking the stalemate and sweeping through Italy."

Odoacer sat forward, his expression changing almost immediately. "Who is this alliance with?"

"A Roman general in Gaul. Eschelus, a former tribuni."

"The one they call the 'Emperor in the North'?" Odoacer asked.

Severus seemed surprised. He had thought that even just the information of Eschelus's existence would be news to the king. "You have heard of him?"

"I have heard stories of him and his knights. The things they are able to do to the Goth armies up there. I had heard he may have gathered an army, and that Tufa is among them."

Odoacer sat back again, looking at his generals around him, all of whom had stopped eating.

"Tufa? Your chief commander?"

"Aye. Him and his son."

"I thought they were dead," one of his generals blurted out.

"As did I, after their surrender," Odoacer replied. "It turns out he is just a fucking turncoat. Say what you will about Romans. At least they have honor. A code."

"I apologize," Severus said solemnly, "I have wasted your time."

"Nonsense," Odoacer answered. "I didn't know that the two armies were working together. This is news, and I am grateful for it. Though I must admit, given what Caecina has told me about you, I am surprised to see you here."

Severus glanced at Caecina again, who was still sitting smugly next to his king.

"What has he said, Your Highness?"

"That you are a member of the loyalist faction in the Senate, attempting to see Roman rule restored."

This was accurate, of course. From the very beginning, Severus had actively contrived against Odoacer's reign in the background. Though it was less out of a desire to see the emperor's return, and more the desire to combat Caecina's influence. Considering Caecina was an expert teat-sucker in Severus's eyes, it hadn't had much effect.

"In my eyes, Your Highness," Severus answered politely, "Roman rule has already been restored. I am an old man now. I have seen several emperors come and go. I have seen the fall of the last one. I have seen you go from a barbarian warlord to a rightful king. You respect the Senate, which is more than the emperors did. It is clear, now, with this alliance, that this general who calls himself Roman is merely an opportunist, siding himself with the next barbarian after the title of king."

"Theodric is a jealous cunt," Odoacer added. "He couldn't get Zeno to give him land, so he decided he wants mine. I was given this territory by the emperor himself. Now he wants to take it from me?"

"Zeno isn't much better," one of his generals added. "He is the one who sent that Goth over here."

"You watch your mouth against the emperor," Odoacer chided. "He is the one who gave us what we have."

Severus could see that he was torn. On the one hand, he certainly was thankful to Zeno for all that he had given him. On the other hand, that same benevolent emperor was now trying to take it away. Severus could see the confusion in his eyes, but he knew Odoacer would never admit it. He couldn't.

Odoacer thanked Severus for the information profusely as they finished dinner. They continued on with the wine until the seemingly limitless supply had turned all but Caecina and Severus into drunken fools who saw themselves off to their chambers. Severus took this rare opportunity with Caecina alone to talk with him one-on-one. Like they used to do.

As Severus approached, Caecina put on a warm but guarded smile. A familiar face that many senators seemed to be able to put on at a whim.

"The man's every word oozes your manipulation," Severus started. "Him blaming other barbarians instead of Zeno for all of this has your name written all over it. I have to admit I am impressed with this creation of yours."

"It took years, but he is coming around," Caecina boasted proudly. "A few years ago this meeting would have ended with him drunk, covered in chicken, and ignoring your every word."

"Well, he certainly still got drunk."

"That I don't think will change even when he is dead." Caecina paused for a moment before erasing his smile. "What is your play here, Severus? Why did you come here?"

"Because it has become clearer to me with each passing day that we are safer and have more influence under Odoacer than we would under Eschelus and his barbarian army."

"Even with me as consul?" Caecina asked curiously.

Severus shook his head. "You just enjoy bringing that up. Let me put it to you in these terms: under Eschelus, who is to say there will even be a consul to be jealous of?"

"The devil you know against the devil you don't," Caecina said. "You are choosing wisely. For once in your life."

"So, what is our great king going to do? He is losing this war, and Eschelus entering doesn't make it any easier."

"I already have something worked out, my friend. What, you think I didn't account for your friend Eschelus realizing that there weren't enough Romans left in Gaul to restore the empire?"

"A plan? Odoacer seemed to have no idea!"

Caecina leaned in to Severus's ear.

"The first rule of being a Roman working for a barbarian king: tell them only what they need to know."

Caecina embraced his fellow senator before turning to leave, deserting Severus in the vast dining hall of the palace to see himself out.

XVIII

Chalcedon Estate, Southern Gaul

The air had been buzzing with anticipation since Eschelus had begun the final rally. Every soldier seemed to know their role in assembling the army, the result of years of preparation. Immediately outside the walls was the bulk of the army, in makeshift tents and bases assembled from local wood. Inside, Eschelus and his most elite guard were organizing the weaponry, which would shortly be distributed.

Gargarus and his family were watching from the doorway of their villa, unable to conceal the worry on their faces. Eschelus had promised to leave them a small expeditionary force, but it wouldn't be enough. The day that the army departed would be the day local barbarian warlords knew that the last independent Roman estate in Gaul was ripe for the taking.

It was a countdown to doomsday, and all Gargarus could do was pray that Eschelus would do what he said and bring the empire back from the ashes.

His entire family had been single-handedly shaken from the news that Eschelus was working with Theodric. The Goths had killed dozens of their friends and family across Europe. Eschelus had assured them that these were a "different" group of Goths than the ones who ended up taking Spain under Alaric, but to his family and to the hundreds of families who suffered under them, it was all the same.

Eventually, out from the door behind them, came the two barbarians Eschelus had brought back with him from that night excursion. The older, Tufa, was one of Odoacer's generals who had surrendered to Theodric early in their war. He was a quiet man who only spoke to Eschelus. Even then, he only spoke when he needed to. His son, Torix, was much more open but his training to become a knight had taken up most of his time since he had arrived.

Now, stepping out of their villa, he was nearly indistinguishable from his fellow knights. His armor, his demeanor…he was one of them, all right. And it gave Gargarus some hope that Eschelus had made the right decision.

"Thank you for your hospitality," Tufa said softly, with a gentle nod toward Gargarus. As he spoke, Gargarus realized that he had never actually heard Tufa's voice. He spoke Latin very well given his background.

"Thank you for what you are about to help do," Gargarus answered.

Eschelus, Michael, Bracchus, and Roman had approached to meet the two of them on horseback.

"Are you and your son ready?" Eschelus asked.

"We are."

"Then it is time. We will be meeting Theodric's army as reinforcements to the main assault." Turning his attention to Gargarus, Eschelus could see the fear in his family's faces. "Gargarus, don't appear so forlorn. It is only temporary. Once Rome is ours again, it will only be a matter of time before I march back north and retake all of this for the empire."

Gargarus didn't reply. They had already said their goodbyes before. He didn't believe Eschelus would ever be back, even if he did retake Rome. It would take all of his army's strength to just hold on to Italy. Today was likely the last they would see of Eschelus and his knights, and it chilled him to his core.

Given how large the army was, the speed at which they managed to get off the property was nothing short of astounding. In what seemed like only minutes, the Chalcedon family's fortunes walked out of their gates, likely never to be seen again.

XIX

Constantinople

The other passengers had woken Orephes up for the approach. They knew he would want to see it.

Rome had been beautiful, but Constantinople was indescribable. Beyond the port the city laid upon a hill, painting the landscape gold in the sun's reflection. Overhead, the archway leading into the city seemed to embrace the vessel as he peered up, the marble glistening in the light. The monuments were magnificent, and stood unmarred by graffiti or wear. It was as though you could see the city's wealth and intellect in the very essence of its towering buildings.

For a brief moment, it felt bittersweet to see. Out west, where the empire had been forged, the very foundations were being eroded by time and malice. Here, in the east, it looked to Orephes what Rome should have looked like. Unwavering. Unsullied. He felt a nostalgia for a Rome that he never got to see.

The west had died for their sins. It was reborn here, in the east, more magnificent than ever.

"The Port of Theodosius," Marius chimed. "Beautiful view, isn't it?" He had a slight smile on his face as he watched Orephes in awe of this place he had been to so many times. It helped to remind him how beautiful this world they had built truly was, after spending so much time in the ugliest parts of it.

There were hundreds of other ships in the harbor, some leaving, some arriving. Many simply tied. In Rome, it simply felt as though people wanted to leave. Here, Orephes could feel a draw to the city. People wanted to be here.

"I always tell people that the empire has one foot in the grave," Marius started again. "This is the other foot."

"You sure you aren't a poet?" Joanna said jokingly.

Marius turned to look at her with that same grin that he always seemed to have. "For someone as skilled in as many things as me, I very well could be," Marius joked back.

He steered the boat into the harbor, avoiding the other ships and docking at a small open sector toward the harbor edge. A few Roman soldiers came over to quickly inspect the ship and make sure the crew weren't pirates. Thankfully, they left satisfied. Marius tied up the ship and gathered his things. Everyone else followed suit.

The four helped each other off the boat, standing on solid land for the first time in several days. Orephes had lost track of how much time they had spent at sea, or away from the villa.

As the crew made it onto the street nearest the port, Marius stopped and turned to face the rest of them.

"This is one of the main streets. Follow it east to the city center, west to head out toward the mainland."

"I suppose this is goodbye, then," Orephes replied, though he didn't want it to be. There was an odd silence among them all, and he could only imagine they were thinking exactly what he was: that this goodbye was a bit premature. Over the course of time they had spent on the boat, the four of them had grown close. Not to mention, these were the only people who knew the true purpose of his mission. In that way, he felt closer to these three people than he did even to his own "family" back home.

"I just need my payment, and then I will be on my way," Marius said. "Then I can pay you, and you can be on yours." He had directed that last line at Joanna, who did her signature eye roll as she stood with her arms crossed.

Antonius took out a few coins from the money satchel that he and Orephes had brought on the trip. He counted the amount that they owed and handed it to Marius, who began to count the coins intently in his palm.

"Let's agree to never do that again, hmm?" Antonius said quietly. "Let's quickly find your parents and then get the hell back to the army."

"Seems to be all here," Marius assured him. He put the coins in his own satchel, save the few that he handed to Joanna. "There, your time has finally been paid for. You realize you could have slept with dozens more of Rome's finest in this time, right?"

"I'm not going back to Rome," she answered happily, taking her coins. Marius let out a snide laugh.

"You can't just decide you aren't returning. You are a whore. Your *lena* will come looking for you."

"She won't. I am a free woman. She has no reason to."

"You are a free woman?" Antonius asked, surprised. "You aren't a slave?"

"I am not," Joanna replied.

"Then why are you a whore?" Marius asked incredulously.

"Because men will pay good money to fuck," she answered. "Why turn it down?"

"It seems like a pretty significant sacrifice for money," Marius replied.

Joanna finished counting her money and looked Marius with a grin. "Who's to say it was a sacrifice for me?"

Suddenly, there were a few loud yells before a large stone flew at Antonius. It hit him straight in the temple, knocking him to the ground. A stone flew at Orephes at well, but it bounced loudly from his chest plate without causing any harm. Before anyone had any time to think, two people lunged at Orephes, attempting to drag him to the ground. Orephes quickly drew his sword, striking one and prompting the second to step backward. As he did, Marius's daggers appeared through his neck and chest. The unknown man fell to the floor, gasping his last breaths.

As Orephes collected his thoughts, he could see all around him groups of Romans running at the guards stationed around the harbor. They ran right past Joanna and Marius, ignoring them as if they weren't even there.

"Are you all right?" Marius asked.

"I am fine. What the hell is going on?"

"The bacaudae," Marius answered grimly.

"Who are they? Why aren't they attacking you?"

"Rebels. I will explain later. They only attack the guards."

"I'm not a guard!"

Marius looked Orephes up and down. Orephes remembered the armor he had on.

"You sure as hell look like one, kid!"

Joanna knelt over Antonius. There was blood pouring out of his head. He was unconscious.

"He isn't looking very good!" she shouted, prompting the two others to kneel next to their friend.

Marius checked his pulse and felt his head where the wound was. "His heart is beating, but that wound is severe," Marius said worriedly. "We need to bring him someplace to rest, and try to heal that thing."

Orephes kept darting his eyes around, making sure that no more of these bacaudae were going to try to make their job getting Antonius out of there more difficult. He noticed another group of guards nearby, just exiting a building and getting surrounded by the rebels. There was a young boy with them, perhaps no more than ten years old.

One of the bacaudae used their same trick, tossing a large stone toward the group of guards. One of them was struck, and the other attempted to grab the boy and run. He was shoved over by one of the other rebels, and Orephes decided he had seen enough.

"Hey!" he shouted, drawing his sword.

"What the hell are you doing?" Marius answered from behind him.

Orephes ignored him and pressed forward, his mind already made up. Most of the bacaudae had turned their attention to him. There was no going back now.

Suddenly, he felt that same feeling as he did on the *Nero*, like a breeze inside his body. This time, though, it felt different. Rather than a breeze simply passing through, this time it felt like a wind was flowing *into* him. He almost stopped out of fear, but he couldn't. Whatever this was inside him, it wanted him to keep moving. It wanted him to fight.

As the first bacaudae reached him, he parried a sword hit and used his other hand to land a punch square in their jaw. There was a loud crack as the rebel fell to the floor, no longer moving. Each bacaudae who came at him was dispatched with equal ease. None of them seemed to even be able to hit him. He lost count as one by one, and occasionally two at once, tried to face him and failed.

The Roman guard and the boy noticed Orephes helping them, and they drew their own swords as reinforcements, taking out one or two of the bacaudae nearest them as the crowd thinned out.

Then Orephes felt it. The cold sting of a blade on his arm, followed by the warm trickle of blood. He turned toward the sword to see a frightened-looking bacaudae, both his hands grasping his weapon. It had barely entered the skin. A minor flesh wound.

Almost as a reflex, Orephes grabbed the blade out of his arm and shoved it backward. The blade's handle struck its owner in the chest. With one final swing, Orephes brought his sword down into the bacaudae's shoulder, slicing through the cartilage and leaving a fountain of blood in its place.

The remaining bacaudae in the area seemed to be retreating, returning to wherever it was they had come from. Disappearing into the urban jungle around them. Orephes hurried to the guards that he had helped. The one who had been struck with the stone was getting back up. Luckily, it didn't seem as though he had been hit as bad as Antonius.

Marius had made his way over with Antonius over his back. Joanna followed him.

"The coast seems clear now," he said, making note that all the bacaudae seemed to have fled. "They won't do another strike like that for several weeks."

Despite the protests, one of the guards, the small boy, hurried over to Orephes, an excited look on his face.

"That was amazing!" the boy shouted. "How did you do that?"

Even for a child, that reaction seemed over the top. It had only been a sword fight. Orephes turned to see what he had done. Around two dozen bacaudae were sprawled across the floor of the harbor, each killed by his hands. He hadn't even noticed how many had fallen. There were a few that he didn't even remember fighting, let alone killing in the manner that they were.

He looked at his bloodied hands and remembered that feeling—the same one from the ship—that he had felt right before the fight. Was that what caused this bloodlust he had felt? How could he have lost control like that, without even remembering it? This hadn't simply been the rush of combat. This was something else.

"Train harder than your last fight," Orephes finally answered the child, "fight harder than your last training." It wasn't the truth, but it was a good lesson nonetheless. Those were the same words Eschelus had used when he told him how he could become like his knights at the beginning of his knighthood.

"I've never seen someone fight quite like that," the wounded guard said. "What is your legion?" He was a surprisingly young man for his authoritative tone. Handsome but rugged. The blood from his wound covered some of his face and wet his short curly dark hair.

"My legion?" Orephes asked.

"Your armor. I assumed you were in the Roman army?"

"In a way. I come from Gaul. The army of Eschelus, tribuni scholae."

"The Emperor in the North," the guard said with a light laugh. "Clearly you have been trained well. The bacaudae are not well trained, but they are no pushovers. You managed to take out more of them than some of us see in our lifetimes."

"We learn to fend for ourselves against awful odds in Gaul," Orephes replied.

The guard nodded. "Aye. It is a tough place up there now. You have traveled quite far. Each of us owes you our lives, and I see you have wounded. We can take you to our station. It isn't far from here, and we can treat him there."

"I don't think that will be necessary," Marius chimed in. "We can take care of him ourselves."

Orephes and Joanna looked at Marius curiously.

"What are you talking about? He needs attention," Joanna answered angrily.

Orephes assumed his hesitation was due to his checkered past. Certainly, the guards here in Constantinople were looking for him in some fashion. Particularly if any of them were crooked and working for his old boss the crime lord.

"She's right. He will not survive without help. We have seen wounds like that before."

Marius shook his head but silently conceded.

"My name is Justin Istok," the guard began as they started walking away. "I am a commander of the Excubitors here in the city. For the harbor sector, which is what I was doing here. This young zealot is my nephew, Justinian."

"My name is Orephes, from the Chalcedon Estate," Orephes answered. He was specific to not mention the Chalcedons as his family anymore. It wasn't true.

The group zigzagged through the city streets. On the way, the crew told Justin their entertaining stories about how they met at a whorehouse, and their subsequent journey across the sea, and their run-in with the Vandal pirates. By the time they reached the Excubitor station, Justin had been brought to tears of laughter at the expense of the crew's poor luck.

Marius and Justin also took time to explain the bacaudae. They explained that they were the poor. Peasants. Slaves. Ever since the empire's recent troubles, the people at the bottom have been hit the worst. Every now and then they organize and try to stage stunts like at the harbor to get the attention of the emperor.

Marius described a few times when he had worked as a bandit for a few bacaudae groups out west, usually in northwestern Gaul. It was so lawless up there, the Goths had simply taken to calling them "the Roman hordes."

Justinian seemed extraordinarily interested in the life Orephes had lived out west. That fellow Romans have such plights as constant barbarian raids, he said, made him very angry.

"He is going to grow up to retake the whole Western Empire," Justin bragged facetiously, usually while ruffling Justinian's curly hair. "Isn't that right?" To which Justinian's response became a predictable "and kill all of the barbarians!"

Justin thought his nephew's outbursts were entertaining. To Orephes, they were a painfully naïve dream that Justin would do well to wipe from his head.

Watching Eastern Romans interact like this was like a look back in time. It had likely been more than half a century since anyone in the West had any dreams of wiping out the barbarians. They had become a way of life for the people there. Something Romans had learned to accept. It was well-known how detached Constantinople was from everything happening in Italy and Gaul. He hadn't expected it to be quite as severe as what he was seeing before him.

Once Antonius was settled, Justin extended the offer to give the worn-out crew the opportunity to sleep in one of the urban villas that the Excubitors owned. They lunged at the opportunity, particularly Marius, and each went their own way to their rooms. Justin held Orephes back a moment after his friends had gone, asking him to have a seat in the main hall next to him.

"Where are you headed?" Justin asked. "I would like to see to it that you get there without harm."

Orephes did not want to explain where he was headed. It might sound alarm bells. The Eastern Empire was becoming far more Christian even than the West, and they took apostasy very seriously.

"You have already done so much for us. Surely, the debt is repaid now."

"Nonsense, you saved my life," Justin guffawed. "More importantly, you saved Justinian's life. Those bacaudae would have loved nothing more than to kill the next generation of Imperial Guards to get their silly point across."

Justinian had taken a seat next to his uncle, his legs kicking in and out from under the seat in calm excitement.

"I must go where I am headed alone," Orephes answered.

"At least help me tell you how to get there safely. Zeno is old, Orephes. He will be dead soon. When an emperor dies, the streets outside of this city often become unsafe."

"I am headed north, to Greece."

"What is your business there?"

"I am looking for my real family. My adoptive father—Tiberius Chalcedon—told me I should go looking for those who dropped me at his doorstep. He said they would be in Greece."

"Odd for him to know all of that. Where in Greece? I know the region well. I am from Thrace."

Orephes hesitated for a moment. Why was he continuing to hide this? What did he have to fear? Justin had done nothing but help them. He was a good man.

"Mount Olympus," Orephes answered. There was a moment of silence as he could see Justin processing the information.

His eyes narrowed and his head tilted slightly. "You are searching for your family on Mount Olympus?" Justin asked. Though it sounded more like an accusation.

"My father told me that I was left at his doorstep by the Gods. The only way for me to be sure if he was simply mad is to go to their supposed home and see for myself."

"The Gods? You mean the Old Gods?" Justin's tone changed. He seemed annoyed. Betrayed.

"Those are the ones my father meant."

"Justinian, go to your chambers," Justin commanded.

Orephes grew worried. There were no guards around, certainly he could take Justin if he needed to. But he didn't want to. Not after everything he had done for him.

"But, Uncle," Justinian protested.

"Go," Justin commanded more sternly.

Once Justinian was out of earshot, Justin turned back to Orephes. He seemed to be thinking for a moment, but soon his look softened.

"I wish you had told me this sooner," he admitted. "I would never have brought you here if I knew you were a follower of the Old Gods. It is not safe for you. Or for me."

"I didn't think it mattered."

Justin looked around, checking if anyone was near. "I have orders to kill Old God worshippers on sight. Everyone in this city does."

Orephes felt a sudden jolt of fear.

"Do you intend on killing me?" Orephes asked blithely.

Justin laughed. "After what I saw today, I am not sure I could even if I wanted to. But a few dozen guards with more orders certainly could." Orephes hung on Justin's every word, just waiting for him to tell him that this would be the end of his journey. "Luckily for you, I won't be giving those orders. Now you can consider us even."

"Should I leave?" Orephes asked.

"You and your friends can stay the night. Then you need to leave, but you don't need to go all the way to Olympus to get your answer."

"How?"

"There aren't many augurs left in the empire. Nearly all of them have been killed. But I can take you to one. He can tell you what you need to know without you having to make such an arduous journey."

"An augur?"

Justinian looked puzzled.

"Did your father never tell you about augurs?"

"I suppose not. I have never heard of them."

Justin looked around again, appearing more uncomfortable with each passing moment.

"The augurs were the priests of the Old Gods. For many years in the early republic and empire, every town had an augur, sometimes several. They watched for divine signs, and claimed to relay the will of the Gods to the people. Some of them were known to be able to do incredible things—we Christians would call them miracles, I suppose. An augur would know whether or not what you say is true."

"How can I find one?"

"There aren't many left. The empire and the church spent years hunting them down and killing them. They went into hiding. There are likely some still alive, but they don't practice anymore. They likely have converted so as to never be found."

"So, how is this helpful to me?"

"There is one left close by. A practicing one. He is hidden, but I know how to get to him. My men have been watching him."

"Justin, I don't know how I could ever repay you for this. This is far too kind." Orephes couldn't believe it. This would significantly cut down his trip. He might even be able to make it back to help Eschelus.

Justin stood from the seat, not looking Orephes in the eyes. He shook his head and started to walk off.

"You can repay me by never coming back here. I will leave a parchment in your room with instructions how to find the augur. Tomorrow morning, you will pack your things, follow those instructions, and never return."

"You have my word."

Justin marched off, not turning back once. Orephes stood to head to his room, and caught movement out of the corner of his eye. It was Justinian, who had been hiding around the corner. He had heard everything. Orephes went to speak with him, but by the time he made it to the corner, the boy was long gone.

XX

Orephes had been in his room for several hours. The sun had been down for most of them, but he couldn't sleep. Not with all this weighing on his mind. He had taken a brief look at the name and address that Justin had written on the parchment left near his bedside. It seemed so odd that this journey was almost at an end so much sooner than he thought. It almost felt wrong, as if something was telling him not to do this. Like it was too easy.

His time alone gave him a pause from the drama of the moment but instead his mind drifted toward his family. At least his adopted one. He thought about Gargarus and everyone else he had left behind with not even so much as a goodbye. What must they think of him now? Would they even accept him if he returned?

He felt a moment of guilt before remembering that Gargarus knew everything. He had never told him, but he knew that he wasn't his true brother. After years of lying, what did Orephes owe him? The truth? Honesty? Honor?

Creak.

A shadow moved across the ceiling as the door to his room shifted. Someone had pushed it, but he didn't see anyone enter. The candlelit room was dim, but it certainly wasn't dark. Nobody had entered.

"Who's there?"

He shot up from the bed. His sword was on the other end of the room, near the door. He maybe had a few seconds to get to it, if whoever was on the other side of that wall was planning on killing him.

"Mr. Orephes?" a faint voice spoke from behind the door. It was Justinian. He peeked his head into the dim lighting, squinting to adjust after the darkness of the hallway.

"What are you doing here?" Orephes asked, walking toward the door. He placed his hand on the boy's shoulder, escorting him into the room while taking a moment to peek outside and make sure he hadn't been followed.

"I needed to tell you something."

"It is very late. Does your uncle know you are here?"

"No."

"I don't want your uncle to be upset. You must go back to your room."

"I don't care if he knows," Justinian said defiantly. "I need to tell you something."

Orephes crossed his arms. The faster this was over with, the faster this kid could go back to his room, and the faster he would no longer have to worry about any of this.

"Well, what is it?"

"The augur that my uncle wants to send you to. He isn't real."

Orephes felt his stomach turn. Those feelings—the ones telling him that something felt wrong about all this—magnified. He uncrossed his arms and sat down on the bed.

"What do you mean he isn't real?"

"The place where they are sending you is a fake augur. They use him as a trap. To catch the people who don't believe in God and Jesus."

"A trap? How is he a trap?"

"People come here from other parts of the empire looking for anyone left who follows the Old Gods. They always end up finding this augur, the fake one, because agents of my uncle lead them there. Old men in pubs. Normal civilians. The agents are everywhere to spread this. When they get there, to the augur's home, they are tortured and killed."

Orephes didn't want to believe the kid, but he knew it was true. Something else was telling him the same. Something that he trusted far more, even though he didn't even know what it was. He couldn't believe that after all of that, Justin still planned to kill him. He could have just done it here, while Orephes was sleeping. Why did he have to send him to this false priest to die?

Perhaps Marius was right. These Imperial Guard types can never be trusted.

"Thank you," Orephes said. "When we leave tomorrow, we will not head that way. I will continue on. To my original destination."

"No. I know where you need to go."

Orephes smiled at the child's adorable audacity.

"And where is that?"

"There is a real augur. One that my uncle and the bishops found a few years ago, but they can't get to him. That is where you need to go."

"Why can't they get to him?"

"Because he is in barbarian territory."

"I grew up in barbarian territory," Orephes mentioned with a smirk.

"He will be able to help you. He is a real augur. The last one that my uncle knows of."

"Thank you. Why are you telling me all of this?" Orephes laughed in his head at the number of times he had to ask that in the past few days.

"Because one day, when I am emperor, I am going to have a huge army and we are going to take over the entire empire again. I need people who can win. Like you. You can't win if you are dead."

Justinian handed Orephes a small parchment before quietly leaving the room. Orephes took a look, and scrawled in childlike Latin was the name of a town and a crudely drawn map. If he was reading it right, it looked like the town was north of Greece, deep in the "barbarian north." He slid the parchment into his satchel and finally drifted off to sleep, his mind feeling at ease.

XXI

*O*rephes.

The voice was different this time. Harsher.

Orephes!

"Father!" Orephes shouted, remembering the last time this happened. He looked around and saw nothing but black. "Father, are you out there?"

Where are you going?

Something was wrong. That final line certainly didn't sound like his father.

But it had to be. This felt exactly like last time. Perhaps this time, he could get to speak with him.

"Where you told me to go," Orephes answered. "Don't you remember?"

There was no voice in reply, but Orephes could make out a faint figure in the distance, appearing in the void of black.

Suddenly, there was a faint whisper and everything became white. Orephes could see himself perfectly. He no longer saw a black abyss but a white one. It extended in every direction, endless and muted.

Then he saw it. The figure. Only unlike everything else around him, the figure had remained pitch-black. He couldn't make out any details other than the figure's outline and his arms and legs as they moved. Why were they moving?

It was coming toward him. Orephes tried to see more detail, but it seemed as though the more he strained, the less he could make out. Instead, it seemed to blur further out of distinguishability. Was it his father? The voice he kept hearing?

Then, suddenly, the feeling. It wasn't how he felt last time, when he heard his father. The warmth that seemed to permeate his skin. No, this time, he felt different. He felt empty—as though whatever this figure was, it wasn't bringing him life, it was taking it from him.

"What are you?" Orephes asked.

There was no reply. The closer the figure seemed to get, the worse Orephes felt. It was like a burden was being added to him with each step it took.

Last time it was only a dream. He had to wake up. He needed to get out of this. It didn't feel right. This felt too real. He tried to smack himself to no avail. Nothing was working.

The figure was only a few feet away now, and Orephes could finally make out a set of eyes, or at least, sockets where the eyes should have been. The feeling was overwhelming. Whatever this was, he wanted to have nothing to do with it.

He drew his sword in his hand and thrust into his own abdomen, just as the dark figure's arm reached out to him. The figure disappeared in a puff of smoke, and Orephes's eyes opened in the bedroom he had fallen asleep. His hands unconsciously flew to his abdomen—no wound. He was drenched in sweat, but he was perfectly fine.

He felt around for the amulet. Last time this happened, the amulet had comforted him. It was as though the amulet had been in there with him. This time, it was nowhere to be found. He shot up and searched, finally finding it in his satchel across the room. Unlike last time, he didn't feel the same connection to it. He almost felt farther from it.

None of it made any sense. He didn't understand what was happening to him, but unless he reached Olympus, he may very well never understand. He put the amulet back into his pocket and went back to bed for a bit before everyone else woke.

Later that morning, he had nearly forgotten the entire experience. Marius had come in to wake him, and Joanna followed shortly thereafter. They had subsequently bickered about both waking him up when the other had already done it. They were much faster to move in the mornings than he was.

Justin hadn't even had the courage to come face the group again before they left. Orephes knew why, but Joanna and Marius assumed he must be busy. They had bid their farewells to the other guards as they headed out, including the young Justinian, who waved happily to Orephes as they left the expansive urban estate to go back into the streets of Constantinople.

Orephes had made the difficult decision to leave Antonius behind. It would be better for him there, among fellow guards and allies to Rome, than on a treacherous journey in his state. Some of the guards feared he may never wake up. They said several of their friends had it—they called it "mind of stone" after the thing that made them that way—and ultimately they had made the decision to kill them as their bodies fell apart from being unable to eat or drink.

In any case, Antonius hadn't even wanted to come this far. Surely, he didn't want to go any farther. This way, even if he did awaken, he could feel free of his obligation to watch over Orephes as though he was some kind of child. He could go back to fight alongside Eschelus, which is what he really always wanted. To go home on his own terms.

Although Orephes promised Justin he would never be back, he left a small note in Antonius's armor for him to find when he did wake up. It let him know that Orephes, on his way back from wherever he was going, would come back this way to get him if he had decided not to leave. Justin be damned.

As the trio made their way onto the street, the sheer prosperity of the city became even more apparent. Rome had a bit of affluence, and certainly many people, but Constantinople had none of the beggars, none of the decrepit structures. It all felt new and expensive. Even the insulae housing everything from the wealthy to the poor seemed more put together. As though there was care put into the design, and it hadn't been haphazardly rebuilt.

At first, none of the three looked at each other as they walked away. Marius, of course, got the first word in.

"I just can't seem to get away from you two," he said with a sigh. "After being nearly castrated by a prostitute, being attacked by both my former employer and pirates, and subsequently being almost killed by the bacaudae, I think this is finally my cue to depart. Orephes, I wish you the best in your trip scaling the mountain of the Gods. Surely, given your luck so far, there is no way you can fail." Orephes detected the sarcasm in his voice, but let it slide if for no other reason than he would miss it. Marius hadn't been there for the chat with Justin, so he had no idea that the destination had changed. "Joanna, it was a pleasure developing this exceedingly platonic relationship with you. You are the first whore I have ever paid to simply spend time with."

"Was it as good for you as it was for me?" Joanna asked.

"If you mean not at all, then yes, of course," Marius answered with his token smile.

"I did," Joanna answered, smiling back. "Though I can still smell the sweet odor of that hideous fur jacket."

"Hey, there are pirates who will pay good money for those jackets," Marius shot back, waving his finger in the air. "Where will you, the enigmatic wandering free citizen prostitute, be heading from here?"

Joanna walked over and stood next to Orephes.

"I am going with him."

Marius and Orephes shared a look of surprise as their eyes shot wide open. Marius stammered a few incoherent lines before finally blurting out, "What do you mean going with him? Removing the simple fact that you live all the way back in Rome, you understand that what he wants to do is insane?"

"What I saw on that boat was insane. But I saw it. Orephes doesn't have Antonius anymore. I won't let him do this alone."

"We got to know each other pretty well on that boat," Marius started, exasperated, "but surely we didn't get to know each other enough that you are willing to die for his crazy theory?"

"Marius, you saw exactly what I did on that boat. Do you think nothing of that? Besides, what do you care where I go?" Joanna's voice suddenly grew contentious. "Aren't I nothing more than the enigmatic slave girl?"

Marius tried to think of something to say before falling silent. If Orephes didn't know better, he would have said that Joanna seemed bothered by the silence.

"He's right, Joanna," Orephes replied. "This is bound to be extremely dangerous. I think it might be best if I do this alone."

"You have very little chance of doing this with some help," Joanna replied, "let alone by yourself. I am coming with you. There is nothing for me back in Rome. Being here with you two has been the most meaning my life has had."

"Us two?" Marius interjected. "I knew that fur coat meant more to you than you were letting on."

"OK," Orephes answered after a deep breath. "But we have to leave now. We have a long way to go."

"Well, good luck with all of that, you two. If you need me, I will likely be alone running from guards and crime lords here in Constantinople."

"Marius, thank you for everything. I couldn't have come this far without you."

Orephes stretched his hand out for a shake. Marius wasn't looking at him, instead his eyes were fixed on Joanna's exceedingly disappointed look. He finally looked at Orephes, the proud young kid who got him into all this mess, standing there like a damn fool wanting his hand shaken as though it meant anything.

Marius shook his head and let out a deep sigh, whispering, "God strike me down now," before finally opening his eyes after a long blink.

"Well, I damn well can't not go on this suicide trip now. I would feel terrible if my primary benefactor of the next month ends up perishing knowing I could have helped. Or at least watched. I'll come, but none of this handshake nonsense. We aren't taking a bet. Well, other than on our lives."

Orephes put his hand down and hid a smile. "The more the merrier."

Marius grabbed his things and joined the other two in heading away.

"You better be careful, Marius," Joanna said. "You are in danger of becoming a good person."

Marius stopped abruptly and pointed backward. "I will turn around right now," he teased angrily. "Don't tempt me!"

As the group neared the city exit, they heard a bell begin to chime. This was followed by increasingly loud murmurs from the citizens, who stopped in their tracks at the very first toll. They started to move, almost in unison, but all seemed to be heading the opposite direction of the group, back toward the city center.

Something had happened, and Orephes couldn't help but feel as though the entire city was in on it except for him.

"What's going on?" Joanna asked nervously.

"Hey," Marius asked, grabbing one of the slower movers walking by. "What happened?"

"The emperor has passed away." They didn't need to say anything else. Marius nodded and let the person on their way.

"Well, I guess Zeno's reign is over," Marius lamented softly. "As far as emperors go, he was all right, I guess."

"What happens now?" Orephes asked.

"They will have a vigil, among other things. We don't have time to worry about it. Death of an emperor only means one thing for us—a tougher trip. Once word gets out, small barbarian raiding parties like to take advantage of the disarray in the capital to make strikes on Roman roads."

"How long do you think it will take for the word to get out?"

"Let's not wait around to find out. You know where we are headed, kid?"

"I do."

"Then let's move."

The three headed out of Constantinople to the continuing chimes of the bells, an ominous, foreboding sound that set the tone as they disappeared into the abyss of stone roads ahead of them.

XXII

Odoacer's Palace, Ad Laurentum, Ravenna

The sound of swords clanking filled the usually quiet dining hall, punctuated only by the occasional shout of "good!" or "no, this way!"

For Odoacer's wife, Sunigilda, seeing her son and husband fight like this, even to train, was torture. All it would take was one missed swing and someone could lose an eye or an arm.

As she stepped into the room, Odoacer lowered his sword. His son kept swinging, and nearly hit him.

"Whoa, boy!" Odoacer shouted, spinning him around by his head to face his mother. "No fighting when your mother is around."

"She is always around," his son joked. "At this rate I will never be the warrior you were. You took Rome, maybe I can take Constantinople!"

Odoacer laughed, though his wife seemed far less amused.

"Go wash up for supper," he commanded to his son, who hurried off.

"You know I don't like this sort of thing," Sunigilda mentioned as her son sped off.

"He needs to learn to fight, Sunigilda," Odoacer replied pleadingly. "I should have trained him when he was much younger."

"You told me we were taking Rome to build a better world. One where our people didn't have to fight for a living."

"All men fight," Odoacer answered. "Some fight for a living. Others for survival. But we all fight."

"Why is our son destined to fight for survival, then?"

"Because others will give him no choice." Odoacer placed his sword down on the table. "You worry far too much." He grabbed his wife by her ass, pulling her closer to him up against the table. As always, he took a moment to think about how gorgeous she was. How amazing the ass that he got to grab every day was. Few barbarian men could claim a wife so beautiful.

"You worry too little."

"We are at war. It isn't strange of me to want our son trained to fight."

"Why can't he be a senator?" she asked, running her hand through his beard.

"Because he isn't Roman."

"Neither are you, yet here you are, patrician and king of Italy."

"I've explained to you before. It is different."

"It is no different, except that you let those old Roman bastards dictate to you. They hold the strings not you."

Odoacer kissed his wife.

"How did I find such a brilliant woman," he said with a laugh. "Everything you say is true. What am I to do about this? Slaughter them all? There would be civil war!"

"Ask them to make your son a senator. What harm can it bring?" Odoacer looked down at his smiling wife as she placed her hands on his chest. She was right. There was no reason he couldn't, unless he was afraid of the consequences. Why should he be afraid of that now? Italy was his. They couldn't take that from him even if they wanted. The Senate had no army. He had been very fair to them. It was time for them to be fair back.

"All right," Odoacer proclaimed. "Next time I am with the Senate, I shall command they accept our son as a senator."

"Really?"

"I promise."

Sunigilda kissed her husband excitedly. Then again, and again, until he turned her around over the table, his hand running up her legs.

Then a cough from the doorway.

"Pardon, sir," a guard said meekly. "I have urgent news."

"This better be the most important news I have heard all year," Odoacer said, spanking his wife as he turned from her. "I'll be back for you in a moment."

"Emperor Zeno is dead, sir," the guard announced.

"When?"

"Just yesterday, sir. He died peacefully in his sleep."

"I don't give a fuck how he died, you fool. Does everyone else know?"

"Just the generals and a few of the elite guard, sir."

"Tell everyone. We shall use this to turn the momentum against that liar Theodric. He will have no legitimacy to attack us now. We will counterstrike to meet their assault. Tell my generals to come now."

"I want to come first," Sunigilda said pleadingly from behind them.

Odoacer grinned as the guard shifted stance uncomfortably.

"On second thought, tell them to come after supper."

"Yes, sir."

The guard hurried off, leaving Odoacer alone with his wife.

"Do you think this will help us win the war?" she asked.

"If the next emperor chooses us over Theodric, then yes."

Sunigilda shook her head.

"Even after the fall of the emperor in Rome, those people still find a way to get tribes to fight each other instead of the common enemy. Betting on who wins and loses with gold while spilling no blood."

"I love it when you talk smart," Odoacer said, grabbing his wife's ass again.

"Who will they choose?" she asked softly.

Odoacer leaned forward over his wife again. He kissed her ear before whispering his answer, "Whoever is winning."

XXIII

Somewhere in Greece

The trio had been traveling for days, stopping at inns and small villages along the way. Marius mentioned that out west it was far more difficult to travel now. Most of the small villages were abandoned and the roads were in disrepair. Here in the east, they still had Roman engineers come out and repair the roads every so often. The Imperial government paid good money to keep the gold flowing into Constantinople. Of course, the massive East Roman army, and its ability to keep the barbarians at bay unlike out west, certainly played a major role.

In fact, despite the emperor's death, the group didn't have a violent incident throughout their trek, though Marius believed it was merely due to the group getting out there before the word could spread.

Eventually, the roads grew sparser and the villages grew farther apart. The area they were going was right outside Imperial territory. They knew they were getting close the farther from civilization they seemed to become.

"I don't remember Olympus being this far," Marius whined. "I know I have been there at least once. I think I was stealing offerings left up there from the Old God worshippers. Told myself I would be back. Never thought it would be like this."

"We aren't going to Olympus."

Joanna and Marius looked at each other, and then at Orephes. They stopped in their tracks.

"When did this change? Why didn't you tell us?" Joanna asked angrily.

"Because I was afraid you wouldn't want to come anymore."

"We opted to join you on a mad quest to the peak of Olympus, and you think going somewhere else would have scared us away? Where are we going?"

"To see an augur."

"What is that?" Marius asked.

"I've heard of those. Old stories about augurs. They were priests, right?" Joanna asked.

"Something like that. I know where the last one is living. He can tell me what I am. I won't even need to go to Olympus."

"This sounds like a much better plan," Marius said happily. "Where does this thing live?"

"Right outside the Imperial border in the north."

"In barbarian territory?"

"That's right."

"On second thought, it might be better if we headed to Olympus."

"Don't be a baby," Joanna shot back. "Like you haven't ever been in areas heavily populated with barbarians before?"

The sound of Marius and Joanna bickering disappeared into the distance as Orephes noticed something ahead on the road. A person, standing alone. No horse or cart. He didn't know why, but he immediately filled with dread the moment he set eyes upon him.

"Look ahead," Orephes said, interrupting the two. "Do you see that person?"

Marius focused his sight ahead.

"The one standing eerily ahead of us? Yes."

"No horse or cart. No village for miles. What are they doing out here?"

"More importantly, why are they standing there looking our way."

"Is it a barbarian?" Joanna asked.

Marius used his hand to block the sun and looked a bit closer. "I don't know. He is wearing something I have never seen before. It doesn't look barbarian or Roman."

The man started toward them, never breaking his stare at the group. He moved with a slow cadence. The group expected him to pick up the pace, but he simply kept moving slowly toward them, never breaking his stare or stride.

As he got closer, the group could finally make out his face. He looked middle-aged, his skin paler than most Greeks. He was clean-shaven, with curly hair and perfect-looking blue eyes. His muscle tone easily outdid even that of Orephes, who had spent months training to be a knight. His strange outfit, complete with tall, tied sandals and what seemed like an armored chest plate over typical Roman robes, seemed like something from a different time.

"Hello, there!" Marius shouted as he came close enough that he could hear. There was no answer. "Well, he certainly isn't polite."

"He is cute, whoever he is. But this is very strange," Joanna said nervously.

"I disagree," Marius said. He pretended to be examining the figure closer. Orephes could tell that he was jealous.

As the man got closer, Orephes became more certain of what he was feeling. It was the same thing he had felt that night in Constantinople. That weight. That shortness of breath. That feeling like someone was telling him something is wrong. This time, he also felt that familiar breeze inside his body. This time, it felt like it was blowing right past him. Through him.

"He isn't a friend," Orephes said quickly. "We need to stay away from him." Joanna and Marius seemed to listen, but they didn't move. "We need to move now!"

It was too late.

Without breaking his stride, the man lowered his hands to the ground, throwing dust and dirt into the air on either side of him. Slowly, the dust seemed to swirl around his hands as he gently moved his fingers, faster and faster until it started to pick up the stones off the ground, as well.

Finally, he lifted his hands. The swirling mix of dirt and stones seemed to first glow yellow before igniting into flames in his palms, slowly transforming before their very eyes from a plume of smoke and stone into a solid object in his hands.

After a few moments it became clear what they were—two swords, one in each hand, forged from sand and stone. The swords looked cracked and dented, each crevice filled with an orange-yellow glow like hot charcoal in a fire. Orephes could see the heat waves coming off them, as well as small pieces of glowing, burning dust falling to the ground.

"Please, for the love of God," Marius started as the man continued his approach, "tell me that you can do something like that."

Orephes drew his sword as the man came before him.

"Whoever you are, we have no quarrel with you," Orephes shouted.

The man answered with the swing of his sword. Orephes felt the hot air as he dodged it, keeping it narrowly missing his face. As it hit the ground, small embers flew off it. It reminded Orephes of striking the floor with a burning log. Though the sound it made as it hit the ground made it clear that this would be a lot more painful.

Marius drew his knives in an attempt to help his friend. Before he could even take a step, he was propelled backward with a flick of the man's wrist in his direction. Joanna suffered the same fate before she could even finish drawing her sword. Orephes wondered why hadn't this man—this thing—simply done the same to him?

They wouldn't be able to help him. Orephes was alone to face whoever this was.

The man slammed his swords together, releasing a flurry of embers. The sound the swords made was unsettling. The sound of metal swords had become so ingrained in Orephes's head, hearing something like this—what sounded like two stones slamming together—simply reinforced the fear driving him.

"Who are you?" Orephes asked angrily. "Why do I feel like I've been near you before?"

"I am Volusian." He had finally spoken. He had a soft voice. Almost soothing. It was a voice Orephes hadn't expected. Perfect Latin with no discernible accent. "But that is irrelevant. Names are irrelevant. The more important question is what I am. Even more important is what *you* are."

Orephes held his sword forward, ready for another swing at any moment. He assumed he must be talking about his secret lineage. There was no other explanation that made sense. But he wouldn't be the one to tell him if it wasn't the case. He would instead play dumb. The two were walking in circles, as to always be in front of each other. Volusian had a smirk on his face as though he was enjoying it.

"Well, what am I, then?" Orephes asked.

"If my suspicions are correct," Volusian replied, "you are something *spectacular.*"

"I am a knight in the army of the Emperor Eschelus in the North," Orephes replied. He would give nothing back. "I am on a special mission."

"Tsk-tsk," Volusian hissed back. He shook his head condescendingly. "Disappointing."

He took another swing, this time landing a blow on Orephes's sword. The blow was forceful; Orephes hadn't been expecting it. It nearly knocked the sword from his hand.

Suddenly, a stone flew at Volusian's head. He turned to it and lifted his hand, dissolving it into embers before it could hit him. Orephes saw Joanna had gotten up and was running back toward the fight.

Orephes took the opening, driving his sword forward. It was met by Volusian's other sword, which pushed both of them backward from the ricochet.

Joanna finally returned and took a few swings, pitting them two on one. Volusian easily and dismissively countered both of them before finally throwing Joanna back again, this time even farther away.

Orephes felt his legs give out from under him as Volusian lifted his arm. His one attempt to stand up was met by a kick to the chest, knocking him back down.

"I will ask again," Volusian pressed. "What are you?"

"It seems like you already know," Orephes shot back. "Go ahead and tell me."

Volusian rolled his eyes and lifted his hand toward Orephes's head.

The next thing Orephes remembered was darkness. He was inside his own mind, powerless as Volusian tore away each and every boundary to learn who he was. What he was. He could feel thoughts leaving him, scooped up in large quantities by Volusian as he hunted for what he wanted. He wanted to scream. He wanted to push back. But he was powerless. Volusian's voice, like whispers, haunted him in the darkness. Images flashed around him of people he didn't recognize being slaughtered by Volusian's flaming swords.

Then, abruptly, he was back. He tore his eyes open as Volusian let out a yell. Marius had leaped up from behind him, sticking his two knives into his shoulders. Orephes took the chance to quickly stand and attempt a swing. Before he could, dirt and dust began to spin around all three of them, carried by a mighty wind, blocking their vision.

"Marius," Orephes shouted. Dust poured into his mouth as he yelled, immediately drying out his tongue. "Are you there?"

As suddenly as it began, the wind and dirt subsided. Volusian was gone, leaving behind only Marius's swords where he had once stood.

Orephes helped Marius up as they coughed up the remaining dust. Joanna had made her way back to the group.

"He's gone," Orephes assured them both. "I can feel it."

At first there was silence. None of them knew how to even process what they had just seen, let alone react to it. This wasn't a happenstance breeze shoving people off a boat. This was someone who can forge swords from the soil. Who can fling people around like twigs.

Marius, always one to break a silence, was the first to speak.

"To add to my list of things that you have brought into my life," he started, "I can now place crazy magic people who can form swords out of the dirt. I always say that anything can be a weapon, but that was a bit absurd."

"That wasn't just some barbarian raid," Joanna added worriedly. "Whoever he was, Orephes, we can't beat him. Not when he can toss us around like feathers in the wind." Joanna, in particular, seemed affected by what had just happened. As though her very reality had been uprooted in front of her.

"Whoever or whatever he is, he has something to do with all of this. Where I am going. I think it means I am on the right track."

"If someone like that is simply walking around the empire… who knows what he has been doing this whole time. What he *can* do." Marius put his hand on Orephes's shoulder. "Listen, kid. I didn't really care much for this stuff before. I am a Christian. I don't believe in superstition. But whatever that was, that was real. That man—that thing—is out there, and it scares the hell out of me. If helping you get to where you need to go helps take something like that off this world…" He seemed to drift away in thought for a moment. "Let's get you to this priest. Let's find out what the hell is going on. Before it is too late."

"We will get there. All of us. Together."

XXIV

Chalcedon Estate, Gaul

They must have been watching much closer than he thought. Either that or there had been a spy in the ranks of the citizens here at the villa. It was the only way they could have known as soon as they did that Eschelus had departed.

Gargarus had received word in no more than three days that the Goths were forming their army. It needn't be too big—they knew that. There wasn't much left in the form of a defense anymore. But they wouldn't want to risk it. They knew that Eschelus's men were some of the most well trained in the world. They would certainly be bringing more than they needed.

The meetings with the older Romans in the villa were becoming increasingly sparse, and at the same time increasingly tense. More and more were leaving, no longer feeling safe without Eschelus's army to help. It wasn't lost on Gargarus that the more who left, the fewer he had to help defend his home. At the same time, the ones who remained have begun challenging him on how to manage his own estate. On several occasions, he had had to tersely remind them that his home is not a republic. This is his home. His property. His rules.

Every now and then he thought again about Orephes. How he had abandoned him here to run the affairs alone. Granted, he was never one for management or politics. But it would have been nice to have someone at his side. Someone he could trust implicitly.

He trusted the group of soldiers that Eschelus had left for him, but there weren't many. All it would take is one strong raid, and he would be without guards and with nobody to keep his home his own.

There was some shouting from the gate. Someone was there.

One of the guards approached him calmly. He didn't seem in a panic.

"Sir, there is someone at the gate asking for you. They seem to be Roman."

"I wasn't expecting any guests."

"He said you would recognize him."

The guard escorted Gargarus to the top of the wall overlooking the gate, where he could see for the first time in weeks the land outside of his own. The endless expanse of green that seemed to simultaneously shrink and grow larger by the day.

There was a Roman standing there, holding his horse and a scroll in his hand. He recognized him immediately, and he certainly wasn't about to let him in.

"Tell my wife to stay inside," Gargarus instructed one of the guards near him. He leaned over the edge of the wall, sneering down at the man in front of him. "What do you want, Erophus?"

"I have been sent by Alaric II, King of the Goths, to deliver your terms of surrender."

"You are working for the Goths now, are you? I half expected to see you here someday. The role of a barbarian king's bitch suits you well." Gargarus could not think of anything other than the scar on his wife's head, hidden by her hair but still in pain when it was cold. The lasting fears she often had of being in the dark or in a locked room.

"Don't be petty, Gargarus. The terms are fair."

A few of the guards snickered.

"This is the last vestige of Rome in Gaul, and it is my home. I will never surrender it."

This time, Erophus snickered. "Listen to you, a man who would steal another man's property, claiming to be friends to the Roman way. You were never a friend to Rome or its ways. You were a selfish bastard, always have been. You used Rome when it suited you, fought against it when it didn't. No better than a bloody baucadae."

He could have shot an arrow right there and killed him had he been a smaller man. Or a better shot.

"She isn't your property. She is my wife."

"Not according to the laws of the Rome you pretend to represent. You should love these barbarians, Gargarus. It is only because of them that I wasn't able to show up here with the local magistrate and tear her from your bed while you slept. Perhaps I would have taken some time to fuck her on the way back to my estate, to reclaim her. To remind her who that cunt of hers belongs to."

He didn't come here to piss him off. He came here for a reason. Gargarus was letting himself get flustered. He needed to stay focused.

"I will never surrender. If your king wants this property, he can take it from our dead hands."

"Perfect. I will relay the message."

Erophus was happy. It was the answer he wanted, though certainly not the answer his king wanted. Erophus wouldn't be on the front lines. It would mean more Goths would have to die to take this place. If it didn't sit near one of the old major Roman roads, they might have just let them be. But they would never stand for insubordination like this.

Erophus departed quickly after that, sparing Gargarus any additional banter. A few of his guards made it a point to try to assure him that they would hold out as long as they could. He was certain they would. It wasn't simply his home they were defending; it was also their lives.

XXV

Northern Italy

It was colder than usual, even for October. Eschelus had trouble masking his hands when they shook in this weather. He had to keep them steadied on the hilt of his sword or on his waist. His men couldn't see it. It was a sign of weakness that he could not afford. Not at this hour.

His men would think it was the cold. They would think him frail. Old. If they knew the truth, they would be far more distraught.

Eschelus could never be sure that his men were as haunted by their kills as he was by those he had killed. Most simply seemed to carry on, and many had killed far more than he had. For Eschelus, every kill weighed on him. Tore at him. Twisted his soul.

He could remember every single one. The first kill in Ravenna almost twenty years ago. The barbarians shortly after. It made him sick. Ruined his focus. It was as though he had caught a plague of the soul, and the only cure would be his inevitable death.

There had been only two men alive who knew, or at least seemed to understand, what he was going through. Both were dead now. Paul had noticed it at the inception all those years ago.

"Blood sickness," he called it. Others called it "war haunted." It had many names across the different cultures, but the symptoms were always the same. He could barely sleep, awoken by the screams of war. He would find himself being startled at the smallest of sounds—a pot falling, his men laughing. They brought him back to those moments. To his sword plunging into the heart of a child younger than him at the time. Watching the life leave their eyes.

Tiberius had been different. He didn't think it was a sickness at all. He believed that those he had killed were with him. Following him. Chipping away at his soul with every additional kill, until one day all that would be left is his body. A hollow, shaking shell unable to function like a normal man. Unable to function at all.

He wasn't sure whose view he ascribed to. Whether this was all caused by a madness inside him or a group of spirits without. He did know that it had been getting worse, and whatever was to happen, it had to happen before he was no longer fit to lead the very army he had built.

He was in with his knights, a bit away from his main camp. The plan was simple. Eschelus would meet the army of Odoacer first, drawing him and his generals out for negotiation in the open. As they did, his knights would come bounding from the east before they could retreat, slaughtering Odoacer and his leadership where they stood. One knight would go to Theodric's camp, farther to the east still, and signal them to begin their attack.

The hope was this would cause Odoacer's army to retreat immediately. If it didn't, the combined armies of Theodric and Eschelus would be more than enough to defeat the demoralized armies before them.

The plan was dirty. Slaughtering generals and a patrician before the battle could even be won was dishonorable. But it had to be done. They couldn't defeat the army one-on-one. Rome itself was at stake. A few of his men had felt uncomfortable with the plan at first. Tufa, the barbarian general that Theodric had given him, helped to quell the unrest.

"He would do the same to us," he claimed. "You are doing your people a service."

Michael was finishing preparing Torix. This would be his first battle, and it was the most important one. Nothing could go wrong.

The other knights had assured the general that Torix was ready. That the plan would go over without a hitch. He trusted them. The knights had never failed him. This was the most important battle of them all. They would be there for him stronger than ever before. They would take Rome back together. They would restore all that had been undone.

The thought was the only thing that kept Eschelus going. All the death he had seen and been a part of. All the destruction. It all paved the way for this moment. For him to be able to retake this land for the people of Rome. It wasn't so much that he would be emperor. It was that there would be an emperor again, in his rightful place.

One of his guards told him that it was time. He embraced each one of his knights, even Torix, before heading back to the main camp. The battle would begin in the morning. One more night to allow Theodric's army to get into position.

The knights, alone again, took a moment to collect their thoughts.

"This is it," Bracchus finally blurted out. "It is finally happening, boys. We are taking back our country."

"I will be honest," Roman added. "I wasn't confident I would ever see the day."

"Neither was I, but we are here now," Michael said. "And we will win."

They recapped the plan. Reminded each other to stick to it. Recounted their number of kills so far, competing with each other as always. Bracchus kept reminding Michael that the person he decapitated after the other shot them with an arrow was *actually* his kill, while Michael kept implying that bacaudae, being fellow Romans, counted as double.

Torix wasn't Roman, but now, as he partied with his fellow knights after months of training, he certainly felt like he was. The knights had embraced him as their own. Even Bracchus, after enough of a struggle. The type of connection that Romans felt to each other and to their country was very different from that which he knew as a Goth. For his people, it was about your family. For Romans, it was about so much more than that. It was about a culture. An entire infrastructure.

His people had watched Rome from afar for generations, envying what they had. This was his chance to be a part, now, of what they could rebuild.

While his comrades celebrated, he sat quietly. He told them he was focusing. Getting ready for the battle. He couldn't tell them the truth of why he was sent there. About his true mission that he was meant to fulfill. He wasn't sure if he wanted to fulfill it anymore. His mind was racing, weighing the pros and cons to himself.

As the knights settled down in their individual tents to sleep, Torix lay awake, knowing what would have to be done. Trying to decide whether or not he could do it. He had one hand on his sword, the other on the cross he carried around with him. Was this right? Was what he was about to do what was best for his people?

He shot up quickly, drawing his sword. There was a stirring outside his tent. Someone was in the nearby bushes, their feet crunching in the dirt. It wasn't any of the other knights. Their tents were on the other side of the clearing. It was far too late for it to be Eschelus.

Suddenly, there was a shadow on his tent. An outline of a person. Someone was out there, and whoever it was, they wanted him.

XXVI

Dacia, Barbarian Territory, Northeast of Greece

Everything seemed different this far north. Even the trees seemed to have less life. The trio had been mainly silent after the fight with Volusian, even while Marius and Joanna seemed to be getting along very well. So well, in fact, that if Orephes didn't know better, he might have thought they even liked each other as more than just friends—or, rather, adventurers. Their arguments about the direction they were headed were entertaining, if not annoying. Orephes was simply happy to have company. It was very possible, even just a few days ago, that he might have been doing this entire journey alone.

Throughout Greece, and thanks to Justinian writing them a letter forging his uncle's signature, the trio had the privilege of using the special designated Imperial postal routes, resting at the handpicked villas along the way. After leaving the security of Roman walls, there was no such thing. They were traveling by foot.

Since leaving Roman territory, they hadn't hit a single village along the road they were following. Even Marius, someone a bit more familiar with the barbarian north, found it odd. He had checked

191

again—this was certainly the right road. Justinian had made it very clear. Even the landmarks he had mentioned could be found along the way. The tree with one branch. The horse painting on a stone. It was exactly as he had written it.

The quiet of the trip kept Orephes thinking about Volusian. About how he had dug into his mind. Pried it open. What had he been looking for? More importantly, what had he found? Worse yet, when would he be back? This all had to be tied together—he just wasn't sure how. Hopefully this augur could explain it. Hopefully this augur was still alive in the first place.

The group stopped when they hit a clearing in the woods. There were remnants of a sign on the side of the road, and ahead, buildings. The first they had seen since leaving Rome. All of them looked abandoned and overgrown. The group looked at each other momentarily before, without speaking, choosing to press forward. Justinian had mentioned the augur lived in an abandoned Roman settlement. This certainly was abandoned. The question was if it was the correct settlement.

As Orephes stepped past the broken sign, he felt a pull. That breeze inside him again, headed toward the town.

"I feel something," he said out loud. His voice sounded thunderous in the silence of the abandoned buildings, echoing off the stone.

"What is it?" Joanna asked quickly. "Volusian?"

"No. Something else."

"Maybe the augur?" Marius asked.

"I am not sure. I haven't felt something like this before. It is a pull. There is something in this town that is…pulling whatever this is that I feel."

"We must be in the right place." Joanna drew her sword. "You can't be too careful. Stay sharp."

They were at the edge of the town and Orephes still felt the pull. The abandoned buildings were certainly still abandoned. Nobody had lived there in years. No sign of fire, barely any signs of looting. There was nothing there except the silent ghostly worn marble buildings still standing where they had been erected, slowly being eroded by nature's green veins of vines and weeds.

"This is the end. Should we go back and keep searching?" Marius asked.

"The road seems to keep going. I think we should continue to follow it. The pull is coming from beyond the next tree line."

They pushed over a hill and beyond the next tree line, where there was another clearing. This time, there was only a single building—a small home of wood and stone. It had similar growths of vine and trees but was clearly not abandoned. Smoke billowed from a small chimney on the roof. Glass still covered the windows. There was a faint smell of burning candles in the air.

As they stepped into this clearing, Orephes felt something new—the pull dissipated, leaving just a pressure. An enveloping warmth that relaxed his muscles yet honed his mind.

"This is it. We are here."

Orephes was the first to step forward, inching closer to the door of the solitary home. Slowly, they made their way face-to-face with the doorway. It was definitely old, with wood rotting away at the ends. From inside, a faint smell of some strange spice permeated the air around them. Orephes stood staring at the shut door, almost fearing what was on the other side.

"Well, what are you waiting for, kid?" Marius asked impatiently. "Give it a knock."

Before Orephes could make his next move, the door creaked open slowly. Staring back at him was a very old man, hunched over and wrinkled. He had a beard that continued down to his chest, white hair that seemed disheveled, and eyes that, while tired, were bright blue and full of life. He was holding himself up with a cane, his tattered and frayed robes hanging over his extended arm. His skin seemed thin, with veins freely appearing through the surface and pockmarks lining each surface.

"Who are you? What do you want?" the old man asked quickly.

"We are looking for an augur. The last augur. I was told that he would be here."

"Augurs?" He seemed almost appalled. "You are mistaken. The augurs are dead."

The man attempted to slam the door shut, but Orephes held it open with his foot.

"We have traveled very far," Orephes pleaded. "I am looking for my family, and I believe that you will know the answer."

"I have lived alone for years in these woods. I don't know your family. Or the augurs." The old man was behind the door now, still trying to shut it over Orephes's foot.

"My father told me that I was the son of a God, and I must know if this is true. I must know if they were real. Please, I need your help!"

"You are mad!" the old man was shouting. "Please, leave me alone. I have nothing of value!"

"This is getting nowhere," Joanna interjected. She placed her hand on Orephes's shoulder. "This must not be him. It is just some old lunatic. Come on, we can keep looking."

"No. This is him. I know it is."

"How do you know that?"

"I can just…feel it." Orephes thought about every other time he had this feeling, and remembered the amulet he had in his satchel. He reached behind him and grabbed it, holding it forward in front of him.

Suddenly, the pushing force from the other side of the door stopped. The door slowly creaked open again, the old man looking much sterner this time. Less senile. Orephes continued to hold the amulet outstretched, and noticed it beginning to glow. It gently lifted from his hand on its own, floating toward the old man, who stretched out his palm as though he was waiting for it.

The old man suddenly stood straight up, releasing the top of the cane he had been holding. Sitting atop the stick was a sphere of metal, glass, and wood that looked eerily like the amulet.

It wasn't a cane. It was a prayer staff. They had found the augur.

"Where did you get this?" the augur asked gently, examining the amulet in his hand.

"The man I previously called my father gave this to me."

"Your father—who was he?"

"Tiberius Chalcedon."

"Tiberius?" A smile creeped across the old man's face. "Now, there is a name I remember." He closed his eyes for a moment, and his face saddened. "He's dead. That is why you are here."

"How did you know my father?"

"Your father was an augur. Like me. A strong one, too." The augur held up the amulet. "This belonged to him. It is called a talisman. Each augur had one, most attached them to their prayer staffs. Some were more adept at using them than others. Your father—at least, the man you called your father—was one of the best in the world."

"On my journey here, this talisman was able to do things. To make me do things, and see things."

"I'm sure it did," the augur said with a warm laugh. "My name is Lucas. You have much to learn. Come inside. All of you. You must be exhausted from that journey. I was just cooking an excellent stew."

"Now, that is the first thing I have heard in this discussion that I recognize," Marius said, perking up. The augur opened the door completely and the trio stepped inside, now surrounded by the smell of spices and meats.

XXVII

The group dug into their stew as though they hadn't eaten in years, devouring Lucas's home cooking with a nearly disrespectful air of desperation. Orephes was the slowest, distracted from the food by the lingering thoughts he had about what was going on here. What his father had really been. The home was quaint and disheveled. Scrolls and books were thrown about, with random piles of fabrics throughout. Most of the small windows were covered with either cloth or wood, with only the smallest one allowing in a smattering of light near a small unmade bed.

"Rather good, isn't it?" Lucas bragged. "It is an old recipe. From the north."

"You could tell me that this was made from human flesh and I would still eat it," Marius said gleefully.

Joanna dropped her utensils and scowled. "What the hell is wrong with you?" she moaned, unable to keep eating.

"I promise you it isn't human flesh." Lucas laughed. Ignoring the continued bickering between Marius and Joanna, Lucas turned his attention back toward Orephes, who had finished his meal. "Orephes, we don't have much time. If you have found me here, others will be here soon. There is much I have to tell you. Much we have to discuss."

"I want to know everything. I want to know the truth about who I am."

"You will. But first, you must learn the truth about everything else."

Lucas stretched out his arm and placed his hand on Orephes's shoulder. Immediately Orephes felt a rush through his body. Then, he felt calm. As though he was exactly where he needed to be.

"What was that?" Orephes asked. "I keep feeling it—first from the talisman, and now I can feel it on my own."

Lucas removed his hand and gave off a friendly smile.

"It's mageia. The spirit of our world."

"Mageia?"

Lucas seemed surprised at the question. "Did your father ever teach you this?"

"No."

"Mageia is the sum of all life on this planet. It is the great spirit that connects all of us. The animals, the plants, the stones. You can't see it, and everyone feels it, but they don't always understand the feeling. When two humans speak. When two humans love. It is there—always being used. Every human soul is connected through it, living or dead. Some of us are more in tune with it than others."

Orephes noticed that Joanna and Marius had begun paying attention, ending their argument as they were glued to Lucas's story.

"What do you mean living or dead?" Orephes thought about the visions of his father he kept seeing in his dreams. Calling to him.

"When humans die, our souls merge with the souls of all who have died before us, and all the life yet to come. They become part of mageia. When followers of the Old Gods burn bodies, the flames destroy the material and transform the soul. In this way, nothing ever truly dies. It all lives on, and for those of us more connected to the mageia—those like you and me—we can still see those who have passed before us. They can see us, too. Protect us. Watch over us. Our ancestors are always there. It is the same for us here as it is in the far east as it is in distant lands yet unknown."

"How? How can we see them?"

"Come. I will show you."

Lucas told Orephes to follow him, and Marius and Joanna followed behind them. They left through a small second door in the rear of the home to the backyard of Lucas's house, where Orephes immediately recognized a small temple, just like the one he and his father had built years ago at the villa.

"Is that a temple?"

"Yes. You have one of your own?"

"My father and I built one on our villa many years ago. It is all that I have left of our time worshiping together. If it is even still there."

The group walked into the temple, and immediately Orephes could feel the mageia inside. It was as though he had stepped into a whirlpool, his mind being tossed around like a leaf in the wind.

"What is happening to me?"

Joanna and Marius, unaffected, stepped in and stepped away from Orephes, who was having trouble standing.

"The mageia is strong in here. Very strong." Lucas got closer, reaching for the talisman. "You are sensitive to it now. You must learn to control how you interact with the mageia around you."

"How?" The room seemed like it was spinning for Orephes. Flickers of different scenes of his life appeared before him.

"Soon, you will be able to do so on your own. For now, you must learn to channel with this." He grabbed Orephes's hand and placed the talisman inside. "This talisman has grown in sync with your inner mageia. It is an extension of you now. Feel where the flow in this room is coming from. Channel it through here."

Lucas saw Orephes continuing to struggle.

"Focus only on the mageia. Ignore your eyes and your ears. Ignore your skin. Ignore your breath."

Orephes shut his eyes and attempted to block everything out, at first futilely. Then he felt something change. What felt like a dizzying breeze from every direction began to feel instead like a slow stream, passing by him gently. Breaking around him. He started to feel the direction—if there was such a thing—as it passed through him. He held the talisman toward where he felt it coming to him, embracing it rather than fighting it.

Within moments, he felt nothing. It was still all around him. like heavy humid air, but it wasn't impacting him. He was part of it. It of him. He opened his eyes. He wasn't in the temple anymore.

He was in a field. In darkness. He could only make out what the moon above him lit in the night. Some trees in the horizon. A small brook that he could also hear a bit away. All around him, on the ground, there was something. Boulders? He couldn't tell. He leaned forward, touching the one nearest him.

It was a body.

It rolled over, its bloodied, decaying face staring at him with wide eyes. Orephes fell backward, startled, onto another body behind him. This one was impaled on a sword, the blood dried around his wound.

Then a dull whisper in the night. *Orephes.*

"Who's there?" he shouted, standing foolishly among the corpses.

These bodies, these men…they were all dead. Perhaps it was the wind? A body to his left caught his attention. He seemed unable to look away. He grabbed it and rolled it onto his back. Staring back at him, lifelessly, was Eschelus. His head was bloodied and deformed, his mouth agape.

"Eschelus?" Orephes asked. The body was cold. He couldn't hear him.

Suddenly, flames erupted all around him. Eschelus's body evaporated from his hands, like smoke being carried away by the wind. He wasn't in the field anymore. He was someplace else. Somewhere he recognized.

He was home, and it was ablaze. All around him the walls his father had built were crumbling, the villa itself burning a few feet away.

"No," Orephes shouted quickly, running toward the burning home. Inside, he heard screaming. Gargarus and his wife. Their daughter, his niece. It was unbearable.

"Gargarus, I am here! I am here!"

He lunged at the door over and over to no avail. Finally, it cracked open and he fell forward.

He woke up inside Lucas's temple, lying on his back. Sweat had built up on his flesh. Marius and Joanna were looking worriedly from afar. Lucas was smiling above him.

"I told you. He is fine," Lucas stated matter-of-factly. It had seemed so groundbreaking to Orephes a moment ago, to be able to tame this force around him. That it was so rote to Lucas—so simple— spoke to how much the man must truly know.

Lucas helped Orephes sit up.

"How do you feel? Do you still feel dizzy?"

"No. I feel fine now."

"Did you see your father?

"No. I saw…" Orephes wasn't sure what to say. He wasn't sure what he saw. Lucas seemed a bit surprised. He had been expecting him to see his father.

"What did you see, Orephes?"

"I saw my friends and family. They were dying. My friends in a battle, my family at our home." The feelings of the vision lingered with him. It didn't feel like a dream, where you awaken and realize that it hadn't been real. Instead, it felt like those emotions were stay- ing with him. Eating at him.

"Mageia is trying to tell you something," Lucas said calmly. "You see what you are meant to see."

"What I saw…is that happening now? Is it real?"

"I don't know. What you saw is for you alone—your soul's per- sonal connection. You must interpret it on your own."

Orephes couldn't shake the feeling that something was very wrong—for both Eschelus and Gargarus. He wasn't sure if the vision had already happened, or would soon. But he knew that it wasn't simply a vision.

"Through temples like these," Lucas started again, "the whole world used to stay connected. Rome. The Eastern empires. The augurs could speak to each other. To the ancestors." Lucas paused for a moment. "To the Gods."

"The Gods?" Joanna asked from the back of the temple. She was holding a statue of Apollo in her hands, longingly. "They were…real?"

"Now they are gone."

Orephes's heart fluttered. If the Gods were real—if Lucas wasn't just some crazy old man—then it was possible that what his father had told him was true. That his father hadn't been mad.

That he was the son of a *God*.

"Where have they gone?" Orephes asked hurriedly.

"Mageia is like a stream," Lucas continued, ignoring the question. "It flows eternally. An endless cycle. It creates a soul, returns to the Earth, becomes a soul again. The Gods were the guardians and the avatars of this cycle—each of a specific component of it. The source and the end of the stream. Their immortality came from worship. When you or I worshipped a God"—he grabbed the statue of Apollo from Joanna's hand, looking at it longingly—"it gave the God power. It sent your mageia to the Gods. It gave them life. It gave them power."

"Without mageia, they die…" Orephes figured out aloud.

Lucas smiled a hollow smile. "Without worship, they have no mageia. Without mageia, there is no immortality. Without their immortality, they die."

"But mageia is still here," Orephes followed up. "So, they are still alive."

"The Gods needed mageia and helped to tame it. Helped to let humans use it. But mageia does not need the Gods. It will be here long after memories of the Gods are forgotten. Long after humans remember how to use it."

"All right," Marius said loudly, standing up. "Don't tell me you believe this nonsense, Orephes."

Orephes seemed to snap out of a trance as he remembered Joanna and Marius were sitting next to them. Lucas turned calmly toward Marius.

"Marius, what is the matter with you?" Orephes asked worriedly.

"We have no clue who this man is," Marius continued. "He could be making all of this up. He lives in an abandoned village, alone, in barbarian territory. If all of this was true, why is he here? He probably drugged your stew with some strange potion to get you to believe this all." Marius went to leave but was stopped by Joanna, who grabbed his arm.

"Marius," Joanna whispered. "What has gotten into you?"

"It's all right," Lucas insisted. "Marius, is it? Are you a Christian?"

"I believe in the one true God," Marius replied sternly. "All of this you are talking about is either nonsense or the work of the devil. I will have nothing to do with this."

Lucas lowered his head, his mouth shaping into a sad smile as he shook it from side to side.

"The one true God," he muttered under his breath with a slight laugh.

"If this is all real," Marius continued, confronting Lucas, "then why didn't these all powerful Gods stop their own demise. Some Gods they are if they can't even seem to keep control of the world they were guardians of."

For a moment, Orephes felt doubt again, like he had when his father passed. Marius was right. If the Gods were real, like Lucas claimed, why are they gone? Why didn't they show themselves to humanity, and ensure that their worship wouldn't end?

"The Old Gods were immortal," Lucas continued calmly, "they were not all-powerful. They were not all-seeing. This myth of an all-powerful God...it was created by Christians. How could any human worship the Old Gods, when they were told the new one was more powerful than all of them combined?"

"A *myth*?" Marius hissed.

"Created by humans to take power away from the Gods. So that humans could finally become their own masters."

Marius laughed and threw his hands to his sides.

"If you two want to sit here and keep listening to this madness, that is for you to decide. I am done."

"Marius, calm down," Joanna pressed softly.

He pulled his arm away from her hand and opened his mouth to say something. He stopped himself. Instead, he silently stormed out of the temple.

"You want to go after him," Lucas said to Joanna. She looked at him in a combination of fear and surprise. "I can feel it. Let him go. It isn't easy for many who live in the world today to hear the truth. It doesn't make sense when people first hear it. In truth, the world stopped making sense many years ago."

"He needs someone," Joanna answered.

"He cares about you, you know. If there is one thing mageia can help one sense, it is when two souls have a connection they may not even feel themselves."

Joanna was silent for a moment. She had a look on her face that Orephes hadn't seen before. He couldn't tell what she was feeling.

"I believe you," Joanna finally admitted. "After what I have seen Orephes do, I believe all of it."

"As do I," Orephes said. "But I must understand: Why didn't the Gods fight back?"

"They tried. Augurs and the followers of the Old Gods fought back for years. But the Christians' message of all being forgiven, of Christ dying for the sins of humanity, it stood in stark contrast to the message that we must always pay tribute to the Old Gods for the rest of eternity. All the while, with each conversion, the strength of the Old Gods was fading. The augurs were powerless to stop it. ur use of mageia was being labeled as witchcraft and the work of the devil. This ancient world and the empire rose on the grace of the Old Gods, and it is falling on the arrogance of humanity. This world we lived in was about so much more than Rome, or the emperor. Every human civilization understood the importance of it all. Of connection with our ancestors. So few people remember or care to understand anymore."

"After the Christians took over, and the emperors converted," Joanna asked, "what happened next?"

"They hunted down every augur, everyone who refused to convert—all of us. They slaughtered us without mercy. The Gods lost the last bit of power they had, until there was nothing left and no way to fight back."

"Why didn't my father want me to fight, then?" Orephes asked. He felt his heart racing at the thought of all that had transpired. If he was the last hope, why was he not allowed to help restore what was ending?

"Tiberius kept you from fighting to prevent your connection to mageia from growing. There are many ways for your connection to mageia to solidify. One of the most rapid is through combat. When you and another are locked in battle, aiming to take each other's lives, there is no greater moment of connection between two souls than that, even if it is one of hate. Preventing you from fighting was to keep you hidden. He was wise to do so."

Orephes wanted to ask again who he was being hidden from, but he remembered the man they had encountered on their journey, who had torn at his mind and created swords from the dirt beneath their feet. He realized he may already know the answer.

"We encountered someone on our way here," Orephes started. "He called himself Volusian. He could do…seemingly impossible things. Who was he? Is he an augur, like you?"

Lucas looked up directly into Orephes's eyes. For the first time since they had arrived, his expression changed. His eyes seemed to grow tired and sad, as though the name brought such great pain to him that he couldn't bear to hear it. Orephes started to feel anxiety, pain, and sadness all at once. Traveling through him, within him. He didn't understand it at first, but as he stared at Lucas's face, it became clear.

The sadness he felt—the weight—was what Lucas was feeling. He could *feel* Lucas's anguish. Lucas eventually took his eyes away from Orephes, staring down at the ground.

"No." He finally answered grimly. "The augurs were human."

Orephes almost didn't want to know the answer to his next question. Lucas could probably feel his anxiety now.

"You said the Gods were gone, so what is he?"

Lucas hesitated for a moment, letting out a deep breath.

"He is one of the Lares. A demigod."

The Lares were something Orephes's father had taught him about—local minor Gods, guardians of the people in their area.

"The Lares…they were demigods?"

"That's why there were so many. Half human, half God. Worship to them fueled them with mageia, but they were never as powerful as their parents. They were not immortal, and like their parents, they are gone."

"I don't understand. If they are all gone, how is he still alive? Was that who Father was keeping me hidden from?"

Lucas let out a long sigh, his old eyes shutting for a moment.

"Humans weren't the only ones jealous of the power of the Gods. Volusian betrayed us all, working with the Christians to hunt us down."

"Why? Why would he do such a thing? What could he possibly gain?"

"As I said, mageia is infinite. Without the Gods to compete, to maintain the balance, Volusian is free to be the sole beneficiary of worship, as a saint. To have unlimited power. To be—"

"Immortal," Orephes cut in, finishing Lucas's sentence.

"Immortal."

"Is that what I am? A Lar like him?"

"If what your father says is true, then yes."

"Is it true?"

"I don't know."

It was a disappointing answer. Orephes had expected this to be the end of the road. That he would leave here knowing how to fix what he was meant to fix. Figure out why he had been hidden.

"You don't know why I was hidden away? What my role in all of this is? You seem to know so much."

"Only you can discover the true answer to that question on your own. You are strong with mageia, that much I know. But there have been many humans born with that gift, myself being one of them."

"How can I know? Where can I learn the truth?"

"The very place you were originally headed."

"Mount Olympus?"

"There you will discover the truth. What your meaning is in all of this."

"How will I know?"

"Because if your father was lying, and you were not meant to be there, you won't make it back alive. No human has ever set foot within Olympus. The mageia there is too strong."

There was his answer. He would either find out who he truly was, or die trying.

For a moment, Orephes wondered if it was even worth it. Why would it matter if he was truly Zeus's son? Was he planning on taking on his mantle? Was he going to try to avenge him? *Perhaps this was a fool's errand,* he thought. Perhaps he was wasting his time.

"I sense your doubt," Lucas said with a knowing smile. "There is no shame in that. You must decide for yourself what is more important to you. Knowing the truth, or living the rest of your life knowing it doesn't matter anymore."

Lucas started back toward his home, giving Orephes a gentle pat on the shoulder.

"If what your father told you is true," he started again softly, "then you are all that is left of the legacy of the Old Gods." He left the temple, leaving Joanna and Orephes alone with their thoughts.

Joanna sat next to Orephes for a while, careful not to break the silence. She figured he needed it after that. A few moments to reflect on all he had just been told.

"Whatever you decide," Joanna said quietly, "I am with you. All the way."

"You heard what he said. I don't even know if I can get up that mountain. We know for sure you can't."

"Then I am with you until we get to where I can't go anymore."

Orephes was obviously grateful for her support and kindness, but he couldn't help but feel wrong about it—as though he was bringing two horses along with him into the sea, where they would surely drown.

Despite all he had just learned, Orephes couldn't shake the feeling that something was wrong—worse than before, even. If he didn't know any better, he would have said the mageia was trying to tell him something. A chill blew past him, leaving his skin in small bumps. In the darkness of the outside forest as the sun began to set, Orephes began to feel uncomfortable. Helping Joanna to her feet, the two headed back into Lucas's humble home, away from the unknown.

XXVIII

Northern Italy

Torix wasn't sure whether to be relieved or disappointed to see his father standing before him behind his tent. At least he could be sure it wasn't someone who wanted him dead. Behind him were two more soldiers. He couldn't be sure whose, but he knew they weren't Eschelus's men.

"Well?" Tufa asked his son. He was aggressive. Harsh. He didn't have patience for the delay.

"It isn't done yet."

"The armies are set to meet at dawn," Tufa chided his son. "How long have you been lying here?"

"Is there no other way, Father?"

Tufa let out a low growl, followed by a smack of his lips.

"So, that is the true answer, then. You are a coward."

"What is the true cowardice, Father? To die in a battlefield with honor or to slaughter men while they sleep?"

Tufa got close to his son, his scruffy, dark jowls no less than an inch away from his face. Torix could smell his breath—a noxious combination of wine and the rot of a human stomach.

"You would do well to watch your mouth, boy. We are here to do one thing, and one thing alone. I thought it might be a mistake letting you get so close to these Romans. Now grab your fucking sword." Tufa shoved his son backward, nearly knocking him over back into his tent.

Torix obliged and grabbed his sword, removing it from its sheath as quietly as he could. He stood there holding it, and saw at its base the notches that the knights had scratched into it with their own swords as his training had ended. To mark that he was one of them now. "So that we each take a small piece of everyone else's sword with us into battle," they had said to him.

"Well?" Tufa's voice startled him, shook him out of his thoughts. "What are you waiting for?"

Torix dropped his sword to the ground in front of Tufa.

"I won't. It isn't right."

Tufa sneered and grabbed the sword from the floor. "You fucking coward."

Without hesitation, he smacked Torix in the face with the blunt end of his own sword, sending him falling backward. Torix lay on the ground helplessly, grasping his nose as his father continued to rain blows down on him from above. Eventually, with one solid kick and a sharp pain to his temple, he stopped struggling, unconscious from a blow to his temple.

Tufa touched the tip of his son's sword—at least he had kept it sharp. He exited the tent, knowing full well what he had to do next. Unlike his son, he would not hesitate.

XXIX

Michael shot up from his bed. He had heard something—some-one—outside the tents. Was it just an animal in the night? He listened for another moment to be sure, pressing his ear against the cloth.

Voices. Whispering. It was unmistakeable. Then the subtle pang of an unsheathing sword. It sounded like it was coming from Torix's tent. Were they being ambushed? He wouldn't put it past Odoacer's men to do such a thing. He should have been more prepared.

He quickly grabbed his sword when he heard a struggle. The sound of flesh being hit, then silence. *Shit*, he thought. *I am too late.*

He ran outside the back of his tent, not bothering to put on his armor. From behind the row of tents, he saw someone leaving Torix's and entering Roman's. This time, he didn't hear the sound of a struggle. Just the clear sound of iron piercing skin. Once. Twice. A third time. Then he lost count.

Next, the figure was moving into Bracchus's tent. He needed to move. He ran as quickly as he could, but before he could reach the tent he heard someone running up behind him.

He quickly lifted his sword, anticipating a swing. The clank of the swords was startling in the otherwise silent night. He knew he was at a disadvantage with no armor, so he was going to fight dirty. He lifted some of the dry dirt off the ground and tossed it into the man's face. It gave Michael the advantage he needed as he thrust his sword into their chest. He covered their mouth so they couldn't scream, tossing them to the ground.

He ran to the back of Bracchus's tent, throwing the rear flap open. Two men were inside, swords drawn above Bracchus who was sleeping silently in ignorant bliss.

"Bracchus!" he yelled as he sprinted inside. Bracchus's eyes shot open as one of the men turned to face Michael. Bracchus rolled off his bed just as Tuva's sword plunged downward, narrowly missing him.

"You treasonous son of a bitch," Bracchus yelled, grabbing Tuva by the legs and knocking him over. His sword flew to his side.

Michael let out a yell as the other soldier gashed his arm, evading his parry. He dropped his sword and held where the blood was spewing. The soldier laughed and held his sword in front of him.

"You knights aren't so tough," he said dismissively.

Bracchus and Tuva rolled on the ground, trading the upper hand as they tried to wrestle control. Bracchus held Tuva down by his throat, pressing harder and harder.

"You fucking barbarian cunt!" Bracchus shouted. He was squeezing as hard as he could.

Tuva stopped trying to pry his hands off, and instead reached to his side. He felt his sword beneath his fingers. With his last ounce of strength, he grasped the hilt and thrust it into Bracchus's side.

"No!" Michael shouted.

Immediately, the hands loosened. Tuva kicked Bracchus off him and caught his breath, gasping and holding his throat.

The other soldier turned to look at Tuva, and Michael took the opportunity to lunge forward, knocking him over. He grabbed the soldier's sword and dug it into his throat.

"Well," Tuva started, sounding hoarse, "a wounded, naked knight against a barbarian general."

"I'd say the playing field is even now, lucky for you."

Michael took a moment to survey his opponent. He was holding his main weapon—his broadsword—at an angle in front of him. Offensive stance but not aggressive. He had something else. He saw on his hilt two throwing knives. If he had good aim, he could sink one of those into Michael before he could even react. Or worse, they could be locked in a sword fight only to have Tuva use the throwing knife as a dagger right into his side. With no armor, he was wholly unprotected for that. That isn't even taking into consideration his wound.

He had no choice. He had to fight.

"After everything we did for your son," Michael said. "After we opened our alliance to you, you would still see us dead?"

"My loyalty is to my people," Tuva said. His answer was so matter-of-fact, so without remorse, that it made Michael regret everything kind he had ever said about barbarians.

"I defended your kind when everyone else thought we were crazy for letting you in. I kept your son alive!"

"Then you are as foolish as you are weak."

Suddenly, Torix appeared behind his father, bloodied and beaten. He drove a sword through Tuva's abdomen, the tip appearing out the other end.

"Only traitors are weak." Torix pulled his sword out from his father, shoving him to the floor. Tuva gasped for air a few times, looking angrily toward his son as he sputtered his final breath.

Michael fell to his knees as he grasped his arm in pain. Torix quickly grabbed the sheet from Bracchus's bed and handed it to him.

"Wrap it, quickly. You have to stop the bleeding."

"Roman?"

Torix replied with a solemn head shake. Michael quickly wrapped his wound and stood up.

"Did you know about this? About the plan to betray us in the night?"

"I tried to stop my father. I no longer wanted to go through with it."

"No *longer*?" Michael shoved Torix to the ground.

"I saved your life!"

"Bracchus and Roman are dead because of you!" Michael shouted at him, holding his sword to the barbarian's neck. "You knew about this last night. Hell, you probably knew about it since you joined us. You could have saved them. Instead, you let them be slaughtered in their fucking sleep like a coward."

Michael spit on him in disgust. "You saved my life, so I will spare yours. But I never want to see you again."

"We need to warn Eschelus."

"I will warn Eschelus," Michael hissed, turning around. "One of his real knights should let him know what happened here."

Michael quickly put his armor on in his tent and happily made the discovery that the horses were still alive. They had probably figured there was no need to kill the horses if the humans would all be dead.

"Michael, wait!" he heard Torix shout from the distance.

Fuck him, he thought. He wasn't going to let him come. He walked next to his horse and felt the ground move beneath him, followed by a snap.

"Shit."

The last thing he saw was a stone flying at him in the darkness.

XXX

Dacia, Barbarian Territory, North of Greece

It was freezing outside, but it didn't bother him tonight. Perhaps it was the adrenaline, perhaps the anger. It didn't matter. He couldn't be inside with them anymore.

He had his knives in each of his hands, twisting them around in front of him as he examined their edges. After he had stabbed Volusian, the ends of the knives were blackened, as though he had stabbed into ash or charcoal. He had tried to wipe them clean, but the dark stain simply wouldn't rub off. The color stayed there as a reminder to him of what he had seen. Of what had almost killed them.

"Are you going to sit out here all night?"

Joanna sat down next to him before he could answer, taking one of his knives from him. She rubbed her hand on the dark stain, just as he had been doing a few moments before.

"They are ruined," Marius said. He dropped his second to the ground in front of him.

"I think it makes them look more intimidating. You could be known as the petty criminal with the black daggers from here to Spain."

"Petty?" Marius laughed.

There was a moment of silence as Joanna grabbed Marius's other blade. He hadn't looked at her since she sat.

"Aren't you cold out here?"

"It is better than sitting in there."

"I know that you are worried that everything he is saying isn't true—"

"I'm not worried that it isn't true," Marius said, cutting her off. "I'm worried that it is."

"You *know* that it is."

Marius finally looked at her. His light brown eyes seemed solemn yet beautiful. She couldn't help but appreciate how handsome his face was. That damn face that kept her from completing her real mission over and over again.

"After Volusian, I didn't want to believe it. I still don't."

"It isn't about believing. It is about what is real and true. You saw what Volusian could do with your own eyes, Marius. He was real. These knives—the black on them—that is real."

Marius was still looking at her. It seemed like the first time he had ever looked into her eyes since they met. Not looked *at* her eyes but into them. As though he wanted to know what was behind them. As though he cared. It was probably all the talk of mageia, but she could almost feel him next to her.

"Who are you really?" he asked abruptly. "What are you doing this far from Rome? Why are you here?"

"What do you mean?" Joanna seemed flustered. The connection she had felt a moment ago seemed severed. She hadn't been expecting this to come up again. She had hoped they had moved on.

"Why have you come all this way? What do you want from all of this? I know it isn't just my money—you could have had that days ago."

She had been trying to hide it for so long she had almost forgotten herself. She debated continuing the lie, but something about this place…he could see right through the lies.

"You wouldn't believe me if I told you."

"Try me."

"I was an assassin."

Marius's eyebrows curled with an amused confusion.

"You're right. I don't believe you."

"Considering everything going on, you would be wise to keep an open mind."

"It would explain how you can fight. Who did you work for?"

"Whoever would pay. Typically the bacaudae."

"I have never heard of you."

"I wouldn't be very good if you had heard of me, would I?"

Marius rubbed his chin, a smirk running across his face.

"Let's say you are telling me the truth. That still doesn't explain how you ended up in that whorehouse, or why you are here."

"What better way to get close to the citizens of Rome than by letting them get close to me? I was here to go after one of my targets."

"Who?"

"You."

Marius's gaze shot quickly to her. He was holding his knife tight. He was nervous. He believed her.

"Eudoc?" he asked.

Joanna nodded.

"You have had plenty of opportunity to kill me. Why didn't you?"

"I don't know. Perhaps I still should," Joanna joked.

"That isn't funny."

"I have a soft spot for what Orephes is trying to do."

"Why? You barely know him."

"When I was very young, my entire family was slaughtered in front of me by a group of religious soldiers on horseback who came in the night. Their necks were cut, and they were strung up from the trees to let the blood drip down into buckets beneath them. They used the blood to paint crosses up and down my father's farm as a warning to those who passed by. Convert or die."

"Your family were followers of the Old Gods?"

"Yes. I feel like somehow being here with Orephes is avenging my family. As though they would have wanted me here helping do this."

"How did you survive? When they killed your family?"

Joanna rolled up her shirt, revealing a large scar up her groin toward her breast. Marius had noticed it at the whorehouse back in Rome, but thought little of it. Many of the women (and men) who worked out of the establishment had wounds and scars that told of a life far less glorious than the patrons.

"They thought I was already dead and I got lucky. They had enough blood for what they wanted."

Marius reached forward and grabbed her hand, his beautiful eyes seeming sincere again. It was maddening to her how he could do that—switch from sly thief to caring companion. She felt the connection come back as he touched her. Her pulse raced.

"I am so sorry."

"It isn't your fault. I can't blame all Christians for what was done to me. Even if they blame all followers of the Old Gods for what used to happen to them."

Marius pulled her coat—the coat he had given her off his boat— farther over her goose bump-covered shoulders.

"You look like you are freezing. Should we head back inside?"

In that instant, Joanna's mind went blank as she leaned forward and kissed him. He hesitated for a moment, unsure how to react, before grabbing her back and pulling her closer. His hands traveled along her hips, to her rib cage, to her breasts, cupping them gently. He had done this before.

His left hand stopped at her scar, running his finger up and down its length. She pulled away, embarrassed.

"What's wrong?"

"I know it isn't appealing…"

"Are you kidding? A woman who can fight and has the scars to prove it. I can't think of anything sexier."

Joanna pulled him close again, tugging at Marius's collar as she landed her lips back on his.

"Guys, I… Whoa! Sorry," Orephes's unwelcome voice boomed from behind them.

They pulled away from each other and attempted to gain composure. Marius rolled his eyes. "You sure have a knack for finding us at *just* the right moment, kid," he joked.

"Lucas says we can stay the night. We head out for Olympus tomorrow."

"We will be ready."

"*We?*" Orephes joked, looking at Marius.

"Enjoy your night, kid," Marius said hurriedly, waving Orephes off. "Try not to interrupt any more big moments on your way to your room."

XXXI

Constantinople

There had been nothing but black for days—possibly weeks, months or, hell, years—he couldn't tell anymore. He could occasionally make out a faint sound, like an echo in the distance. Either he was alive or in hell. There was no way a divine afterlife could be so void. An eternity in blackness, with only a wind-like whisper on the horizon, was certainly no paradise.

"Antonius."

It wasn't a whisper this time. It was clear. It was definite—thick enough that he felt like he could reach out and grab it.

Then, in the blink of an eye, the blackness around him changed. He was standing at a wall, fire burning beyond it. Dozens were screaming all around him, but he couldn't see them. All he could see were the bricks in the wall before him and the smoke billowing above it.

"Antonius." The voice called again, from behind him this time.

He turned around. It was Orephes. He seemed different, almost magnanimous. He could tell it was him, yet he couldn't fully make out his face. He seemed to be behind a glowing, comforting haze.

"Orephes?"

"You have to help them, Antonius."

"Who?"

"Gargarus and those remaining at the villa. Beyond the wall."

The screams continued in the distance. They tore at him. He felt an urgency, as though he was wasting time. "How? How do I help them?"

Orephes stepped forward until he was right in front of him. He reached out his hand and rested it on his chest. A warmth coursed through him unlike anything he had felt before.

"Wake up."

The words seemed to echo in his mind as the scene before him seemed to spin away from him in a flurry. The black returned in an instant.

Then his eyes opened.

He shot up quickly, his face covered in sweat. He wasn't sure where he was or how he had gotten there. The bed was comfortable, the room well decorated. It was certainly someplace wealthy.

A servant stepped into the room, holding towels and some water.

"Oh!" she gasped in surprise. "You are awake!"

"Where am I?"

"The Imperial Palace in Constantinople."

"Constantinople? How did I get here?"

"You have been unconscious a very long time, sir. I will fetch the guards. They will better be able to answer you."

Guards? That was never a good sign. No matter how he had arrived here. As the servant left, he shot out of the bed and looked around for his armor. The robes he currently wore certainly wouldn't be suitable for where he was headed.

He wasn't sure how or why, but he knew Orephes needed him. The villa needed him. He had to get back to Gaul as soon as possible.

As he passed a mirror, he noticed for the first time the enormous gash across his head. It had mostly healed, but it was certainly unsightly. He couldn't remember what had happened to him, and that was likely the culprit. Had the guards done this?

The guards walked calmly into the room, one of them smiling as they saw him scurrying about searching for his armor.

"So, you are awake," one of them said. "Take it easy, or you will find yourself back on your ass."

Neither of them had their hand on their hilt. They weren't planning anything—yet. He could relax.

"I apologize. I don't remember how I got here."

"You got smacked with a brick the size of your fucking head," the guard answered. "You've been out for weeks. Some of us didn't think you were ever going to pop back. We were thinking of doing the merciful thing and slicing your neck."

"Thankfully that won't be necessary," Antonius assured him. "I need my armor. I need to get back to Gaul."

"All due respect, sir, your head is still rightly fucked up. I doubt that you would make it that far."

"I will."

The guards looked at each other, as if they were wondering whether they should let Antonius go. After a moment, the first one nodded.

"All right. Your armor is in the next room. Be careful out there, the Blues and the Greens have been causing some mayhem after Anastasius was named the new emperor. Wouldn't want to see you back here again. At least, not in those circumstances."

"Zeno is dead?" Antonius asked, dumbfounded. "I missed a lot in these few weeks!"

Antonius put his armor back on and saw a small parchment fall out of it. He picked it up and saw a note from Orephes letting him know that, if he woke up or not, he would be back for him. How ironic that he ended up being the very reason he woke up and would end up getting out of here.

Even though he had been asleep, and hadn't seen Orephes in weeks, he felt closer to him now, after that dream or vision, whatever it was. It was as though he could still feel him with him, guiding him to get back to Gaul.

He wouldn't let him down.

"Don't worry, Orephes," he said out loud as he left the Imperial Palace. "I got your message."

XXXII

Bishop's Cathedral, Central Gaul

Martel's hands ran over the parchment in a frustrated frenzy. He had been trying for years, but he still couldn't see it. He still couldn't see what was missing.

Some of them, he knew, such as Volusian, were born with it. Their manipulation of mageia was something that he could never replicate. Nor did he want to. The seemingly divine nature of their ability to leech mageia from man's worship was one step too far from the new world introducing Christianity had set out to create.

The augurs, however...their abilities were not divine. They were men, like him. Men who learned how to use the powers of the Gods for themselves. Unfortunately for them, they never used it to advance their own people. Only the will of the Gods. And because of that, they ended up perishing. Disappearing into the world they had helped maintain.

He would not make that mistake. He would find a way to make mageia his own, just as the augurs had done. And when he did, it wouldn't be to progress the will of the Gods.

No, it would be to progress humanity. To allow them to transcend the mortal prisons the Gods had given them and the Christians sought to maintain.

"Archbishop," Peter said, opening his door.

Martel shot up from his seat, attempting to shield the parchment on his desk.

"What is it, Peter?" Martel responded angrily.

Peter looked at the parchment on Martel's desk, understanding that he wasn't meant to see it. He gave the archbishop a suspicious look. "Is everything all right, sir?"

"Did you have something important, Peter? You are wasting my time."

"Everything is prepared to leave for Rome, assuming you finish your reading."

"You watch your place, Peter," Martel hissed.

"I know my place, Archbishop," Peter replied softly, bowing. "Forgive me."

Martel knew there was sarcasm in his voice. He didn't care. He simply wanted him out of his quarters. He was getting reckless. He couldn't risk being seen studying these incantations and spells. At least, not yet.

Not until he understood what he needed to do. Then, it would never matter again.

XXXIII

Orephes woke up in a cold sweat. His eyes adjusted to the light from the window invading the darkness of his room. In a faint echo, he almost thought he could still hear Antonius's voice.

His door creaked open slowly. Lucas stepped inside, that same calming look on his face.

"I heard you talking in your sleep."

"I had a vivid dream."

"For Lares like you, there is no such thing. A vivid dream is either mageia's way of telling you something or your way of using mageia to tell something to someone else."

"Is that possible? To talk to someone through mageia?"

"It's not only possible, it often happens out of your control. Mageia is a powerful force, Orephes. Who you connect with, who connects with you, and how those connections interact—we may never fully understand it."

Suddenly, Lucas's expression changed—serenity replaced by confusion and pain. He fell forward onto his prayer staff, which he was using as a cane. Orephes ran forward to help hold him up.

"Are you all right?" Orephes asked worriedly.

"There is something coming," Lucas said quietly after a pause.

Orephes felt something, too. He didn't quite understand yet what mageia was always trying to tell him, but he knew that the mageia around him had shifted, as if it was making room for something else. There was also a coldness to it—a familiar feeling that gave him a recognizable sense of unease.

"You need to leave," Lucas said quickly, regaining his strength. "Now."

Orephes followed him out of his quarters into the living area, where Marius and Joanna were already up.

Joanna immediately noticed the worried look on Lucas's face. It worried her.

"What is going on?"

"All of you need to get out. Orephes, get to Olympus. Everything will be answered for you there."

"I don't think I am ready," Orephes answered. "I need more time. There is so much more to learn from you."

"You aren't. But there is no more time. Get your things. Quickly."

"Well, this was a complete reversal," Marius said. "Did the old man suddenly remember who he was?"

There was a noise in the distance. A pattering sound was getting louder and louder. At first only Orephes seemed to hear it, but soon the others noticed, too.

"Horses," Marius said quickly. "Coming from the west, from the sounds of it. Quickly. I assume these aren't our friends, then?" Marius asked Lucas, who simply ignored him.

"We are too late."

Orephes could feel it more closely now. He knew the feeling. It was Volusian. He was coming for him.

"No. I won't run from him."

Joanna and Marius looked at each other. They knew who he was talking about.

"It is wise to understand when to fight, and when to flee," Lucas said.

"You don't think I can beat him?"

"No." Lucas's answer was quick. He believed it. "Not yet. You aren't ready for this fight."

The horses were closer now, the sound of hooves smacking the ground beneath them became a chorus in the distance.

"Sounds like ten horses or so," Joanna said, grabbing her sword. "He isn't alone."

"Orephes, if you can't make it to Olympus, then all is lost."

"He will kill you if we leave."

"You can't help that now."

Joanna drew her sword as Volusian and his crew approached the home. Marius felt his waist, realizing that he didn't have his knives.

"Shit," he shouted. "Do you actually believe what you said about him sparing us?"

"Not a chance," Joanna answered. "Where are your knives?"

"It doesn't matter. I always believed that anything can be a weapon. You just need to know how to use it." Marius grabbed a pot off Lucas's shelf, spinning it in his hands.

"You must be joking."

"Would you rather give me your sword?"

There was a crash from the rear entrance to the house. Two armored knights stormed into the home, swords drawn. There were gold crosses emblazoned on their black chest plates, which belied the purpose of their visit. Orephes remembered those crosses vividly—an old memory flickering on and off in his mind. The memory of his father dying. The soldiers in the yard. The hooded man against the wall.

It had been Volusian, all that time ago. There. At his home. Hunting his father.

Before anyone could react, the front door flew open, nearly ripped off its rusting, fragile hinges. Six or seven more knights broke into the home, taking positions surrounding the four occupants. Marius and Joanna gave each other a look that said "we are fucked," but they didn't want to say it. Joanna knew from experience that this many men with this much armor wasn't something people got away from. Marius knew from experience that she was right.

"What is the meaning of this?" shouted Lucas, though he already knew why they were there.

The sound of slow, meaningful footsteps was the only remaining sound after the knights had entered the home. As the steps came closer and closer, Orephes could feel the mageia in the room shifting. It was as if the air around him was screaming for him to flee. Screaming at him for still being there.

Volusian stepped through the broken front door, wearing a hooded robe and the same, old-looking footwear on his legs. Unlike the rest of the men around him, he didn't have any armor or weapons. Everyone in the room, except perhaps some of his own entourage, knew why. They had seen what he could do.

Volusian seemed surprised as he took his first look inside.

"Lucas. You're alive." He spoke with a weight behind him—an almost palpable sense of derision directed at the old man. It was clear to the trio that these two knew each other.

"Yes, though certainly not without effort," Lucas shot back.

The fact that Volusian was here reaffirmed Lucas's commitment to getting Orephes to Olympus. It meant he had sensed it, too—that Orephes was exceptional. Volusian looked at Joanna and Marius for a moment before focusing on Orephes.

"So predictable," he chided Orephes. "You and I have unfinished business."

"Leave him alone," Lucas said. There was anger in his voice, but it was measured. Calm and collected. Even in the face of Volusian, Lucas seemed to be unaware of the danger around him.

"You know why I am here, Lucas," Volusian continued.

"He's not what you think he is, Volusian. I had hoped the same when he arrived."

Volusian closed his eyes and lifted his head, feeling the mageia around him.

"Mageia betrays you, Lucas. I sense more to him than a rich boy from Gaul." Volusian smiled as he felt Lucas's indignation. "You have grown weak with your age."

"It's me you want," Orephes said. "Leave him alone." He was upset at how immature he sounded compared to Lucas. Almost childlike and innocent.

"Martel's orders were to kill everyone, sir," one of the Inquisitor knights, presumably a commander, said quickly. "Why are we wasting time?"

Lucas smirked and shook his head. "The leash rears its ugly head again," he said calmly.

For the first time since Volusian stepped into the room, Orephes felt the mageia change again. It was coming from Volusian and it was anger. Lucas's comment had dug into him.

"I may be old," continued Lucas, "but nobody controls me."

Orephes felt it right before he moved, in a shift of mageia in the air. Volusian lunged forward, in an uncharacteristic moment of personal weakness, but was thrown backward by Lucas, who had raised his now glowing prayer staff into the air. In another moment, streaks of white lightning were flung from the staff's head aimed at each of the Inquisitors in the room, striking them into convulsions and ultimately collapsing into smoking, lightly charred corpses.

"I am so glad he is on our side," Marius said enthusiastically, twirling the pot in his hands.

Volusian rose quickly to his feet. He was angrier than before, his eyes growing darker and more bloodshot. In a swift movement, he flung his arm forward, tearing apart the front of Lucas's home and shooting a ball of flames and stone forward at them. Marius, Orephes, and Joanna flinched, expecting the debris and fire to hit them, but turned to see Lucas holding his brightly glowing staff high, disintegrating Volusian's attack before it could reach them.

As the smoke cleared, leaving Volusian standing with his back now toward the outdoors where several horses stood, Orephes felt him growing angrier still.

"You might fool the idiot Christians who flock to their churches and the poor souls trapped in the war zone that was once Rome, looking for something to hope for or something to fear," Lucas said as he lowered his staff. "But you are no God—and you will never be worshipped as one."

"In a Godless world," Volusian said angrily, "I am all that is left." He pointed his finger at his own chest, convincing himself more than anyone else.

"Not yet."

Lucas lifted his staff again and shot his hand forward. Volusian, who had appeared about to move toward Orephes, seemed held in place as the staff pulsed. Mageia began swirling in the room with a deafening fury, like the howling wind of a storm.

"Orephes, go now!" Lucas shouted. "Hurry!"

Orephes could see wrinkles growing on his face with each passing moment. He wasn't sure what he was doing, but he knew that it was draining him. His eyes grew yellow and his body thinner.

"There isn't any more time, go! Get to the mountain. You are all we have left now. Remember the task ahead of you is *never* as great as the power behind you."

Everything in his body and in the air around him was telling him to listen. He looked at Joanna and Marius, who nodded and followed him out the back door, quickly mounting the cross-adorned horses that had been left behind. They hurried off into the distance, not turning to look back.

Slowly, Volusian regained control of his body. His face was contorted with rage as he slowly stepped forward to the increasingly frail Lucas, fighting the mageia that pushed him back. By the time he managed to move the several feet to reach him, Lucas was on his knees, using what seemed like all his energy to keep his staff lifted.

Volusian pulled the staff from his hands, knocking Lucas back onto the ground in front of him. With a quick, sudden movement, Volusian smashed the head of the staff on the ground, which erupted into an explosive crack of bright light.

He picked Lucas up by the neck, which had become thin and frail. Lucas seemed to be gasping, as if to speak, but was too weak even to push out a word.

"Mageia was a tool for you," Volusian started with derision, "nothing more than a sword or a shield to be wielded." He held Lucas close to his face, noses nearly touching. "Mageia is *my birthright,* and it will not be you, or that boy, or *anyone* who will keep me from it! Everything I did, I did for the sake of freeing you from the ungrateful claws of the Gods who despised everything about what you were. This is how you *repay me?*"

Volusian shook Lucas, as though he wanted him to speak. To say *anything*. Lucas's mouth opened to say something, but all that came out were pained groans.

"What is it?" Volusian shot angrily. "What do you have to say for yourself?" He was shaking him more aggressively now, privately hoping he would snap his neck.

"Your father…was right about…you," he finally managed to squeak out weakly. "He always…was."

Volusian threw Lucas to the ground, and quickly launched a line of flames at him from his arm, engulfing the dying old man in a fast-burning inferno.

As the rage left Volusian's body, he looked down at the charcoal and dust that his anger had left behind. At first, he simply felt pity for the old man. Then, as if coming to a sudden realization, he realized what he had just done. The body was gone, burned away. Lucas had baited him into burning his body.

"No," he whispered to himself. "No!" He kicked Lucas's dust in front of him and tossed the still standing table in the kitchen into the wall.

"Sir," a faint voice said from behind him. One of the Inquisitors had survived. "Help me. Please."

Volusian raised his arm in disgust, and the Inquisitor's head tilted sharply to one side with a snap, breaking his neck.

He knew where Orephes would be heading. There would be no more distractions. No more Inquisitors or interruptions from Martel. He had no *leash.* He was a Lar. He was the *last* Lar—at least, he would be soon, once this young aristocrat from Gaul was out of the way once and for all.

XXXIV

Northern Italy

The soil was damp from early morning rains. The horses plodded instead of galloped, their hooves getting sucked ever so slightly into the mud with each step. The soldiers were faring no better, coated in a sheen of water and their own oils from time on the march.

Eschelus was in front, flanked by his top men. They were adorned in armor to make it appear that his knights were flanking him, but these men by his side were nothing more than highly talented foot soldiers. His knights were at a different camp. One that was far enough away from the battle but close enough so that they could make their entrance quickly.

Behind Eschelus, one of the men on horseback was holding high the purple flag of the empire—an older, outdated relic, but one that got the point across nonetheless. It was adorned with the Imperial eagle, and the letters *S.P.Q.R* flanking its wings.

The Heruli tribe didn't wear armor. They typically carried a sword and a single shield so as to not weigh themselves down. Contrastingly, his men were more adequately prepared, having gathered

235

all the remaining Roman armor north of Italy. But he wasn't so naïve as to believe that he would be battling only the Heruli. Odoacer was their chieftain, but he was now king. Patrician. He would have an army behind him that rivaled the Imperial legions of old. He couldn't afford to underestimate him.

He had hoped to have more cavalry—long gone were the days of long columns of Roman legionnaires with their long shields as the devastating supremacy on the battlefield. His men weren't trained horsemen. They were farmers, traders, fathers, and sons from across what was left of the empire.

Eschelus and his guards made it atop the nearest hill, his full army a few paces behind. In the distance, atop a second hill across a grassy valley, was Odoacer's army. Their armor gleamed in the sun, which was emerging from behind the clouds. These weren't the Heruli tribe of years ago. This was a Roman army.

His hands started to shake on the reins of the horse. In an instant he was back on that wall seventeen years ago, watching Rome crumble in front of him. It flickered in and out, teasing him. A taste of a past that molded and scarred him. That held him back while giving him the strength to press forward.

Like always, next came the sweat. It was beading down his head, and surely his men, many cold from the chill outside, would notice. He wiped his brow and kept focus. It wouldn't distract him. Not today.

"Sir," one of his men said, motioning out toward the shallow valley. Odoacer and a few of his men, carrying flags behind them, were riding forward, detaching from the bulk of their army.

"Let no more of Rome die today!" he shouted, turning to his men. They responded in unison. He turned back forward. "Let's go."

The group in front galloped forward, taking care not to appear too aggressive. It was not time for that. Not yet.

As they came closer to meeting their opponents face-to-face, he kept thinking of the plan and its execution. If one part failed, the entire plan fell apart. It was a risk he had been willing to take, but his body was regretting. He couldn't quite understand why, but something in the air was telling him that something was wrong.

After a few moments of discussions, Eschelus's knights would come soaring over the hill from the east. They would descend and, with Eschelus's group, corner Odoacer and his generals and slaughter them, leaving the opposing army leaderless.

It was immoral. It was against everything he had been taught about the rules of war. But the world had long since stopped making sense. This was what was needed to set the course right again.

Shortly after, he imagined Odoacer's army would charge. Leaderless, and with morale shattered, it would be easy for Eschelus, even with fewer numbers, to break them. With Theodric's men, they would outnumber them and make quick work, which is precisely why their allies had yet to arrive, in order to fool Odoacer into thinking he had the numerical advantage.

At last, their horses met a few feet apart in the base of the valley. Eschelus immediately noticed an unexpected face to Odoacer's right. A senator, as evidenced by the insignia on his armor—custom designed for the rare to the point of nonexistent occasions that members of the ruling class decided to grace the battlefield with their presence.

Theodric had said it, but he hadn't believed it. He had thought perhaps his message hadn't been received yet. This wasn't right. The Senate was supposed to be backing him. He was certain that Severus had received his message. He was certain they knew he was coming. Did they not want Roman sovereignty restored?

His brain fluttered, cycling back and forth with anger and disbelief. This senator would be slaughtered like the rest when his knights marched down into the valley. It would be a declaration of war not just against Odoacer and his "kingdom" but the Roman Senate.

But they are traitors, as well, he thought. *To back a barbarian over a Roman makes them no better than the bacaudae.* He convinced himself of the point, but he couldn't shake a thought that was eating away at his mind. Pecking at the creases in his brain like a woodpecker feeding on a tall pine.

The cause is lost. Peck.

The cause is lost. Peck.

He felt the sweat forming on his head again. He couldn't show weakness. Not here. Not in front of the self-proclaimed king of Italy. Not where it counted.

None of this mattered. Once his knights came down that hill, it was over.

"So," Odoacer finally spoke, snapping Eschelus out of a trance, "here you are. The Emperor in the North. Your reputation precedes you."

"And yours, you," Eschelus answered respectfully.

Odoacer was wearing a rudimentary crown, an ugly thing emblazoned with pretty stones but nonetheless appearing to have been forged just for the occasion. It read atop *King of Italy and Rome, and Patrician of the Roman Empire under the Emperor*. The crest on the senator's armor read *Consul*.

"I will give you and your men one last chance to surrender," Odoacer proclaimed heavily, ensuring that it sounded regal. It was as though his consul next to him had taught him what he would say, and how he would say it. "You are outnumbered, and your cause is futile. As you can see"—he motioned at the senator—"Romans are respected and living well under my reign. I am recognized as the sovereign of these lands by the emperor himself. If you truly respect the legacy of your people, you shall leave this field in peace with your fellow Romans." He waved behind him now, indicating that his army to his rear were the "fellow Romans" that Eschelus sought to battle.

"His Majesty is being immensely generous based on your commitment to Rome," the consul finally spoke, in a quieter, more refined tone. "On behalf of the Senate of Rome, we would like to grant you free return to Rome as a respected general of the army, to serve beneath His Majesty and the emperor once again."

For the briefest of moments, Eschelus felt his mind considering the proposal. Why sacrifice the lives of so many Romans, on both sides, if Rome was existing peacefully somewhere just over that hill?

What was the aim? For he himself to become emperor? To enter the never-ceasing game of purple robes? Of betrayal and of conquest?

His cause was noble, not of conquest. Why, then, did he insist on fighting?

He looked for a moment at the men behind him, their faces tense and filled with derision as they looked at Odoacer and his barbarian generals next to him. This battle wasn't simply about who got to sit in Rome as the sovereign of Italy. No, it was about a way of life. About centuries upon centuries of history, evaporating like dew off the grass on a dry, warm summer morning with each passing day of Odoacer's rule.

It was his people who had destroyed Rome. It was his people who had slaughtered innocent woman and children as they coursed through Gaul, raiding for food.

"Our fates will be decided on the battlefield," Eschelus answered.

Odoacer shook his head, amused. "I have heard many things about you, Eschelus," he stated, "that you were a fool was never one of them. It seems I have overestimated you."

Eschelus felt his eyes darting from left to right as he looked for his knights. They should have been here by now, coursing down into the valley. His men behind them had their hands on their swords, ready for them. Where were they?

"Are you looking for someone?" Odoacer asked. He had a smirk on his face, and it was like a punch to his gut. "Your knights, perhaps?"

Eschelus felt bile rising into his throat. Odoacer knew. He knew everything. He had been betrayed. He felt anger but that immediately subsided into disappointment. The thousands of men standing behind him just minutes ago looked to him as a leader. As someone who would develop a strategy and execute it. Someone who would win battles.

He had failed them. He had failed Rome. Again.

His hands immediately started to shake once again. The consul whipped his horse's reins, pulling away from the group with a disappointed sigh. Odoacer's generals placed their hands on their hilts.

Odoacer raised his sword, and immediately a cloud of arrows shot overhead toward the Roman soldiers. Eschelus raised his sword in return, turning quickly to his army, but it was too late. Dozens were killed in the volley, dozens more wounded. Those remaining let out shouts as they began running forward, matching the calls of Odoacer's men likewise piling into the valley, arrows flying overhead in both directions now.

Eschelus flew forward as his horse stopped short beneath him. He saw several arrows had pierced the poor beast, which lay dying in the mud. Eschelus stood up quickly, grabbing his sword and turning back to Odoacer.

The barbarian king had hopped off his horse on his own volition, spinning his sword in his hands. Despite everything, he seemed regal in his clean armor, in comparison to Eschelus's worn-out, muddied attire that squeaked as he walked forward.

Around them, their armies had met and the battle had begun. Shouts of men and clanks of swords overpowered his senses. What sounded like loud explosions as horses smacked into each other sent him flinching.

Rome flickered in front of him again, shouting at his men, all odds against them, to hold the wall.

He came back to reality as a Herule ran in his line of sight, who he quickly dispatched with a slice to the neck. Odoacer flung his gasping, dying countryman out of the way, swinging his broadsword at Eschelus. The two parried several times, with Odoacer laughing the entire time.

Eschelus felt slow, as though the mud was sucking him in for an early grave. Odoacer was using every inch of his body in the fight. From his arms swinging the sword to his shoulders, which knocked him back.

"You disappoint me, General," Odoacer shouted. "All of this talk of your military prowess. You can barely lift that sword in your hands. How far Romans have come from the soldiers I fought seventeen years ago."

Odoacer, of course, had no way of knowing that Eschelus had been in the very battle he spoke of. He was simply some no-name soldier back then. Today, here he was, face-to-face with the very embodiment of the plague that had conquered the West. He couldn't give up. Not yet.

Eschelus swung again, this time with more force. Odoacer parried and grabbed his arm with his other hand. Eschelus barely saw Odoacer's armored elbow strike his nose. Once. Twice. A third time, with the worst crack yet. He tasted blood before he felt the pain, falling backward into the mud behind him as Odoacer pulled his sword from him.

He looked around him and saw his army fighting valiantly but futilely. They were vastly outnumbered. He couldn't be certain that Theodric's men were coming, not after the betrayal. All seemed lost.

One or two of his men—perhaps more, he had lost count in his dizzy, wounded state—attempted to reach him. Odoacer dispatched each with a merciless precision that only a barbarian—only someone weathered by mistreatment, by cold and hunger—could muster.

Odoacer let out a shout as he pulled off his armor, revealing his muscular, hairy, scarred torso.

"I want you to see," he shouted at Eschelus, pointing at him. "I want you to see who it is who defeated you. That Roman armor—that isn't what beat you. No. It was *me*. A *barbarian*. You, with all your scheming and attempts to be immoral, to kill us during negotiations—and you failed. Just as your emperor before you."

Eschelus attempted to stand, reaching for the nearest sword. He was certain he looked pathetic, scrambling around with a bloodied nose. Certainly not inspiring for the men around him, who began fleeing the scene. They knew the same as he did. It was over.

Odoacer kicked the sword away, leading Eschelus to lunge at him. It was futile, and Odoacer tossed him aside like a side of beef.

"Here," he shouted, grabbing the crown off his head. The battle around them had died down, the bulk of the remaining fighting now taking place near the top of the hill where his men had been stationed. "This is what you wanted, isn't it? This crown?"

He placed the crown on Eschelus's head upside down, so that the sharp tips of the crown dug into his head. It was too small and barely fit. He felt his head begin to bleed.

"There, does that feel better? Does it feel like you wanted it to?"

Eschelus spit a bloody ball at Odoacer's face.

"You will never be emperor. You will always be the bitch of some Roman in Constantinople."

Odoacer took the blunt end of his sword and slammed it repeatedly into the crown on Eschelus's head, bringing it down over his face like a bloodied set of knives digging down along his flesh.

He did it until the crown was over Eschelus's mouth, blood coursing down from the rest of his head. He put Eschelus back on his knees, and drew his sword.

"Go to hell, you Roman cunt."

He sliced through Eschelus's neck, decapitating him. His head fell straight to the ground, rolling a bit farther into the valley. Odoacer reached for it, ripping the crown off the face, tearing much of the remaining flesh away.

He looked toward the battlefield. He had won handily. His men were finishing off the last stragglers. It hadn't even been a competition.

XXXV

Chalcedon Estate, Southern Gaul

Gargarus tapped his fingers on the wooden table in front of him. It was solid wood. He found himself thinking that it was the type of craftsmanship you couldn't find anymore. What a silly thought that was. Little things like that—how nice your furniture was and who sat on it—seemed so irrelevant now. So far detached from reality.

How he and his family—indeed, how all the empire—had taken so much interest in such trivialities was beyond him now. He would easily sacrifice this table, the gold on the furniture, all the elements of sophistication to help save his family and his home.

"Gargarus," Castella said, stepping into the room. She glanced around, a confused look on her face. "Where is everyone else? They haven't arrived yet?"

"Or they simply aren't coming," Gargarus replied, motioning for his wife to take one of the several empty seats around the table. "They are likely scrambling to either learn to fight or find a way to flee before it is too late."

"Surely it is already too late," Castella said worriedly. "The army is already on its way."

"We sat at this table and decided as a group for years what was best for this place, our home. Together, with those whom we allowed to live here. Father gave them a say, unlike so many others in Gaul. This is how they repay us."

"Last time you all did that, Gargarus, it nearly ended in a fight. It is no wonder they don't want it to happen again."

In the distance, a horn blew. Gargarus and Castella shared a knowing, worried glance to each other.

"Get Mara inside the main house. Hide her."

"Gargarus," Castella said, placing her hands on her husband's shoulders. She rubbed for a brief moment, and for that instant, it felt like it did years ago after he had first found Castella. When it was just the two of them. "I love you."

"I love you, too."

The mood was tense outside the home. The few soldiers Eschelus had left behind were scrambling around, making an effort to appear prepared for what was about to come. He made his way down toward the south gate to make sure it was sealed as he had ordered the night before.

On his path he saw the old temple his father and Orephes had built, still standing in its audacious defiance against the Christian world surrounding it. It likely wouldn't survive the attack once the Goths made their way through the walls. He had been inside only once, when it was first built. His father had wanted to show him, but he hadn't expected him to pray or follow. All of that had been reserved for Orephes, though he never knew why.

He wiped a bit of dust off the door handle. He wasn't sure what for. He flung the door open and walked inside, immediately taken in by the intricacies decorating it. The miniature busts of who must have been the Old Gods. The attention to detail on the prayers written into the walls. The arrangements of candles around the walls.

In the dust and dirt on the floor, he saw footprints leading to an empty spot on a shelf. On the floor below it were the shattered remains of one of the Old Gods covered in a layer of gray, lifeless coating.

Orephes and his father had spent countless hours in here, his father teaching his young brother all the intricacies of a dead faith from the time he could speak. There was something nagging at him—something that didn't seem right about the whole thing. Why was only Orephes taught this, and he had been left to determine his own faith?

Standing up against the side of the entryway was Orephes's prayer staff. Gargarus recognized it from the few times he had interrupted his brother praying in here. He had never noticed how intricate the head of it was. So gleaming, he could see his own reflection in either glass or polished stone.

It was all enough to make him miss his brother again. In spite of his naïve attachment to this superstitious nonsense, he was family. Perhaps had he been around, things might have ended differently here at the villa. Or perhaps it would have all gone the same. Either way, he would have had his brother.

He held the staff in front of him, as he had seen Orephes do in the past when he was engulfed in prayer. He had never prayed before, but it certainly wasn't a bad time to start.

"Father Mars, I pray that you watch over my family and my home," he said, trying to pull the prayer he had heard in the past from memory. He wasn't sure he said it right, but hopefully, he thought, Mars wasn't too picky.

He placed the staff back against the wall, and just as he did, something seemed to pass through his arm and into his chest. A warm feeling that immediately forced out of his mouth two words, as though by reflex: "He's all right."

He wasn't sure why he had said those words, but he knew it was about Orephes. He could feel it like a nagging thought in his mind. His brother was out there somewhere. He was OK. He might even someday come home.

Outside, Gargarus saw the other esteemed Romans who lived at his home heading toward him. They were all together, so he wasn't sure why they had missed the meeting he had requested.

"Gargarus," an older woman named Eres said from the front of the group, "we have been looking for you."

"Had you been at the villa court meeting, you would have found me," Gargarus replied sternly.

There was a small contingent of soldiers following behind the group. They seemed anxious. Something wasn't right.

"We want to thank you for your hospitality. And your father's." She wasn't able to look him in the eyes. Something was happening here, something he wouldn't like. He just wasn't sure yet what it was. "You must know that we can't win this fight, Gargarus. It is hopeless."

"We have made it out of hopeless situations before," Gargarus answered calmly. "We shall do it again."

There was a pause while Eres looked to the other villa inhabitants for support. She turned back and raised her head.

"We have decided that we must surrender to the Goths. It is the only way we will survive."

It took Gargarus a moment to understand what she was suggesting. This was his home. His property. Who were they to decide that they would surrender? Who were they to make that decision in his absence?

"How dare you." It was all Gargarus could manage to say. It was raw emotion.

"Gargarus—"

He cut her off. "This is my home. My property, as it was my father's before me. You have no right to surrender it. If you choose to surrender, you can leave."

"We have been living here for years, Gargarus. This is our home now, too."

"You are a guest!" Gargarus shouted. He felt himself getting angry. "A guest in *my home.* On *my property.*" He could tell he wasn't convincing anyone. The guards behind him stayed locked on him.

Prepared to make a move if they had to. "The barbarians will only accept surrender from the owner of the property. I will never do so."

One of the men behind her stepped forward, holding a parchment. He looked Gargarus in the eyes as he handed it to him. Gargarus unfolded it and read it from top to bottom, where a line sat for his signature. It was a contract, shifting ownership of the estate from himself to a man in the group named James. It already contained barbarian terminology, renaming the estate and placing it within one of the "counties" they so often spoke of. It also swore fealty to the king of the Goths.

"Once you sign this, it will no longer be your home. It will give us the authority to turn the estate over to the barbarians." Eres placed her arm on Gargarus's shoulder. "We have already made arrangements. Your family will be safe; we will be kept safe. You will all be allowed to live here. Nothing will change."

"I will not sign this," Gargarus said, tossing the paper to the floor. He wasn't just angry at them. He was disgusted.

Eres shook her head and looked down before looking back at the crowd around her. She let out a sigh as she pointed at the guards.

"We didn't want to have to do this, but you have left us no choice."

Two of the guards stepped out from behind the crowd. One was holding Mara in his arms, the other was holding Castella by the neck, forcefully pulling her forward toward him. She looked at Gargarus with fire in her eyes. She hadn't been crying; she was too strong for that. She shook her head at him as if to say "don't do it." Mara was crying next to her, each shriek making his hair stand.

Gargarus went to step forward as one of the guards drew his sword.

"Don't do it," he said, holding the sword to his wife's neck. "I don't want to have to do this."

Gargarus felt his will evaporate through his relaxing jawline. It didn't matter what Castella said. He couldn't let them hurt her or Mara. He let out a deep sigh as he picked the parchment back up off the ground.

"Gargarus," Castella hissed. "Don't do it."

"Give me a stylus."

Eres handed him a metal stylus that he immediately recognized as his father's. The irony that his father's stylus would be the very thing to etch his signature into the parchment giving their home away wasn't lost on him. His hand shook and Castella argued as he signed away his family's life, destined to be forever a subject to His Majesty, the king of the Goths.

Eres immediately took the parchment away and handed it to a guard.

"Get this to the barbarian army now," she said quickly. "Let them go."

Castella sprang from the guard's arms and grabbed Mara from the second one. She ran toward Gargarus, who embraced them both. The crowd that had gathered quickly dispersed, finding hiding places in case things didn't go according to plan.

"Did they hurt you?"

"Don't be silly, Gargarus."

"When I saw you in their arms, I…"

"What have you done?" Castella lamented quietly.

"I saved our lives. I had to. They would have killed you both."

"We better pray that the Goths keep their word and allow us to remain here."

The family held each other close for a few more moments, the two parents taking a moment to each understand what had just happened.

"Gargarus?" A familiar voice called to him from behind them. He stood quickly, positioning himself between the voice and his family.

He saw the armor first, gleaming in the sun above them. It was the armor of Eschelus's knights. Gargarus let out a low laugh.

"Antonius. Impeccable timing."

"Good to see you again, friend," Antonius said with a smile. "We have much to discuss."

XXXVI

Northern Italy

The air was thick with the smell of blood and rotting flesh. Theodric was sitting atop the hill; he couldn't imagine the stench his men were wading through as they searched below. The disparity in the dead hadn't gone unnoticed. Eschelus's men far outnumbered Odoacer's on the ground, and the armies hadn't been that different in number when they met. It had been a massacre.

He wasn't sure whether it was Tufa who had betrayed them, or one of Eschelus's knights, or someone else. But he knew that someone had kept Tufa from signaling his army to march forward, letting him know the battle had begun. He also knew that Eschelus's knights had never entered the battle, as their corpses, which would have been adorned with armor, were nowhere to be found.

It had all gone to shit, and Odoacer still sat on the throne of Italy. With Eschelus's defeat, the hope of barbarians and Romans living together, ruling together, ushering in a new world...all of that was destroyed.

One of his men marched up from the valley, carrying something under his arms.

"Sir," he said as he came near, "we found him."

The soldier held out Eschelus's head, bloodied and torn apart. The sight of a man whom he had regarded so highly—who had seemed so strong only a few weeks earlier—was so staggering, even though he had seen it over and over again.

Theodric held what was left of Eschelus in his hands, looking at the senseless expression on his muddied, bloodied face. He was livid. He dropped the head to the ground and wiped the blood on his pants. He didn't have the men he needed to beat Odoacer outright. But he had more than Eschelus, and more than enough to draw him out. Odoacer wouldn't get away with this. He couldn't.

"Any sign of the knights?"

"No, sir. None."

He tried to piece everything together, but something wasn't adding up. Someone betrayed someone, but he wasn't sure who. He was certainly sure that Odoacer had something to do with it. The brutish oaf was sacrificing their chances for a new world where Romans and barbarians could live in peace, and for what? The seat of king?

"Issue the order to pull back. There is nothing more we can do."

"Where are we headed, sir?"

"To Odoacer's fucking gates."

XXXVII

Outskirts of Ravenna

The wood creaked beneath Martel's feet as he made his way to the front of the church. It was a small, provincial building, very unlike the stone churches of the wealthier cities. It hearkened back to the days when Christians had to hide their faith, building small, unassuming churches that were a far cry from the cathedrals that adorned the walled Roman cities of the rest of the peninsula. Martel liked this architecture far better than the exuberance some of the other bishops clung to. The wealth and size of the larger churches was a holdover from the high Roman era—an era he wished to see wiped from the face of the Earth. The church was unassuming enough, he thought, to be somewhere that nobody would look.

His Inquisitors took their positions like a reflex, making sure that access to the entrances and exits would be a privilege that only Martel could order. Gaius took his position next to his bishop, still unconvinced that there was any reason to be hiding in this collapsing, country church that reeked of old candles and molding wood.

Martel could sense Gaius's doubt. It hung over the pair of them like a cloud. Perhaps he hadn't waited long enough to bring the

251

young priest into his fold. It was one thing to commit to the life of a Christian. It was another entirely to commit to the life Martel had planned for them. As far as most of these people were concerned, mageia wasn't even something thought about. If it was, it was merely through the lens of mythology. To be reintroduced to a system that redefines existence is nothing short of staggering.

That he handled it so well for a while impressed Martel. He had seen many of the so-called miracles he had Volusian perform—he had no choice but to believe. It was one of the reasons he had made him his right hand. Other men would have broken at the sight. But that strength was also a liability. Gaius was a free thinker. The son of a wealthy patrician. He could just as easily reject Martel's desire for mageia as their Christian ancestors before them had rejected mageia as a whole. It was that singular thought that kept Gaius always at a distance.

"He's here," a guard shouted, entering the church. He was followed by a pair of barbarians. They seemed weary and unkempt.

"Tufa," Martel started with a smile, "I trust all went well?"

"It's done. Even better, I've heard word that it worked. Eschelus's army was defeated."

Martel smiled and nodded. "I knew I could trust you."

"At least someone does." Tufa seemed aggravated. Martel cocked his head, like a surprised hound hearing a foreign sound. "I sacrificed my reputation for this," Tufa continued angrily. "I am going to have to live the rest of my life hiding."

Martel smirked at his brazen, laughable insinuation that he should have any care about this barbarian's fate.

"A fate worse than death," Martel assured his guest. "Hopefully I can make this right."

"I am glad we are on the same page. Give me my payment and I will be on my way."

"Our Lord in heaven shall reward you when you arrive at his gates." Martel was calm and precise as he raised his hand, directing the two nearest Inquisitors to grab the arms of Tufa and his associate. He struggled with the ferocity of a trapped animal, foaming as he shouted obscenities at the archbishop standing in front of him.

Martel approached and laid his hand on Tufa's wriggling forehead.

"In the name of the Father"—he slowly ran his hand down to roughly his eyebrow—"the Son"—now to the left and right—"and the Holy Spirit."

"Fuck you! Fuck you and all of your bullshit!" Tufa spit at Martel's feet, narrowly missing them.

"Your sins are forgiven. Amen."

The Inquisitors sliced through Tufa's neck, sending blood flying forward. Martel stepped out of the way just in time to keep his white robes from becoming soiled. He had a meeting to attend.

"What was this barbarian's role in the bigger picture, Father?" Gaius asked Martel, speaking over the gurgling of the dying men near them. He had seen enough of it to perfect his volume and pitch to be heard over it. "Why did we bother with intervening in that silly war for the throne?"

"Eschelus was an enabler and friend of Orephes, the one I told you about."

"The Lar?"

"The *possible* Lar. But certainly a follower of the Old Gods. A user of mageia. You know what we must do."

Gaius nodded without fully understanding. He knew the plan was to isolate Orephes. Keep him from his friends and family to keep his powers from growing. Keep his story from spreading. Keep his connection to mageia shallow and weak. It was all some elaborate plan, using every connection Martel had. An obsession. But he would be lying if he pretended he knew how it all worked. This was Martel's game, and he was simply a pawn in it.

XXXVIII

Village of Litochoro, Base of Mount Olympus

They called this place the "City of the Gods." It certainly wasn't because of it being grandiose but rather because of its location at the base of the mountain. It was a small village, with scattered homes and a makeshift wall that likely kept no barbarians at bay. It was the only place that had a trail leading up the stony mountain, and for this it had gained notoriety. Olympus had been visible for miles back on their journey, and as they got closer the fact that the task he was preparing to take on became more daunting than anything he had ever done. This wouldn't be training with Eschelus to become a knight. This would be fighting the elements to climb to the top of a mountain, against powerful mageia that existed to keep people like him out. It didn't help that Marius insisted on reminding him, constantly telling him that he was crazy.

Or, he thought, perhaps not. If he was who his father said he was—whom he now believed he was—then perhaps the ancient power sitting on this mountain wouldn't be against him but instead help to guide him. A fleeting happy thought, immediately evaporated by the anxiety again.

"Are you planning on going up the mountain?" an old woman asked from a stool in front of a small mule cart as they entered the village.

"How did you know?" Orephes asked. He didn't actually need to. Why else would he be here? This was a small village. They probably had foolish explorers here all the time, and they would know anyone who wasn't a local.

She replied with a distant smile. "Because you don't look at the mountain with awe. You look at it with fear."

Orephes replied with a warm smile and went to continue on, but the old woman kept talking.

"Many have tried before you," she cautioned. "None have returned." She pulled back a curtain on the cart behind her, revealing an enormous parchment filled with names and dates. Those who had gone before him. Good people who didn't know what was waiting for them up there.

"He is different," Joanna said as a matter of fact. "He will make it there and back. I know it." She was looking at Orephes and he could tell she believed it. It empowered him, and not just because it boosted his confidence. Her belief shifted just a small amount of mageia toward him.

"You sure that you don't want us to come with you?" Marius asked worriedly. "We have been through a lot together. We work well as a team."

"No. I have to do this alone. The journey would kill you. It might not kill me."

"Might not." Marius shrugged and laughed. "You are a braver man than me, Orephes, with odds like that."

"Or stupider."

"You said it, not me."

Orephes extended his hand for a shake, but Marius leaned in and embraced him. He slapped his back a few times before letting him go.

"Remember everything I taught you when you get up there."

"How to steal a boat?"

"You never know when it will come in handy."

Joanna leaned forward and gave him a hug, too. It felt comforting, like a hug a mother would give to her son. It made Orephes appreciate the companionship that the two had given him on this journey.

"We will be here when you get back," she said softly. "Get up there and make things right again."

Joanna's innocent sentence drove home the importance of what he was about to do. This was no longer just about him finding out the truth. He wouldn't be sure whether or not he was who his father said he was until he got there. But the fact that the Gods were real, that mageia, something he could have never imagined, was all around him…all of this meant that what he was about to do was about so much more than himself. This was about a way of life older than Rome itself. About preserving an essence of the planet on the cusp of being wiped away forever.

He finished saying his goodbyes and left the town through what they called the "Gate of the Gods," a rickety old gate with arches that led to a path up the mountain. He could tell it was once supposed to look majestic, so much so that he would have liked to have seen it in its prime. It was on the far side of the small village, and as the gate creaked open, he saw the locals watching him with a look of both awe and amusement. They were likely thinking he was a foolish young man trying to attain glory like so many before him.

There was a stone portion of the arches as he passed through, covered in paint and graffiti. Names of former climbers littered the stones, as well as a few unsavory messages. "There are no Gods," one message said, next to a large black Christian cross. Christians and followers of the Old Gods seemed to have traded barbs here, but the paint was old. Nobody had cared or bothered to deface this gate in years.

The path on the other side of the gate led up into a stone pathway that was carved into the side of the mountain. It was steep but manageable. He slid his belt—sword and all—around his shoulder to give himself more flexibility. As he took his first steps onto the stone path, he turned to look back at the village, where Marius and Joanna were standing on the other side of the gate watching him. He gave a single wave back to them before disappearing around the corner, out of the realm of man and into the realm of the Gods.

XXXIX

Rome

The familiar sound of war could be heard in the distance. The crashes and shouting that had become commonplace on the Italian peninsula were once a rarity. Before Severus's time, and his father's before him, nobody had dared attack Rome at its heart. Those days were over. He had no faith that they would ever return. Outside the city walls, two armies, both ostensibly Roman but clearly barbarian, clashed to decide who would run the West.

His once pristine home had been torn apart by his aides taking what they could once he said he would not be returning. He had expected as much, though he hadn't expected them to turn so quickly. Only one or two remained to help him travel to Ravenna, where he promised to pay them handsomely. After all, the city had been under siege for years. It would not be easy to reach. He stepped over a few parchments and reached into his closet, which had remained untouched. He threw aside a few robes and opened a hidden compartment. He pulled out a prayer staff, which he grasped with both hands.

He strode gently to the center of the room and sat quietly on the floor, stretching the prayer staff out in front of him. He began to whisper under his breath some of the old prayers that he remembered, from the days when the Senate were the last defenders of the Old Faith. Back when they had forced the emperors to return the shrines and statues dedicated to preserving the old ways, and thus preserving the very thing that had kept Rome dominant for centuries.

"Give me guidance," he said at last, releasing his prayer staff so that it stood on its own in front of him. He closed his eyes so that he was unable to see the stone on his staff give a dull, pulsing glow as the room around him transformed to black.

He welcomed the vision, opening his eyes and watching as two armies materialized in front of him. He had seen this vision before, the armies clashing outside Ravenna. He knew he had to be there. He just needed to know what had to be done.

He heard a whisper surrounding him. He tried to focus, to understand what mageia was trying to tell him. It lasted only a few moments before the vision ended. He opened his eyes again to see he was back in his room, his prayer staff lifeless on the ground before him. He understood now what had to be done.

He summoned his final two remaining aides and asked them to prepare his transport. It wouldn't be right to Ravenna he would be traveling. No—it would be to Theodric's encampment, where he would do his part to end this war.

He took a candle that he had lit earlier in the day and held it to the wooden part of the prayer staff, igniting it in a bright flame that quickly popped and dissipated. He wouldn't be needing it anymore.

XL

Mount Olympus

He felt like he had been scaling the mountain for days. His body was already weak by the time the trail had become simply jagged stones. He now was as exhausted as he had ever felt, scaling a vertical wall of stone.

He was surrounded by clouds or fog, he couldn't be sure which, and he couldn't see more than a few feet in front of him or the ground below him, if it was even still there. He couldn't be sure if he was going the right way or if he was still on the right path. He just had to keep going up.

The eeriest part of the climb was the silence. The fog and lack of wind combined to provide mute air surrounding him. He could hear his own breath, feel his heartbeat. He was alone with his thoughts. And, he had to remind himself, with mageia. As long as he had that, he was never alone.

As he closed his eyes to center himself, he felt the stone beneath his right hand pull out of the mountain. He felt for another, but there was nothing. He felt his body start to fall. His mind flickered with thoughts that he couldn't control. He wasn't sure how high he was or where he would end up or if he would even realize he made it there, killed upon impact.

The first thing he noticed was the color green before his body crashed into the ground beneath him. He felt grass and dirt under his hands, and as he looked around he could see that the fog and clouds had dissipated near him. Above him was the stone wall he had fallen from, which disappeared into the clouds that he had just been sitting inside.

He was in a small cove of grass; an oasis of life within a column of stone. He wasn't sure how he had missed it when he was climbing, but somehow he had been lucky enough to land here when he fell. He noticed his amulet sitting in front of him, having fallen off him during the plunge. It reminded him that it wasn't luck guiding him. He picked up and restrung it around his neck, thanking mageia in his mind for keeping him safe. The phrase startled him at how quickly he became used to the thought of mageia being around and within him.

The cove was small, surrounded by the stone walls of the mountain on all sides. There didn't seem to be a way out.

He finally made it to his feet, when he heard a rustling behind him.

He drew his sword and turned quickly, half expecting to see Volusian and half expecting to see nothing. Instead, he was standing face-to-face with his father, Tiberius.

"Is that how you say hello to your father?" His words were like a warm blanket. Orephes had longed to hear that voice again for so long.

"Father," he said softly, feeling his defenses dropping. He nearly dropped his sword and embraced him but stopped short. Something didn't feel right. A nagging, tugging on the hairs on the back of his neck. Mageia was trying to tell him something.

He looked into the eyes of his father in front of him. They looked hollow and glazed over. They weren't his father's eyes. They weren't anyone's eyes.

"Aren't you happy to see me?" his father spoke again, his face transforming to a look of concern.

His father stepped toward him, and Orephes felt his defenses fluctuate. He felt like something was wrong, despite his longing to see his father again. He kept his sword raised.

"Isn't this what you wanted?" his father continued. "To see your father? I am here. You have made it." There was a hint of joyful desperation in his voice. "I have wanted to see you, too. You don't understand what it is like to watch you from afar and be unable to speak to you."

Orephes closed his eyes and centered himself again. He felt the mageia around him. It was fluctuating, coarse. Something was disrupting it. The mageia coming off his father was unnerving. There was something wrong here. He was sure of it. This thing, whatever it was, wasn't his Tiberius Chalcedon.

"You aren't my father," Orephes said, finally accepting it himself. "Tiberius Chalcedon is dead."

His "father" looked surprised.

"Orephes, mageia connects you with your ancestors, with the dead. Didn't the augur teach you this?"

"I was taught to trust in mageia," Orephes answered coldly. "You are not my father."

His "father" suddenly changed, his face turning manic, eyes black as he let out a screech. He lunged at him.

Orephes closed his eyes and grabbed the amulet, directing the mageia around him to push his "father" away.

He opened his eyes and the spirit was gone. A hole had appeared in the stone wall in front of him. A doorway. The mageia around him had calmed. He gently kissed his amulet and tucked it back into his shirt. The grass in the cove was gone now, revealing a stony patch of dirt littered with human remains—whatever that had been, it certainly was meant to keep people out. He remembered what he had been told; that there would be old mageia here, meant to keep out people since long before the Roman empire.

Onward, he thought, walking into the doorway of stone that had opened in front of him.

His eyes had to adjust to the darkness within the cave. It was cold, stony, and lifeless. Certainly not a home he would have expected for the Gods. This couldn't be where he needed to be. It must be deeper.

He reached the back of the cavern, where he was met with another stone wall.

"Between a rock and a hard place," he whispered jokingly to himself. He wasn't sure where to go from here. The mageia in the cavern felt muted and still. There was no guidance anymore, as though he was where he needed to be.

He felt along the wall until he noticed a small circular groove. He felt along the inside of it and detected a pattern that felt familiar to his hand.

It was the pattern of the stone and glass as it interwove on his amulet. He nervously withdrew his amulet again from his shirt, placing it into the groove in the same direction as the pattern.

There was a sudden pulse of light that illuminated the cave around him and the wall in front of him seemed to evaporate into ash. The amulet returned to his hand, as though magnetized to him, and the light momentarily blinded him. As he recovered, he saw that the chamber around him had transformed from dirty stone to majestic bright marble.

There were twelve seats in a semicircle surrounding him, with one large one at the center, which had gold-and-purple stone plating on the armrests. Behind the main chair was another chamber, which appeared to have a balcony that overlooked the base of the mountain. The mageia around him was palpable—it weighed him down. This was it. Mount Olympus. The home of the Old Gods. And they were gone.

As the sheen of the moment faded, he came to understand the implications of what he had found. The Old Gods were truly gone. Perhaps a small part of him believed he would reach this place and find them—his real family—asleep or otherwise neglecting their duties. That his journey would end with the Gods returning from their hiatus and striking down the traitor Volusian and restoring the world to its rightful place.

Instead, here he stood, not in the presence of greatness, but instead in the presence of failure and abandonment. The mageia here was strong, but the will apparently had not been.

Orephes got closer to one of the chairs, placing his hand on the marble as though he wanted to remember having sat there himself. He saw what looked like black streaks of burn marks along some of the stone. Old wounds on the marble from a different time. Many of the seats, and some of the walls, seemed to be decorated with these ominous signs of a prior life. A prior battle—or slaughter.

"I'm proud of you for making it this far," a voice boomed throughout the chamber, sending Orephes turning quickly to face behind him.

Volusian was standing at the entrance to the chamber, a callous smirk across his face.

XLI

Ravenna

It had been a city under a seemingly uninterrupted siege for years. Most of the civilian population had either fled or retreated to the higher ground forts and villas around the city. Weary soldiers lined the streets, enjoying their reprieve—one they couldn't be sure would last.

Theodric hadn't had the forces to beat Odoacer outright, nor could Odoacer fight off the invading army. The stalemate on the peninsula would have gone on forever. That Theodric had called for a truce had appeared to be divine intervention. The question was, on whose side was the intervention for?

Ad Laurentum, the old Imperial Palace built by Emperor Honorius in the high Imperial days, had become a home for Odoacer in a way more comfortable than he had expected. In the setting sun, and in the presence of a peaceful city for the first time in years, it was beautiful. Rome's people may come and go, but its beauty would never change.

Odoacer held his wife's hand as they entered the dining room of the palace, flanked by his guards. His young son trailed behind them, their entire family beaming with an exuberant joy that perhaps after years of conflict, they had found peace. They took their seats at the table, smiling at each other as the guards and servants arranged the plates.

Without fanfare, Theodric entered from the opposite side of the room, flanked by a few guards of his own. He was smiling, a rare sight since the death of Eschelus. Odoacer stood and shook his fellow general's hands as he entered.

"Who would have guessed," Odoacer blurted out, breath already thick with wine, "that here in the house of the emperors, two barbarians would be negotiating peace."

"It is our time now," Theodric agreed. "Our time to make peace and to make a new empire in our vision."

"Come, sit," Odoacer invited. "Let us eat."

The courts of each of the generals began to enter the room, a few of their captains and family members leading the way. Odoacer's acclaimed consul, Caecina, took a seat next to him, opposite his wife.

Odoacer was surprised to see a senator seated in Theodric's delegation, as well. An older senator whom he recognized, but was not able to remember his name.

"Severus?" Caecina asked loudly from across the table.

Severus nodded with a gentle smile, waving his old wrinkled hand as if to greet his old rival without any recognition of Caecina's surprise.

"So, this is the senator who helped negotiate the peace," Odoacer proclaimed, raising his glass to Severus, "to you we are all thankful!"

"It is my pleasure to bring peace to my home," Severus said softly, raising his own glass without taking a sip.

Caecina looked around. Everything seemed normal, but this didn't seem right. Severus always had a plan, and certainly his plan wasn't simply peace. He didn't trust him, but he could not afford to make a scene here. If he was wrong, then Odoacer would certainly have his head for disrupting this chance for peace.

The food began to be served and he could see Severus still sitting, so at peace. Not an ounce of worry in his body. It drove Caecina mad. He noticed that Theodric's guards around the outside of the table seemed on edge, in stark contrast to Odoacer's men, who were feasting and drinking. Something was wrong.

He excused himself and stood up, noticing Theodric's men follow him with their eyes as he walked into the hallway. Once outside the dining room, he grabbed a few loyal guards and told them to follow him. They headed outside of the palace, where they saw a few more of Theodric's men looking to enter the palace. All heavily armed.

"Both sides are equally represented," Caecina protested. "There is no need for more men inside."

Theodric's men looked at each other, as though they hadn't been expecting to see Caecina, before walking back down the stairs of the palace. It seemed too easy. He saw more of Theodric's men meandering around the palace, watching him and the guards like wolves watching sheep. Was this all just paranoia?

Inside, the two kings feasted on lamb and wine. Theodric and Odoacer laughed about old tales of Romans, the Emperor in the East, and about battles they had fought. Severus sat quietly and patiently, at peace with his place.

"You keep looking at the doors, Theodric," Odoacer said without concern, noticing his colleague's eyes. "You waiting for someone?"

"No," Theodric assured him. "Simply awaiting the delicious dessert."

"As am I! Where is that cake?" Odoacer shouted, his servants hurrying to find something to put out.

Severus's smile faded as he noticed Theodric looking at the doors, as well. Theodric glared at the old senator, a fire in his eyes that he hadn't seen earlier in the night. His patience had worn out.

Theodric stood up, throwing his chair back behind him as he leaped onto the dinner table in front of him. Before anyone in the room had time to react, he lunged across the table with his sword drawn, striking Odoacer in the collarbone. His sword dug deep into his bones and cartilage. It took all his strength to pull it out, sending blood flying across the table.

Odoacer's wife screamed as she stood up, trying to run backward but falling over her chair. She told her son to run as she tried to get up, her twisted ankle betraying her. Theodric's men quickly killed all Odoacer's men in the room before heading after her.

"Where is God?" Odoacer shouted helplessly, blood pouring from his mouth.

"The Gods are dead," Theodric replied, kicking the dying Odoacer down in his chair.

Outside, Caecina heard commotion from inside. Before he and his guards could move, Theodric's men surrounded them, slaughtering the guards one by one before only the consul was left.

"Please, have mercy," he pleaded, going to his knees. "I am a senator of Rome!"

"There will be others," one of the guards said, stabbing Caecina through the heart.

Odoacer's wife pushed past the men, attempting to run to the street. She saw Theodric's men slaughtering her husband's.

"Let none of them live!" one was shouting.

She felt a sudden pain as a stone struck her temple, sending her falling to the ground. She began to weep not from the pain, but for her son, who would never know the peace she had so hoped for him. Then another stone. Then another. The soldiers had finished with the enemy army; they took turns stoning her, laughing as they did.

Inside the palace, Theodric found Odoacer's son attempting to flee out of the rear. He grabbed him by his collar and tossed him back.

The boy pulled out a small knife, which Theodric knocked away. His expression changed.

"You aren't like your father," Theodric said. "You have courage." He lowered his sword. "You are hereby exiled to Gaul. Leave this city and never return. If you ever attempt to step foot here again, you will be killed."

The boy didn't question anything, instead fleeing out the way he had been trying to escape.

Across the city, Theodric's men slaughtered Odoacer's army wherever they could be found. Peace had come back to Rome, and it smelled of blood.

XLII

Mount Olympus

The red glow from Volusian's stone blade illuminated the right half of his body, contrasting the blue light of the sky hitting him on the other side. The blade fizzled and popped like a flame, the warm air warping around it. Orephes felt inadequate in comparison, holding his man-made metal sword that reflected the sunlight from behind him.

"How did you find me?" Orephes finally asked, breaking the silence.

"All of us are connected through mageia. You and I, even more so. Years ago, there would have been thousands of us, scattered across the world, all connected. You wouldn't believe what it was like back then."

The mageia in the room swirled, Volusian's presence disturbing the heavy, ancient presence within the room. It was as though the mageia in here recognized him. Wanted to avoid him. Like oil sitting atop water. Orephes didn't feel as frightened by it this time. He felt an almost subtle recognition, as though their own respective auras recognized each other as the relatives that they were.

Having finally made it here, so far, and standing in the presence of the Gods—he finally felt a connection to the story Lucas had told him. He felt his fear shift to anger and back again, watching Volusian's smirk slowly dissipate from impatience. This wasn't some phantom attacking him in the desert this time. This was Volusian, the Lar who had betrayed the Old Gods. Who had betrayed the old world. Techni-cally, his own flesh and blood as a fellow demigod from a pantheon of Gods all of whom were related themselves who was directly responsible for everything he had suffered. That his family had suffered.

"How could you do this? To the other Lares? To your own *family*. To *our* family."

"I tried to save my family," Volusian shot back quickly. His tone shifted to manic and he pointed his sword forward. "It was *them* who cared nothing about family. Certainly, not to the Gods, whose im-mortality made them callous. Not to the other Lares, whose rejection had made them *equally* callous." Volusian's tone returned to normal. "I was here long before you were born, Orephes. You didn't see the world as it had become. You and I— half God, half man—we think ourselves something extraordinary. That is only because of the world I have helped to build. Lares—we demigods—were loathed in the old world. Too powerful to be human, too weak to be Gods. Condemned to be bastard children for all eternity."

"So, your answer was to slaughter everyone you knew and loved? Everyone who believed in the Old Gods?"

"It was only a matter of time before humans decided that the infallibility of the Gods was not something they could accept forever. When they did, I chose to side with the side of the family who raised me. Just like the human family that raised you. Unlike the Gods, *they* accepted me. There are millions of humans and only dozens of Gods. I chose to give this world to those who rightfully should own it."

For a moment, Orephes bought Volusian's tale of noble self-sacrifice. It seemed genuine and he could feel his emotions were raw. But his rise to power didn't happen in a vacuum. He was only part of the story.

"You knew that with the Gods gone, nobody could challenge your control of mageia. That is why you did this. You wanted the power that you could never have when the Gods were here."

"A side effect," Volusian said dismissively, hiding a smirk, "not a cause."

"I don't believe you."

"I don't need you to." Volusian lifted his hand, tossing Orephes backward with mageia toward the room that overlooked the mountain behind him. Volusian slowly walked forward, admiring the seats where the Gods had once sat.

"It has been centuries since I have been in this room," he started again. "I have been back to Olympus hundreds of times, each time trying everything I could to break the seal that they left here. The missing key was what I needed, and there it is, around your neck."

Orephes touched his amulet, remembering it was there. He tucked it back into his shirt as he stood up, holding his sword forward. He kept preparing himself for Volusian to throw the first blow, but it never came.

Volusian approached one of the twelve chairs that remained in the room, rubbing his hand on the armrest.

"This is where my father sat once," he said finally, longingly. "Ares to the Greeks. Mars to the Romans. Something else entirely to those out east or across the vast oceans. The name didn't matter. What mattered was the worship." He took a seat, looking almost petulant in the grandiosity of the chair. It was as if everything about his body didn't belong there. Not the clothing, not his skin, none of it. "He would have been driven mad seeing me sitting here."

"Ares was your father?"

"He was. Though he wasn't a very good one. All he left me was the ability to forge weapons from the Earth. My mother, on the other hand, was the greatest person in my life, raising me despite everyone in her life telling her to leave me behind. I was a constant reminder to her of the fact that the Gods were not what she thought they were. A constant reminder of that miserable night and what he did to her. Becoming a Lar and having to face him and the rest of them every day…" Volusian's voiced trailed off, his hand clenching the armrest. "They used to take you. It didn't matter if you were ready. If you wanted to stay with your human family. As a Lar, you were property of a system outside of your control."

Then, as though suddenly remembering where he was, he looked back at Orephes.

"That makes you some type of uncle or cousin to me," he said, laughing. "Well, as long as you truly are the son of my grandfather, Zeus. That amulet you wear is certainly his. Don't you want to know once and for all if he is your father? Why you were left behind?" His sword dissipated into thin air, the smoke it left behind swirling around him and disappearing. He hopped off the chair and approached Orephes, who lowered his sword, sensing that he was not in danger. "Is that not why you came here?"

"It is."

Volusian placed his arm around Orephes's shoulder, turning him to face the solitary room overlooking the mountains below.

"Have you heard of Zeus's lightning?"

Orephes nodded.

"I thought you might have. It isn't what you would expect. Most envision him sitting up here tossing lightning bolts down from the sky. Such a human fantasy. The truth is that what humans called his lightning was in fact a weapon—a rudimentary sword forged from ancient mageia right here in this mountain. He wielded it not against man but against the Gods.

"It is the only thing that can kill a God. As long as he had that weapon, he could keep the Gods in line, keep mageia in line, and keep the world order preserved. Though he certainly didn't count on his power—all of their power—waning slowly as humans shed their foolish superstitions. But there is another part to that weapon. It was also the only thing that could *create* a God—ending one's mortal life and tying them forever to mageia."

Volusian turned Orephes to face him. They looked at each other eye to eye for the first time since they had met.

"When they fled this place and sealed it off forever," he finished, "some said Zeus left it behind."

Orephes wasn't sure whether or not to believe him at first. It didn't make sense. Something as powerful as that…why wouldn't he take it with him to his grave?

"Why would he do that?"

"We can't be sure, but why else would he leave this place sealed? What power was sitting in here for someone to take? And who was meant to take it? These were things I pondered for years, as I sat outside that stone wall trying my best to break it. Now, here you are. The boy who just walked right in."

Orephes looked into the vacuous chamber at its triangular floor with its tip pointed out into the horizon. Below the end of the chamber was nothing but the sky, waiting for someone to stand and face the world below. There was nothing in it at all. No seat, no throne, not even a mural or statue as adorned some sections of the other room. Just a stone chamber with a magnificent view. He knew from this journey, however, that looks could be deceiving. Mageia could play tricks on the mind.

"I feel so much mageia in there," Orephes said finally, sensing pulses from the room.

"I feel it, too," Volusian agreed. "This chamber belonged only to Zeus and those whom he gave permission to enter. That mageia you feel was able to keep out even the most powerful of the Gods unless granted permission. For Lares like us, stepping into a place like that would evaporate us in an instant. Unless, of course, we were given permission."

"Have you ever been given permission to enter?"

"Never. Unfortunately, it is too late to ever get that permission now."

"So then why go through all this effort to shield this place?" Orephes asked. "Nobody can grant entry to here anymore. What would be the point of keeping everyone out?"

"Excellent question. I suppose we should find out."

Volusian shoved Orephes forcefully toward the chamber while his guard was down. He fell face first into Zeus's chamber, feeling the mageia in the room begin ripping at his flesh.

XLIII

The burning seemed to subside immediately, but he could still feel the mageia swirling around his body. He could hear it roaring around him, like the winds in a storm. Streaks of blue lightning flew from the walls and the ceiling, striking him as he rose to his knees. They continued until he was nearly engulfed by the strikes, each one more powerful than the last.

He let out a yell as his arm felt like it was thrust out from under him, made to stretch out by powers out of his control. He could see the lightning like an endless current running up and down his arm. Suddenly, all the energy striking his body seemed to pool together at his palm, all the streaks of lightning suddenly striking in one place.

There was a bright flash, and then there was silence. Orephes opened his eyes to see a strange-looking sword in his hand that hadn't been there before, having appeared out of thin air. It was heavy, both with weight and mageia. It wasn't shaped like any sword he had seen. It was misshapen and jagged, with a blade that looked more like the lightning that had just been striking him than a sword forged by man. There was neither a cross guard nor formal hilt, merely an area of the metal that was a bit more rounded for him to hold.

He stood up, holding the sword firmly in his hand. He turned to look at Volusian, whose eyes were beaming at him.

"You truly are the son of Zeus," he said, a sincere smile plastered on his face. "The last great hope for restoring the balance of mageia, bestowed to a small boy in Gaul." He laughed dismissively.

Orephes didn't feel as though the laugh was directed at him but rather at the Gods who left this to him.

"Orephes, you and I are family. There is no reason to fight any longer. Let us together rule over this world. Two raised by man but with the blood of Gods. With that weapon, we can create a new pantheon. One made in our image."

Orephes looked at the sword in his hand and suddenly it all hit him. He was the son of Zeus. He was the last living heir to the legacy of the Old Gods. He was the one thing standing between the end of mageia and the rise of the new world, with humans who are more than happy to fill the void with false religions and war.

He believed Volusian was sincere in his offer. It might have been his awe of the weapon that Orephes now held, but something had changed in the last few moments. Volusian sincerely didn't want to fight him. He could feel it. He wanted them to work together, to become like brothers and reign for all eternity now that nothing was in their path. It was as though Volusian thought that this must be how his own story ended, now that his last roadblock was cleared, and because Orephes had held the key, he owed it to him to bring him under his wing.

Perhaps it was because of the sincerity of the offer that Orephes considered it for a moment. Without guidance, it was clear the world that humanity had forged for itself was collapsing upon itself. The Roman empire of his ancestors was gone. The world was brutal and barbaric now, so much so that people retreated to villas and castles, signing their lives away to work under the protection of noblemen who could provide for defenses. A world of city-dwellers and wealth and senators and excess had given way to a world of far-flung forts, barbarian raids, poverty, and destruction. It wasn't lost on him that the changing world coincided with the loss of the Old Gods. Perhaps he had a duty to help restore balance to this world. Perhaps the sword he held was a chance to start fresh. A new pantheon freed from the sins of the fathers and mothers of the past.

It was likely what Zeus had left this here for him to do—to find this weapon and create the new pantheon.

But the old world didn't die only because it was invaded from without—it had been invaded from outside for centuries. No, the old world died from within. Perhaps the system, as it had worked for centuries, as it was explained to him by Lucas, was designed to fail. Perhaps it was the will of mageia itself that the Gods fell. Maybe in their quest to manage the system, they became inhibited by it. Blinded by its regiment. Volusian was not a product of Christianity. Volusian was a product of the old ways, who sought only to restore the past but with himself—and presumably Orephes—at the top of the same chain as before.

The life Volusian was offering was not the life he wanted. It was not the life he believed he was meant for. Zeus—his true father—hadn't left the sword here for him to anoint the very Lar who betrayed them all. He would not choose to betray his legacy. He would not betray his family's legacy.

"No." Orephes walked forward, empowered by Zeus's sword in his hands. He thought about Joanna and Marius, who had joined him so far, against all odds, despite no attachment to the old world at all. "Ruling over this world is your desire, not mine. The world I wanted to live in is long gone, but there are good people in this one. People worth protecting from someone like you."

"No. No!" Volusian raised his clenched hands. The response was more passionate than Orephes had anticipated. The moment Orephes had rejected him, the mageia around him pulsed outward. Rage and sadness permeated the room. A lament he had not expected. Volusian took a deep breath and returned his hands to his side, taking a deep breath. "You are making a mistake," Volusian said softly. "You are not the first to reject this offer. But you are different from them. Unsullied by a memory of how things used to be. Nobody understands how it feels like we do, to be what is left of a world that no longer exists. The loneliness." He shook his head. "This is your last chance. We can create a new family."

Orephes closed his eyes for a moment to think, opening them to see his reflection in Zeus's lightning. He hadn't seen his reflection since leaving the villa. He looked worn and tired. He saw a very different, haggard version of himself from the one he remembered. The one he had left behind. He saw the amulet around his neck, feeling its weight pulling down on him. The one left to his father, hidden away for decades, by the very Gods who used to inhabit this mountain. The ones who could no longer rule because they allowed their own reign to end.

"My answer is the same. You murdered our family. You have wanted nothing but power, and will do the same to me the minute you need to. It is time for the memory of the Old Gods to end. It is not our place to rule this world anymore."

Volusian let out a seething laugh, like a hiss through his teeth. It was the laugh of both disappointment and derision.

"So be it." Volusian's sword suddenly reappeared in his hand from dust that swirled around him. "If you will not join me, then you are nothing more than another follower of the Old Gods standing in my way, who will soon be destroyed like the rest of them." He pointed his sword forward. It left behind a trail of soot and ash as the embers flew from it. "That sword that you hold is mine. Give it to me."

"This sword was my father's," Orephes responded, holding it firm. "Now it belongs to me."

"You do not deserve a weapon as powerful as that."

"Neither do you."

Volusian lifted his arm and Orephes felt the sword tug at his hand. He was trying to pull it from him. Orephes centered his thoughts around the amulet and focused his mageia, grabbing the sword tight and keeping it in his hands.

There was a crack as the two swords collided when Volusian lunged forward. Both swords were the product of strong mageia but only one the product of the Gods themselves. Their swords met as they parried each other, each time sending out pulses of the mageia used to forge them.

Orephes could feel weight behind each of his opponent's blows. This wasn't just fighting some barbarian—each moment was a constant battle between their conflicting control of the mageia around them. The weapons Orephes held were more powerful, but Volusian's mastery was more refined. He had years of practice, much of it against far more powerful Lares than himself.

Each time Volusian attempted to use mageia against him—to throw him back or pull him forward—it took everything in him to focus on the mageia within the amulet and around him to counter him. It left him open to attack. A fight like this hadn't been something that the knight training could ever have prepared him for.

Volusian raised his open arm, sending stone and dust flurrying toward it in a dizzying whirlwind. In a moment, he lowered his hand and sent a wave of flame and ash hurling toward him. Orephes held the amulet in front of him, sending the flames curling around him as they knocked him backward to the edge of the room, where he could see the sheer length of the drop below him. He went to stand, but Volusian was already standing over him, his sword swinging down on him.

As a reflex he threw Zeus's lightning forward with both hands to defend himself. His opponent pressed all his strength into the sword, sending embers and sparks flying into each of their faces as their weapons scraped against each other at close quarters. Orephes could see Volusian's face behind the red glow of his sword, eyes locked on to his.

Suddenly, Volusian's other hand appeared from behind him, holding a small flaming dagger. Orephes felt the heat coming for his neck, turning quickly so that it only grazed him.

There was a short tearing sound, and the necklace that held the amulet around his neck was sliced in half. The amulet fell, first hitting the edge of the floor before cascading down the stony side of the mountain. The sound of it bouncing, clanking along the rocks, each farther than the last, sent a chill down his spine. He immediately felt less mageia around him. He felt alone.

Almost immediately Volusian was able to push through his meager defense, sending Zeus's sword flying to the center of the room with the force of his swipe. Volusian let out a laugh as he tossed the exhausted Orephes aside, grabbing Zeus's lightning off the floor.

Without the amulet, Orephes felt drained from the mageia that had been giving him strength. He attempted to stand but was overwhelmed by the energy surrounding Volusian, which he was using with no effort to keep him down.

"I've wanted this for so long," he said, a look of awe on his face. "You, of all people, have given it to me."

Just like that, he had failed. His entire journey here ended with his birthright falling into the hands of the very person who had slaughtered them all. He had lost the sword. He had lost his amulet. It was all over. He tried to push himself up again, this time making it to his feet. He drew his normal sword, having been sheathed the entire time, and pointed it forward.

Volusian took a moment from admiring Zeus's sword to look at Orephes. He seemed amused to see his cousin standing there, pathetically holding his sword as though he could do anything to stop him. There was no way he would let Orephes leave here alive. He was the only threat left to his domination, even if it wasn't a realized threat yet. With him out of the way, he could ascend to the role he wanted—a new God for a new world. The mageia in the room began to swirl again, sending dust and stones flying around Volusian like a tornado.

"You could have been a part of this," Volusian shouted over the howl of the wind. "The Christians made me a saint. I have thousands worshipping me. *Fueling* me. Now that I have this weapon, you have nothing—not even a record of yourself—and you will die with nothing, as invisible to history as the Gods who left you."

Instantly, the swirling stones and dust transformed into a massive beam of fire from Volusian's palm. Orephes raised his arms in a futile effort to shield himself but was engulfed within seconds. He felt the flames ripping at his skin, burning his flesh—and then immediately, felt nothing. He heard nothing.

He opened his eyes and saw himself, arms still raised in defense, standing in a white abyss.

XLIV

He lowered his arms and looked around. He seemed to be alone here in this white void. Was he dead? Was this the afterlife— some strange plane where he would live the rest of his eternity?

"Orephes," a voice called out behind him. He turned to see, once again, his father—his human father, not Zeus—standing before him. He had a warm smile on his face. "My son. I am so proud of you."

He was immediately wary, given the last time he had seen his "father" he nearly ended up dead on the side of Olympus, but something felt different this time. It felt warm and good—this whole place did. It didn't feel wrong to see his father this time. He looked into his eyes—the eyes he had once known so well. They didn't feel like a vision or a distant memory. They were his eyes. He was here with him. This time, it was real.

He stepped forward and embraced his father, who warmly hugged him back.

"Father," Orephes said, laughing with a combination of surprise and joy. "How? Where are we?"

"We are in the plane of mageia," Tiberius said, releasing his son. "We are everywhere and nowhere, all at once."

"Am I dead?"

"No," another voice said, a hand appearing on his shoulder. He turned to see Lucas, seeming spry and attentive compared to the version he had met, standing before him. "But we are."

"This is where we go when our bodies are burned, and our souls are allowed to reunite with mageia," Tiberius continued. "I have been watching you—been alongside you—this entire time."

"I knew you were," Orephes answered. "I could feel it. I wasn't sure what it was at the time, but I felt you there with me. I saw you in my dreams."

"You have done well," Lucas said. "You have come so far."

"But the job isn't done," a third voice boomed behind him. This voice he knew before looking.

"Eschelus?" Orephes said worriedly as he turned around. There he was, in an easily recognizable armored state, standing in front of him. Orephes was of course happy to see him but knew this meant he was dead, too. "No…no it can't be. Not you, too. How?"

"None of that matters now," Eschelus shot back. "All that matters is here. Now."

"I can't beat him," Orephes lamented. "He has been doing this for years. Against people far more powerful and in tune with mageia than me."

"His strength isn't your weakness," Lucas started. "Have I taught you nothing? You believe because you lost your amulet and your weapon that you are powerless. That is your weakness."

"Orephes," Tiberius said, "I will always love you as my son. But you must accept who you truly are. You are the son of Zeus, King of the Gods—the God who was so powerful, he could control all the others. You don't need an amulet or a sword. You have everything you need here." He lifted his hands, showcasing the bright, endless void around him. "The challenge ahead of you is never as strong as the power behind you."

Orephes noticed the room around him begin to darken, reforming the cavernous hall of the Gods he had been in moments ago.

Each of the spirits around him placed their hands on him.

"Make us proud." Eschelus was the last to speak before they disappeared, seemingly diving into him, as his body contorted to match his fearful, defensive hand raise as Volusian's flames struck him.

Instantly, he was engulfed by the flames. He closed his eyes and centered his mind and freed his thoughts of the pain. *This is all mageia,* he thought. *It is about control, not strength.*

He opened his eyes and saw the flames surrounding him yet he felt no pain. He stretched his arm out, flames licking his skin as he did, and yet he felt nothing. This fire was built from mageia—and Volusian's mageia wasn't hurting him anymore.

He raised his arms and felt himself push the flow of mageia in the other direction. The flames around him changed from the bright red they had been to a soft white as the control of the mageia changed before their eyes.

Orephes walked forward, transforming the entire beam of flames to a bright holy-looking white as he passed through like a boulder pushing through a stream. Volusian's stunned face was victory enough, but as he reached the other Lar, he reached forward and grabbed Zeus's lightning from his hands before he could react. The stream of fire ended, as Volusian realized it no longer had any effect.

"That's impossible," Volusian shouted, forming his sword again. With a faint crack he swung the sword forward. Orephes caught the blow with his hand, squeezing his fist to crack the once formidable weapon to pieces.

Desperate, Volusian formed the sword again, this time wasting no time to begin swinging. Orephes could feel him using his mageia now as he formed his weapons. He centered on the flow toward Volusian's hands and pulled the weapon away, dissolving it into the millions of dust particles it really was.

"What is this!?" Volusian seemed rabid with anger, flinging fireball and stone at his opponent without care. Orephes slowly and meticulously reached him, finally holding him against the wall by his neck.

"This is for my family."

Orephes plunged Zeus's lightning into Volusian's abdomen. His body instantly fell limp to the ground as the mageia evaporated off him, like steam off morning dew. The half of him that the sword could affect—his God half—was returning to the natural flow where it belonged. On the ground, his body contorted and aged before Orephes's eyes. The mageia from his God bloodline had been keeping him young. Without it, he was simply a human who had lived far past his time.

After a few moments it was over. Orephes was standing alone again in the room of the Gods, Volusian's aged human body at his feet. He fell to his knees, not out of weakness so much as out of shock. With Volusian's death—at his hand—he was truly the last Lar alive.

The irony was not lost on him that he had finished Volusian's job for him. By killing him, he had done exactly what Volusian would have wanted. There wasn't room for two demigods in his plans, despite him pretending that there was. Was what he had done no better than what Volusian had done? Should he have kept him alive?

The mageia in the room seemed calm now in his presence, a far cry from the swooning pressure he had felt upon his arrival to this place. He gently waved his hand over Volusian's dead body, focusing mageia on that single point and igniting it into flames.

XLV

Rome

Pope Gelasius I was one of the last of the "old guard," as Martel called them—the high-level Christians who remembered what the true mission was. Increasingly, the church was populated with sycophants and theologians. To be sure, it was a natural progression of a religion's followers to evolve to match its preaching. But it was a precarious balance between those who toed the Biblical line while understanding why Christianity spread in the first place. Why Constantine had elected to push this religious sect of the Jewish faith at a time when the Old Gods were at their strongest.

The pope greeted Martel warmly as he entered his chambers. They embraced and shared kisses on the cheek—an old greeting—before taking their seats across from each other.

"I have heard of your activities in Gaul," Gelasius said, biting into a piece of cheese on the platter next to him.

"I am ceaseless in my devotion," Martel said proudly.

"You always have been." The pope sat back and looked down at Martel from his raised seat. "However, it is time for them to end."

289

The words sent a shock down Martel's spine. He tilted his head, sure he had misheard.

"My lord—" Martel began, but he was cut off.

"The fight is over, Martel. We have won. Your Inquisitors bounding around in Gaul are doing more to damage the image of Christianity than helping."

Martel immediately grew angry at his old mentor. Here he was, cushioned in Rome, tucked away from any and all open followers of the Old Gods, claiming that the war was over?

"With all due respect, Father," Martel said, bowing his head, "you and I both know that the end goal was to eradicate the Old Gods and remove mageia's influence over humanity. I do not believe that is complete."

"I do," the pope replied, "and that settles the argument. After you, very few of the bishops even remember the old fight. Christianity has taken over. People are following it voluntarily. The Old Gods are seen as superstitions. As sinful."

Martel's anger was less about the fact that the pope was wrong; rather, it was about that he was right. There was no need to maintain a legion of Inquisitors or keep someone like Volusian—a dangerous ally that Gelasius believed was already dead—around to fight the now nonexistent wielders of mageia.

But Martel's work—the one he had decided for himself—that work was not complete. Without the guise of hunting down the augurs, his continued prying into the old magic would be increasingly suspect.

It was no longer about eradicating mageia. No, it was about taming it. About giving humans something they never had before. Power over their own fate, and the fate of the world around them. Something that the Gods had kept to themselves for centuries. Why would humans absolve their own potential power simply to deny the Gods the same? There was a way to find it. He would be the one to do it.

"Am I clear, Martel?" the pope pressed.

Martel looked at his old friend and smiled politely. "Of course." He stood and left the room quickly. Gaius was waiting for him outside, eager to hear what wisdom the pope had shared with his liege.

"Well?" Gaius asked.

Martel took a moment to look at the other bishops and cardinals around them, mindlessly drinking wine and so content with their lives. Christianity had certainly won. These "men of the cloth" have displayed the exact same Roman exuberance that they had claimed to be against. He supposed it made sense, given that they had recruited nearly all the remaining wealthy Romans to the cause, selling it as the only way to preserve their way of life.

"Come," Martel said quickly, walking out of the chambers. "We are leaving."

"Sir?" Gaius asked worriedly. "But we have only just arrived."

"There is nothing left for us here. Our friends here have lost their way."

Returning to his carriage, Martel took a moment to ensure that his parchments—each filled with myths and legends of the Old Gods, lines everywhere in places he had scribbled—were still there. He tucked them away again and signaled his guards to begin the ride home.

XLVI

Litochoro, Base of Mount Olympus

A rooster was crowing somewhere in the village. It was incessant, despite the sun barely having risen.

"That fucking rooster," Marius moaned, meandering out of bed. He peered out the small window in the room. He could see the thing stretching its neck into the air as it made that ear shattering sound a few homes away. "If I had an arrow, I would kill you. Fucking cunt."

"Marius?" Joanna asked from the bed, rolling over to see him in the window. "What are you doing?"

"Admiring the local wildlife," he answered. "Don't get up for me. I'm coming right back."

"I half expected you to be gone this morning."

"It's not morning yet," Marius joked. "Don't tempt me."

"Marius, listen." Joanna sat up, crossing her arms. "About last night."

In a rare moment of compassion, Marius sat down on the bed next to her, holding one of her hands.

"Joanna, before you speak," he started, "if you never want to talk of it again, I understand."

293

"Oh." Joanna seemed surprised. "Well, certainly, if you don't want to, we don't have to."

"Me? I would tell the world if I could. Me, a lowly criminal with a sexy assassin." Marius smiled and ran his hand up her arm. "I am not ashamed. I understand if you are."

"You are not just a lowly criminal to me. Certainly not to Orephes either." Joanna took his hand off her arm and held it close to her chest. "I don't want to never speak of this. I want us to try to make something work between us. Something even more."

"That is the sex talking," Marius dismissed. "I'm not someone that people want to make things work with."

"Not before, but I have seen a different side of you. I..." She paused for a moment, understanding that he might think this next line foolish. "I feel something different about you. Something that draws me to you."

Marius shook his head. "Joanna, from the moment I laid eyes upon you I thought you were the most beautiful woman I had ever seen. At the very least the most beautiful whore in the brothel."

She slapped his arm—jokingly but hard enough that he knew she meant it.

"What do you say?"

Marius looked into Joanna's eyes and saw that same beautiful color he had seen back in Rome. He had meant what he said. She truly was one of the most beautiful women he had ever seen. She was also one of the most compassionate, tough, and spirited women he had ever had the pleasure of knowing. Being with her these past few months had been like a gift.

"I've never fallen for a woman before," he said finally, "so I can't be sure this is what it feels like. But OK. Let's try it. You and me. It won't be easy. I am a wanted man, you know."

"I don't expect it to be." She smirked.

It turned him on, like that smirk of hers always did.

"Have I mentioned yet how gorgeous you are?" He put his lips to her neck and started to kiss her up and down, feeling her smooth skin get transformed by goose bumps under his breath. She slowly reached down his chest, slowly going farther down. And farther…and…

There was a sudden knock on the door, startling them both. They looked at each other, confused. Marius stood, attempting to conceal his erection behind his sword sheath. He went to look out the window but before he could, the door swung open.

Orephes walked in, looking rested and strong. A strong smile spread across his face. Marius let out a long sigh and shook his head.

"You, my friend, have the worst timing of anyone I have ever met in the empire."

"Is that Orephes?" Joanna said excitedly, jumping from the bed and embracing her friend. She looked at Marius and gave him a knowing nod. They both knew what it meant that he had made it back here. "You look fantastic! What happened up there?"

"Well, I looked him in the eyes and haven't turned to stone," Marius answered, "so we know that he hasn't gained that ability."

Another smack in the arm from Joanna.

"The Gods are truly gone," Orephes said quietly. "So is Volusian."

Marius and Joanna wanted to ask so many more questions, but they could tell that Orephes didn't want to talk very much. Not yet, anyway. There would be stories for another day. Marius peeked behind Orephes and saw all the villagers surrounding their small cabin, in awe of Orephes having made it back down from the top of the mountain. The trio stepped outside, hearing the commotion.

The old woman from when they had first arrived there made her way to the front of the group. Orephes looked around at the awe on their faces and remembered what Volusian had said. That the belief that people had put in him—the prayer and worship—as a saint for the Christians had directed mageia toward him. If Orephes was to fix this world, he would need the same. But not behind the guise of Christianity. No, he would do it as he really was. He would inherit the mantle that Volusian had left behind but use it for the greater good, not for genocide.

"What is your name?" the woman asked.

"My name is Orephes, son of Zeus, last of the Lares," Orephes said loudly, so that the crowd could hear him. "I made it to the top of the mountain." The crowd began to murmur loudly, one or two shouting "liar" and "blasphemy," before the old woman noticed Zeus's lightning sheathed in Orephes's hilt.

"There," she shouted, "in your hilt. A weapon of the Gods!" She looked awestruck as she fell to her knees. "You will become legend, Orephes, son of Zeus, for what you have done here."

"Take it out," Joanna whispered to him. "Show them that the Gods were real. That you are real."

Orephes pulled out Zeus's lightning and held it above his head. As he did, a bit of mageia swirled around him, sending dirt flying in a spiral to the sky. The crowd immediately stopped murmuring and fell to their knees, as well.

Orephes turned to look at a similarly awestruck Joanna and Marius.

"Don't expect me to kneel," Marius said, pointing at him forcefully.

"Never," Orephes joked.

"Where are you headed now?" Joanna asked him softly, asking not only out of curiosity, but for her own sake. Would she join him wherever it was?

"Home. My family needs me. I can feel it."

XLVII

Chalcedon Estate, Southern Gaul

The day was cloudy and miserable. A fine mist hung in the air, coating everything, including the sword hilts in a cold sheen of water. The two Gothic guards stood outside the villa walls, leaning lazily against it as they discussed the end result of their latest pillage—a small river town to the south, recently open for razing after the collapse of Odoacer's kingdom and the power vacuum there.

They would certainly rebuild—they always did—but each raid was one more chip off the Roman trunk. Eventually, the barbarians hoped, there would come the final ax swing that would bring the whole bloody culture down. It had already happened in the north. It would happen in Italy, the empire's heart, too. It was only a matter of time.

Their musings were interrupted by the approach of someone on horseback in the distance. The plodding, muddy sounds of the hooves splashing their way toward them. Eventually, the figure was close enough that they could make out a male figure on horseback. He was hooded.

"Who goes there?" one of them shouted. The hooded figure slowed his horse and gently turned his head to look at each of the guards before him. "Oy, did you hear me? State your business?" They drew their swords.

The fools.

Their swords flew from their hands. Shortly after, the two flew to each side of the gate, slamming into the stone walls before falling to the floor. The gates swung open as though struck with a battering ram, crashing backward into the inner walls.

The occupants of the villa ran outside at the noise, the guards a mix of Romans and Goths. The civilians looked worn and tired.

The man hopped off his horse, pulling back his hood. There were murmurs among some of the older people in the villa who recognized him, before someone finally stepped forward to face the invader. He was a short, stocky armored fellow who seemed to have a hard time holding up his armor. He spit a wad of mucus as he approached.

"I am Count Amfalgr of the Gothic Kingdom. This is my property." He snorted, swallowing some mucus. "What business do you have here?"

"My name is Orephes, son of Zeus, last of the Lares. This is my home. I have come to take it back."

"I don't remember seeing any Orephes on my deed," the count said defiantly. "I'll give you one chance to get back on your cunt fucking horse and get off my property."

"Orephes?" He heard a faint voice call from the back of the crowd. It was Castella, Gargarus's wife. She was in chains, being led out of the front of the house carrying a basket. She looked worn and beaten, with bruises on her arms and legs. Behind her was a slave driver—this one, a Roman—looked angry that she had stopped. She dropped her basket from the surprise, leading to the slave driver behind her delivering a blow to her back.

"Pick that up!" he shouted, but Orephes could barely hear it, rendered deaf by his anger.

He twisted his hand, effortlessly breaking the count's neck with mageia. He lifted his arms and pulled the weapons from all the guards, the swords clanging at his feet. Many of them began to run.

In the commotion, he lifted his arm and pulled the slave driver to him, his neck landing in his hand. He squeezed once, breaking his larynx and tossing him to the floor. A few of the guards futilely attempted to stop him, each of their fates ending worse than the last.

Orephes ignored the rest of the people in the villa—some of them shouting "demon" and "witch!"—until he reached Castella, who was crying on the floor. He could sense from her mageia that it was a happy cry.

"Thank you for coming back," she said through her tears, falling into his arms.

"Where is Gargarus?"

She stood up, as though she was remembering a mission, and quickly led him to the basement of the villa, where Gargarus, Antonius, and Michael were sitting naked, wasting away on the wet floor. Orephes ripped open the cell doors with no effort, walking in to see them open their eyes.

"Orephes?" Gargarus said weakly. "Is it you? Am I dreaming again?"

"It is me, brother," Orephes said, a tear running down his face as he embraced him. "I'm here. I will not leave you again. This is our home. It will always be our home."

Sitting in the temple, Orephes reflected on the previous month, when he had returned the villa to his family and the violence that had overcome him as he did. He prayed.

As he did, the world turned to white around him. He opened his eyes to see his father, Lucas, and Eschelus standing before a veritable army of his ancestors in the mageia plane, each with wisdom to share as he moved forward. Here in the temple, others thought he was alone. But he was never alone. Here, and everywhere, those he loved were with him. Through mageia. And they always would be.

A new figure appeared to his right. Volusian, exactly as he remembered him, stood next to Eschelus with a smile on his face. They were family, after all. And here, in mageia, they were all equal—and there, in mageia, they were ready to help Orephes build this world better than the one that had left them behind.

ABOUT THE AUTHOR

Chris Hackett was born in Brooklyn, NY, but was raised in Union, NJ for most of his life where he attended the public schools. He attended Rutgers University in New Jersey where he received a M.S. in Biotechnology and Genomics. He is a mixed-race Dominican American. He currently lives with his wife and three children in Hunterdon County, NJ. He enjoys history, particularly the Antiquities, and writing books that blend real history with fiction and fantasy.

Follow updates from the author at: http://www.chrishackettwrites.com

Follow the Author or Invicta Series on social media…
https://x.com/invictaseries
https://twitter.com/chackettwrites
Instagram/invictaseries